ANDREW GROSS

Before turning to full-time writing, Andrew Gross was an executive in the sportswear business. Andrew has co-authored five novels with James Patterson, all of them reaching Number One in the *NY Times* Bestseller list. He currently lives in New York with his wife, Lynn, and has three children.

Visit www.AuthorTracker.co.uk for exclusive updates on Andrew Gross.

Novels by Andrew Gross and James Patterson

THE BLUE ZONE

Andrew Gross

HARPER

Harper
An imprint of HarperCollins*Publishers*
77–85 Fulham Palace Road,
Hammersmith, London W6 8JB

www.harpercollins.co.uk

Published by HarperCollins*Publishers*

1

A catalogue record for this book is
available from the British Library

ISBN 978-0-00-783401-3

Typeset in Palatino by Palimpsest Book Production Ltd,
Grangemouth, Stirlingshire

Printed and bound in Great Britain by
Clays Ltd, St Ives plc

The manual of WITSEC, the U.S. Marshals agency that oversees the Witness Protection Program, describes three stages of agency involvement.

The *Red Zone* – when a subject is held in protective custody, while in prison or on trial.

The *Green Zone* – when that subject, along with his or her family, has been placed in a new identity and location and is living securely in that identity, known only to his WITSEC case agent.

And the *Blue Zone* – the state most feared, when there is suspicion that a subject's identity has been penetrated or blown. When he or she is unaccounted for, is out of contact with the case agent, or has fled the safety of the program. When there is no official knowledge of whether that person is dead or alive.

PROLOGUE

It took just minutes for Dr. Emil Varga to reach the old man's room. He had been in a deep sleep, dreaming of a woman from his days at the university a lifetime ago, but at the sound of the servant's frantic knocking he quickly threw his wool jacket over his nightshirt and grabbed his bag.

"Please, Doctor," she said, running upstairs ahead of him, "come quick!"

Varga knew the way. He had been staying in the hacienda for weeks. In fact, the stubborn, unyielding man who had held off death for so long was his only patient these days. Sometimes Varga mused over a brandy at night that his loyal service had hastened his departure from a lengthy and distinguished career.

Was it finally over . . . ?

The doctor paused at the bedroom door. The

1

room was dark, fetid; the arched, shuttered windows held back the onset of dawn. The smell told him all he needed to know. That and the old man's chest—silent for the first time in weeks. His mouth was open, his head tilted slightly on the pillow. A trickle of yellow drool clotted on his lips.

Slowly Varga stepped up to the large mahogany bed and put his bag on the table. No need for instruments now. In life his patient had been a bull of a man. Varga thought of all the violence he had caused. But now the sharp Indian cheekbones were shrunken and pale. There was something about it that the doctor thought fitting. How could someone who had caused such fear and misery in his life look so frail and withered now?

Varga heard voices from down the hall, shattering the calm of the dawn. Bobi, the old man's youngest son, ran into the room, still in his bedclothes. He stopped immediately and fixed on the lifeless shape, his eyes wide.

"Is he dead?"

The doctor nodded. "He finally gave up his grip on life. For eighty years he had it by the balls."

Bobi's wife, Marguerite, who was carrying the old man's third grandchild, began to weep in the doorway. The son crept cautiously over to the bed, as if advancing on a slumbering mountain lion that at any moment might spring up in attack. He knelt down and brushed the old man's face, his tightened, withered cheeks. Then he took his father's hand, which even now was rough and coarse as a laborer's hand, and gently kissed it on the knuckles.

"Todas apuestas se terminaron, Papa," he whispered, gazing into the old man's deadened eyes.

All bets are off, Father.

Then Bobi rose and nodded. "Thank you, Doctor, for all you've done. I'll make sure word gets to my brothers."

Varga tried to read what was in the son's eyes. Grief. Disbelief. His father's illness had gone on so long, and now the day had finally come.

No, it was more of a question that was written there: For years the old man had held everything together, through the force of his own will.

What would happen now?

Bobi led his wife by the arm and left the room. Varga stepped over to the window. He opened the shutters, letting in the morning light. The dawn had washed over the valley.

The old man owned it all for miles, far past the gates, the grazing lands, the glistening cordillera, three thousand meters high. Two black American SUVs were parked next to the stables. A couple of bodyguards, armed with machine pistols, were lounging on a fence, sipping their coffee, unaware.

"Yes," Varga muttered, "get word to your brothers." He turned back to the old man. *See, you bastard, even in death you are a dangerous man.*

The floodgates were open. The waters would be fierce. Blood never washes away blood.

Except here.

There was a painting over the bed of the Madonna and child in a hand-carved frame that Varga knew had been a gift from a church in Buenaventura, where the old man was born. The doctor wasn't a religious man, but he crossed himself anyway, lifting up the damp bedsheet and placing it gently over the dead man's face.

"I hope you are finally at peace, old man, wherever you are . . . Because all hell is going to break loose here."

I don't know if it's a dream or if it's real.

I step off the Second Avenue bus. It's only a couple of blocks to where I live. I know immediately something is wrong.

Maybe it's the guy I see stepping away from the storefront, tossing his cigarette onto the sidewalk, following a short distance behind. Maybe it's the steady clacking of his footsteps on the pavement behind me as I cross over to Twelfth Street.

Normally I wouldn't turn. I wouldn't think twice. It's the East Village. It's crowded. People are everywhere. It's just a sound of the city. Happens all the time.

But this time I do turn. I have to. Just enough to glimpse the Hispanic man with his hands in his black leather jacket.

Jesus, Kate, try being a little paranoid, girl . . .

Except this time I'm not being paranoid. This time the guy keeps following me.

I turn on Twelfth. It's darker there, less traffic. A few people are talking out on their stoop. A young couple making out in the shadows. The guy's still on me. I still hear his footsteps close behind.

Pick up your pace, I tell myself. You live only a few blocks away.

I tell myself that this can't be happening. If you're going to wake up, Kate, now's the time! But I don't wake up. This time it's real. This time I'm holding a secret important enough to get myself killed.

I cross the street, quickening my pace. My heart's starting to race. His footsteps are knifing through me now. I catch a glimpse of him in the reflection of a store window. The dark mustache and short, wiry hair.

My heart's slamming back and forth off my ribs now.

There's a market where I sometimes buy groceries. I run in. There are people there. For a second I feel safe. I take a basket, hide between the aisles, throw in things I pretend I need. But all the while I'm just waiting. Praying he's passing by.

I pay. I smile a little nervously at Ingrid, the checkout girl, who knows me. I have this eerie premonition. What if she's the last person to see me alive?

Back outside, I feel relief for a second. The guy must be gone. No sign. But then I freeze. He's still there. Leaning aimlessly against a parked car on the other side of the street, talking into a phone. His eyes slowly drift to mine . . .

Shit, Kate, what the hell do you do now?

Now I run. An indistinguishable pace at first, then faster. I hear the frantic rhythm of quickening footsteps on the pavement—but this time they're mine.

I grope in my bag for my phone. Maybe I should call Greg. I want to tell him I love him. But I know the time—it's the middle of his shift. All I'd get is his voice mail. He's on rounds.

Maybe I should call 911 or stop and scream. Kate, do something—now!

My building's just a half a block away. I can see it now. The green canopy. 445 East Seventh. I fumble for my keys. My hands are shaking. Please, just a few yards more . . .

The last few feet I take at a full-out run. I jam my key into the outer lock, praying it turns—and it does! I hurl open the heavy glass doors. I take one last glance behind. The man who was following me has pulled up a few doorways down. I hear the door to the building close behind me, the lock mercifully engaging.

I'm safe now. I feel my chest virtually implode with relief. It's over now, Kate. Thank God.

For the first time, I feel my sweater clinging to me, drenched in a clammy sweat. This has got to end. You've got to go to someone, Kate. *I'm so relieved I actually start to cry.*

But go to whom?

The police? They've been lying to me from the beginning. My closest friend? She's fighting for her life in Bellevue Hospital. That's surely no dream.

My family? Your family is gone, Kate. Forever.

It was too late for any of that now.

I step into the elevator and press the button for my floor. Seven. It's one of those heavy industrial types, clattering like a train as it passes every floor. All I want is just to get into my apartment and shut the door.

On seven the elevator rattles to a stop. It's over now. I'm safe. *I fling open the metal grating, grasp my keys, push open the heavy outer door.*

There are two men standing in my way.

7

I try to scream, but for what? No one will hear me. I step back. My blood goes cold. All I can do is look silently into their eyes.

I know they're here to kill me.

What I don't know is if they're from my father, the Colombians, or the FBI.

PART ONE

CHAPTER ONE

Gold was up two percent the morning Benjamin Raab's life began to fall apart.

He was leaning back at his desk, looking down on Forty-seventh Street, in the lavish comfort of his office high above the Avenue of the Americas, the phone crooked in his neck.

"I'm waiting, Raj . . ."

Raab had a spot gold contract he was holding for two thousand pounds. Over a million dollars. The Indians were his biggest customers, one of the largest exporters of jewelry in the world. *Two percent.* Raab checked the Quotron screen. That was thirty thousand dollars. *Before lunch.*

"Raj, *c'mon*," Raab prodded. "My daughter's getting married this afternoon. I'd like to make it if I can . . ."

"Katie's getting married?" The Indian seemed to be hurt. "Ben, you never said—"

"It's just an expression, Raj. If Kate was getting married, you'd be there. But, Raj, c'mon . . . we're talking gold here—not pastrami. *It doesn't go bad.*"

This was what Raab did. He moved gold. He'd owned his own trading company near New York's diamond district for twenty years. Years ago he had started out buying inventory from the mom-and-pop jewelers who were going out of business. Now he supplied gold to half the dealers on the Street. As well as to some of the largest exporters of jewelry across the globe.

Everyone in the trade knew him. He could hardly grab a turkey club at the Gotham Deli down the street without one of the pushy, heavyset Hasids squeezing next to him in the booth with the news of some dazzling new stone they were peddling. (Though they always chided that as a Sephardi he wasn't even one of their own.) Or one of the young Puerto Rican runners who delivered the contracts, thanking him for the flowers he'd sent to their wedding. Or the Chinese, looking to hedge some dollars against a currency play. Or the Australians, tantalizing him with uncut blocks of industrial-quality stones.

I've been lucky, Raab always said. He had a wife who adored him, three beautiful children who made him proud. His house in Larchmont (a whole lot more than just a house) that overlooked the Long Island Sound, and the Ferrari 585, which Raab once raced at Lime Rock and had its own special place in the five-car garage. Not to mention the box at Yankee Stadium and the Knicks tickets, on the floor of the Garden, just behind the bench.

Betsy, his assistant for over twenty years, stepped in carrying a chef's salad on a plate along with a cloth napkin, Raab's best defense against his proclivity for leaving grease stains on his Hermès ties. She rolled her eyes. "Raj, still . . . ?"

Benjamin shrugged, drawing her eye to his notepad where he had already written down the outcome: *$648.50.* He knew that his buyer was going to take it. Raj always did. They'd been doing this little dance for years. *But did he always have to play out the drama so long?*

"Okay, my friend." The Indian buyer sighed at last in surrender. "We consider it a deal."

"*Whew,* Raj." Raab exhaled in mock relief. "The *Financial Times* is outside waiting on the exclusive."

The Indian laughed, too, and they closed out the deal: $648.50, just as he'd written down.

Betsy smiled—"He says that every time,

doesn't he?"—trading the handwritten contract for two glossy travel brochures that she placed next to his plate.

Raab tucked the napkin into the collar of his Thomas Pink striped shirt. "Fifteen years."

All one had to do was step into Raab's crowded office and it was impossible not to notice the walls and credenzas crammed with pictures of Sharon, his wife, and his children— Kate, the oldest, who had graduated from Brown; Emily, who was sixteen, and nationally ranked at squash; and Justin, two years younger—and all the fabulous family trips they'd taken over the years.

The villa in Tuscany. Kenya on safari. Skiing at Courchevel in the French Alps. Ben in his driver's suit with Richard Petty at the Porsche rally school.

And that's what he was doing over lunch, mapping out their next big trip—the best one yet. Machu Picchu. The Andes. Then on a fantastic walking tour of Patagonia. Their twenty-fifth anniversary was coming up. Patagonia had always been one of Sharon's dreams.

"My next life"—Betsy grinned as she shut the office door—"I'm making sure I come back as one of your kids."

"Next life," Raab called after her, "I am, too."

Suddenly a loud crash came from the outer office. At first Raab thought it was an explosion or a break-in. He thought about triggering the alarm. Sharp, unfamiliar voices were barking commands.

Betsy rushed back in, a look of panic on her face. A step behind, two men in suits and navy windbreakers pushed through the door.

"Benjamin Raab?"

"Yes . . ." He stood up and faced the tall, balding man who had addressed him, who seemed to be in charge. "You can't just barge in here like this. *What the hell's going on . . . ?*"

"What's going on, Mr. Raab"—the man tossed a folded document onto the desk—"is that we have a warrant from a federal judge for your arrest."

"*Arrest . . . ?*" Suddenly people in FBI jackets were everywhere. His staff was being rounded up and told to vacate. "What the hell for?"

"For money laundering, aiding and abetting a criminal enterprise, conspiracy to defraud the U.S. government," the agent read off. "How's that, Mr. Raab? The contents of this office are being impounded as material evidence in this case."

"*What?*"

15

Before he could utter another word, the second agent, a young Hispanic, spun Raab around, forcing his arms roughly behind him, and slapped a set of handcuffs on his wrists, his whole office looking on.

"This is crazy!" Raab twisted, trying to look the agent in the face.

"Sure it is," the Hispanic agent chortled. He lifted the travel brochures out of Raab's hands. "Too bad." He winked, tossing them back onto the desk. "Seemed like one helluva trip."

CHAPTER TWO

"Check these babies out," Kate Raab muttered, peering into the high-powered Siemens microscope.

Tina O'Hearn, her lab partner, leaned over the scope. *"Whoa!"*

In the gleaming luminescence of the high-resolution lens, two brightly magnified cells sharpened into view. One was the lymphocyte, the defective white blood cell with a ring of hairy particles protruding from its membrane. The other cell was thinner, squiggle-shaped, and had a large white dot in the center.

"That's the Alpha-boy," Kate said, slowly adjusting the magnification. "We call them Tristan and Isolde. Packer's name for them." She picked up a tiny metal probe off the counter. "Now check this out . . ."

As Kate prodded, Tristan nudged its way

toward the denser lymphocyte. The defective cell resisted, but the squiggle cell kept coming back, as if searching out a weakness in the lymphocyte's membrane. *As if attacking.*

"Seems more like Nick and Jessica," Tina giggled, bent over the lens.

"Watch."

As if on cue, the squiggle cell seemed to probe the hairy borders of the white blood cell, until in front of their eyes the attacking membrane seemed to penetrate the border of its prey and they merged into a single, larger cell with a white dot in the center.

Tina looked up. *"Ouch!"*

"Love hurts, huh? That's a progenitive stem-cell line," Kate explained, looking up from the scope. "The white one's a lymphoblast—what Packer calls the 'killer leukocyte.' It's the pathogenic agent of leukemia. Next week, we see what happens in a plasma solution similar to the bloodstream. I get to record the results."

"You do this all day?" Tina scrunched up her face.

Kate chuckled. Welcome to life in the petri dish. "All *year.*"

For the past eight months, Kate had been working as a lab researcher for Dr. Grant Packer, up at Albert Einstein Medical College in the

Bronx, whose work in cytogenetic leukemia was starting to make noise in medical circles. She'd won a fellowship out of Brown, where she and Tina had been lab partners her senior year.

Kate was always smart—just not "geeky" smart, she always maintained. She was twenty-three. She liked to have fun—hit the new restaurants, go to clubs. Since she'd been twelve, she could beat most guys down the hill on a snowboard. She had a boyfriend, Greg, who was a second-year resident at NYU Medical School. She just spent the majority of her day leaning over a microscope, recording data or transcribing it onto digital files, but she and Greg always joked—when they actually *saw* each other—that one lab rat in their relationship was enough. Still, Kate loved the work. Packer was starting to turn some heads, and Kate had to admit it was the coolest option she'd had for a while.

Besides, her real claim to distinction, she figured, was no doubt being the only person she knew who could recite Cleary's *Ten Stages of Cellular Development* and had a tattoo of a double helix on her butt.

"*Leukoscopophy*," Kate explained. "Pretty cool the first time you see it. Try watching it a thousand times. Now check out what happens."

They leaned back over the double scope. There

was only one cell left—larger, squiggle-shaped Tristan. *The defective lymphoblast had virtually disappeared.*

Tina whistled, impressed. "If that happens in a living model, there's got to be a Nobel Prize in this."

"In ten years, maybe. Personally, I was just hoping for a graduate dissertation." Kate grinned.

At that moment her cell phone started to vibrate. She thought it might be Greg, who loved to e-mail her funny photos from rounds, but when she checked out the screen, she shook her head and flipped the phone back into her lab coat.

"If it's not one thing it's a *mother* ..." she sighed.

Kate led Tina into the library, with about a thousand recorded iterations of the stem-cell line on digital film. "My life's work!" She introduced her to Max, Packer's baby, the cytogenetic scope worth over $2 million, which separated chromosomes in the cells and made the whole thing possible. "You'll feel like you're dating it before the month is through."

Tina looked it over with a shrug of mock approval. "I've done worse."

That was when Kate's cell phone sounded

again. She flipped it out. Her mom again. This time there was a text message coming in.

KATE, SOMETHING'S HAPPENED. CALL HOME QUICK!

Kate stared. She'd never gotten a message like that before. She didn't like the sound of those words. Her mind flashed through the possibilities—and all of them were bad.

"Tina, sorry, but I gotta call home."

"No sweat. I'll just start the small talk rolling with Max."

With a jitter of nerves, Kate punched in the speed dial of her parents' home in Larchmont. Her mom picked up on the first ring. Kate could hear the alarm in her voice.

"Kate, it's your father . . ."

Something bad *had* happened. A tremor of dread flashed through her. Her dad had never been sick. He was in perfect shape. He could probably take Em at squash on a good day.

"What's happened, Mom? Is he okay?"

"I don't know . . . His secretary just called in. Your father's been arrested, Kate. *He's been arrested by the FBI!"*

CHAPTER THREE

They took the cuffs off Raab inside FBI head-quarters at Foley Square in Lower Manhattan, leading him into a stark, narrow room with a wooden table and metal chairs and a couple of dog-eared Wanted posters tacked to a bulletin board on the wall.

He sat there staring up at a small mirror that he knew was the two-way kind, like on some police drama on TV. He knew what he had to tell them. He'd rehearsed it over and over. That this was all some kind of crazy mistake. He was just a businessman. He'd never done anything wrong in his entire life.

After about twenty minutes, the door opened. Raab stood up. The same two agents who had arrested him stepped in, trailed by a thin young man in a gray suit and short, close-cropped hair, who placed a briefcase on the table.

"I'm Special Agent in Charge Booth," announced the tall, balding agent. "You've already met Special Agent Ruiz. This is Mr. Nardozzi. He's a U.S. Attorney with the Justice Department who's familiar with your case."

"My *case* . . . ?" Raab forced a hesitant smile, eyeing their thick files a little warily, not believing he was hearing that word.

"What we're going to do is ask you a few questions, Mr. Raab," the Hispanic agent, Ruiz, began. "Please sit back down. I can assure you this will go a lot easier if we can count on your full cooperation and you simply answer truthfully and succinctly to the best of your knowledge."

"Of course." Raab nodded, sitting back down.

"And we're going to be taping this, if that's okay?" Ruiz said, placing a standard cassette recorder on the table, not even waiting for his response. "It's for your own protection, too. At any time, if you like, you can request that a lawyer be present."

"I don't need a lawyer." Raab shook his head. "I have nothing to hide."

"That's good, Mr. Raab." Ruiz winked back affably. "These things have a way of always going best when people have nothing to hide."

The agent removed a stack of papers from the

file and ordered them in a certain way on the table. "You've heard of a Paz Export Enterprises, Mr. Raab?" he started in, turning the first page.

"Of course," Raab confirmed. "They're one of my biggest accounts."

"And just what is it you do for them?" the FBI agent asked him.

"I purchase gold. On the open market. They're in the novelty gift business or something. I ship it to an intermediary on their behalf."

"Argot Manufacturing?" Ruiz interjected, turning over a page from his notes.

"Yes, Argot. Look, if that's what this is about—"

"And Argot does what with all this gold you purchase?" Ruiz cut him off one more time.

"I don't know. They're manufacturers. They turn it into gold plate, or whatever Paz requests."

"Novelty items," Ruiz said, cynically, looking up from his notes.

Raab stared back. "What they do with it is *their* business. I just buy the gold for them."

"And how long have you been supplying gold to Argot on Paz's behalf?" Agent in Charge Booth took up the questioning.

"I'm not sure. I'd have to check. Maybe six, eight years . . ."

"Six to eight years." The agents glanced at

each other. "And in all that time, Mr. Raab, you have no idea what products they make once they receive your gold?"

It had the feel of a rhetorical question. But they seemed to be waiting for an answer. "They make a lot of things." Raab shrugged. "For different customers. Jewelry. Gold-plated stuff, desk ornaments, paperweights . . ."

"They consume quite a lot of gold," Booth said, running his eye down a column of numbers, "for a bunch of desk ornaments and paper-weights, wouldn't you say? Last year over thirty-one hundred pounds. At roughly six hundred forty dollars an ounce, that's over thirty-one million dollars, Mr. Raab."

The number took Raab by surprise. He felt a bead of sweat run down his temple. He wet his lips. "I told you, I'm in the transaction business. They give me a contract. All I do is supply the gold. Look, maybe if you tell me what this is about . . ."

Booth stared back, as if bemused, with a cynical smile, but a smile, it appeared to Raab, that had facts behind it. Ruiz opened his folder and removed some new sheets. Photographs. Black-and-white, eight-by-tens. The shots were all of mundane items. Bookends, paperweights, and some basic tools: hammers, screwdrivers, hoes.

"You recognize any of these items, Mr. Raab?"

For the first time, Raab felt his heart start to accelerate. He warily shook his head. "No."

"You receive payments from Argot, don't you, Mr. Raab?" Ruiz took him by surprise. "Kickbacks . . ."

"Commissions," Raab corrected him, irritated at his tone.

"In *addition* to your commissions." Ruiz kept his eyes on him. He slid another sheet across the table. "Commissions in the commodities market run, what? One and a half, two percent? Yours go as high as six, eight percent, Mr. Raab, isn't that right?"

Ruiz kept his gaze fixed on him. Raab's throat suddenly went dry. He became aware he was fiddling with the gold Cartier cuff links Sharon had given him for his fiftieth birthday, and he stopped abruptly. His glance flicked back and forth among the three agents, trying to gauge what was in their minds.

"Like you said, they use a lot of gold," he answered. "But what they do with it is their business. I just supply the gold."

"What they do with it"—Agent Booth's voice grew hard, losing patience—"is they export it, Mr. Raab. These *novelty* items, as you say, they aren't made of steel or brass or gold plate.

26

They're solid bullion, Mr. Raab. They're painted and anodized to make them look like ordinary items, as I suspect you know. Do you have any idea where these items end up, Mr. Raab?"

"Somewhere in South America, I think." Raab reached for his voice, which clung deep in his throat. "I told you, I just buy it for them. I'm not sure I understand what's going on."

"What's going on, Mr. Raab"—Booth leveled his eyes at him—"is that you've already got one foot in a very deep bucket of shit, and I guess we just want to know, regarding the other, if it's in or out. You say you've worked with Argot for between six and eight years. Do you know who owns the company?"

"Harold Kornreich," Raab answered more firmly. "I know Harold well."

"Good. And what about Paz? Do you know who runs that?"

"I think his name is Spessa or something. Victor. I met him a few times."

"Actually, Victor Spessa, whose real name is Victor Concerga"—Ruiz slid a photo forward—"is merely an operating partner in Paz. The articles of incorporation, which Agent Ruiz is laying out for you, are from a Cayman Islands corporation, BKA Investments, Limited." Ruiz spread out a few more photos on the table. Surveillance shots. The men looked clearly Hispanic. "Are any of these faces familiar to you, Mr. Raab?"

Now Raab grew truly worried. A trickle of sweat cut a slow, cold path down his back. He picked up the photos, looked at them closely, one by one. He tremulously shook his head. "No."

"Victor Concerga. Ramón Ramírez. Luis Trujillo," the lead FBI man said. "These individuals are listed as the key officers of BKA, to whom the simple household products your gold is converted into are consigned. Trujillo," Ruiz said, pushing across a surveillance shot of a stocky man in a fancy suit climbing into a Mercedes, "is one of the leading money managers for the Mercado family in the Colombian drug cartel."

"*Colombia!*" Raab echoed. His eyes bulged wide.

"And just to be clear, Mr. Raab." Agent Ruiz winked. "We're not talking the B-school here."

Raab stared at them, his jaw in his lap.

"The gold you purchase, Mr. Raab, on behalf of Paz, is melted down and cast into ordinary household items, then plated over or painted and shipped back to Colombia, where it is reconstituted into bullion. Paz is just a sham operation. It is one hundred percent owned by the

Mercado drug cartel. The money they pay you . . . for your 'transactions,' as you call them, is derived from the business of narcotics distribution. The gold you supply"—the agent widened his eyes—"is how they ship it home."

"No!" Raab leaped up, this time eyes fiery, defiant. "I have nothing to do with that. I swear. I supply gold. That's all. I have a contract. This Victor Concerga solicited me, like a lot of people do. If you're trying to scare me, okay, you got my attention. It's working! But Colombians . . . *Mercados* . . ." He shook his head. "No way. What the hell do you think is going on here?"

Booth just rubbed his jaw as if he hadn't heard a word Raab had been saying. "When Mr. Concerga came to you, Mr. Raab, he said he wanted to do exactly what?"

"He said he needed to buy gold. He wanted to convert it into certain items."

"And *how* was it that in order to do that he was first introduced to Argot Manufacturing?"

Raab recoiled. He saw it now. Clearly. Where this was starting to lead. Argot was owned by his friend. Harold. *He* had introduced them.

And for years Raab had been paid handsomely for having set up the deal.

That was when Nardozzi, the Justice

Department lawyer, who had to this point remained silent, leaned forward, saying, "You understand the definition of money laundering, don't you, Mr. Raab?"

CHAPTER FOUR

Raab felt like he'd been punched in the stomach. His face turned totally white.

"I didn't know anything!" He shook his head. Sweat was suddenly soaking through the back of his shirt. "All right, I . . . I did take commissions from Argot," he stammered. "But that was more like a kind of finder's fee—not a kickback. I was just a go-between. People do it all the time. But I swear, I had no idea what they were doing with the gold. This is crazy." He searched the agents' faces for an understanding eye. "I've been in business twenty years . . ."

"*Twenty years.*" Ruiz clasped his hands across his stomach, rocking backward. "That's a number we're going to be coming back to from time to time. But for now . . . you say Concerga came to you first?"

"Yes. He said he wanted to manufacture some

items of gold." Raab nodded. "That I would be the broker of record for him, if I could find someone. That it would be very lucrative. I put him in touch with Harold. I never even heard of BKA Investments. Or Trujillo. Harold's a good man. I've known him since we first got into the business. He just needed work."

"You're familiar with the RICO statutes, aren't you, Mr. Raab?" The U.S. Attorney unlatched his case. "Or the Patriot Act?"

"*RICO* . . ." The blood drained out of Raab's face. "That's for mobsters. The Patriot Act? What the hell do you think I am?"

"The RICO statutes state that all it takes is knowledge of a criminal enterprise or a pattern of involvement in one to constitute a felony, which your brokering of the arrangement between Paz and Argot—not to mention the stream of illicit payments you've received from them over a period of years—clearly represented.

"I might also draw your attention to the Patriot Act, Mr. Raab, which makes it illegal since 2001 not to report checks in excess of twenty thousand dollars from any foreign entity."

"*The Patriot Act?*" Raab's knee shot up and down like a jackhammer. *"What the hell are you saying here?"*

"What we're saying," Special Agent Booth cut

in, casually scratching at the short orange hairs on the side of his head, "is that you're pretty much fucked and fried here, Mr. Raab—pardon the French—and what you ought to start thinking about now is how to make this go your way."

"My way?" Raab felt the heat of the room under his collar. He had a flash of Sharon and the kids. How would they possibly deal with this? How would he even begin to explain . . . ? He felt his head start to spin.

"You don't exactly look so good, Mr. Raab." Agent Ruiz pretended to be concerned. He got up and poured him a cup of water.

Raab dropped his forehead into his hands. "I think I need my lawyer now."

"Oh, you don't need a lawyer." Agent in Charge Booth stared wide-eyed. "You need the whole fucking Department of Justice to make this go your way."

Ruiz came back to the table, pushing the water across to Raab. "Of course, there might be a way this could all work out for you."

Raab ran his hands through his hair. He took a gulp of water, cooling his brow. "What way?"

"The way of keeping you out of a federal prison for the next twenty years," Booth replied without a smile.

Raab felt a pain shoot through his stomach. He took another sip of water, sniffing back a mixture of mucus and hot tears. "How?"

"*Concerga*, Mr. Raab. Concerga leads to Ramirez and Trujillo. You've seen the movies. That's the way it works here, too. You take us up the ladder, we find a way to make things disappear. Of course, you understand," the FBI man added, rocking back with an indifferent shrug, "your buddy Harold Kornreich has to go, too."

Raab stared at him blankly. Harold was a friend. He and Audrey had been to Justin's bar mitzvah. Their son, Tim, had just been accepted to Middlebury. Raab shook his head. "I've known Harold Kornreich twenty years."

"He's already history, Mr. Raab," Booth said with a roll of his eyes. "What you don't want to happen is for us to pose the same questions to him about you."

Ruiz maneuvered his chair around the table and pulled it up close to Raab in a chummy sort of way. "You have a nice life, Mr. Raab. What you've got to think about now is how you can keep it that way. I saw those pictures in your office. I'm not sure how twenty years in a federal penitentiary would go over with that pretty family of yours."

"Twenty years!"

Ruiz chuckled. "See, I told you we'd come around to that number again."

A surge of anger rose in Raab's chest. He jumped up. This time they let him. He went over to the wall. He started to slam his fist against it, then stopped. He spun back around.

"Why are you doing this to me? All I did was get two people together. Half the people on the fucking Street would have done the same thing. You throw the Patriot Act in my face. You want me to turn on my friends. All I did was buy the gold. *What the hell do you think I am?*"

They didn't say anything. They just let Raab slowly come back to the table. His eyes were burning, and he sank into the chair and wiped them with the palms of his hands.

"I need to speak with my lawyer now."

"You want representation, that's your decision," Ruiz replied. "You're a cooked goose, Mr. Raab, whichever way. Your best bet is to talk to us, try and make this go away. But before you make that call, there's one last thing you might want to pass along."

"And what is *that*?" Raab glared, frustration pulsing through his veins.

The FBI man removed another photo from his file and slid it across the table. "What about this face, Mr. Raab? Does it look familiar to you?"

Raab picked it up. He stared at it, almost deferentially, as the color drained from his face.

Ruiz started laying out a series of photos. Surveillance shots, like before. Except this time they were of *him*. Along with a short, stocky man with a thin mustache, bald on top. One was through the window of his own office, taken from across the street. Another of the two of them at the China Grill, over lunch. Raab's heart fell off a cliff.

"Ivan Berroa," he muttered, staring numbly at the photograph.

"*Ivan Berroa*." The FBI man nodded, holding back a smile.

As if on cue, the door to the interrogation room opened and someone new stepped in.

Raab's eyes stretched wide.

It was the man in the photo. Berroa. Dressed differently from how Raab had ever seen him. Not in a leather jacket and jeans, but in a suit.

Wearing a badge.

"I think you already know Special Agent Esposito, don't you, Mr. Raab? But should your memory need refreshing, we can always play back the voice recordings of your meetings if you like."

Raab looked up, his face white. They had him. *He was fucked.*

"Like we told you at the beginning"—Agent Ruiz started picking up the photos with a coy smile—"these things seem to go best when the person has nothing to hide."

CHAPTER FIVE

Kate barely caught the 12:10 train at Fordham Road to get back to her parents' home in Larchmont, squeezing into the last car just as the doors were about to close.

All she'd had time to do was grab a few personal things and leave a cryptic message for Greg on the way: "Something's happened with Ben. I'm heading up to the house. I'll let you know when I know more."

It took until the train pulled away from the station and Kate found herself in the midday emptiness of the car for it to hit her—*body-slam* her, was more like it—just what her mother had said.

Her father had been arrested by the FBI.

If she hadn't heard the panic in her voice she would have thought it was some kind of joke. *Money laundering. Conspiracy.* That was crazy . . .

Her dad was one of the straightest shooters she knew.

Sure, maybe he might finagle a commission here or there. Or put a family meal on the company tab once in a while. Or fudge his taxes . . . Everyone did that.

But RICO statutes . . . abetting a criminal enterprise . . . the FBI . . . This was nuts. She knew her father. She knew what kind of man he was. There was absolutely no possible way . . .

Kate bought a ticket from the conductor, then leaned her head against the window, trying to catch her breath.

Reputation was everything to her dad, he always said. His business was based on it. He didn't have salesmen or some fancy arbitrage program or a back room filled with hustling traders. He had himself. He had his contacts, his years in business. He had his reputation. What else was there beyond his word?

Once, Kate recalled, he had refused to handle a large estate sale—it was well into seven figures—just because the executor had shopped it to a friendly competitor on the Street and Dad didn't like the appearance that he'd been bidding for the job against his friend.

And another time he'd taken back an eight-carat diamond he'd brokered in a private sale after two years. Just because some shyster appraiser the buyer had found later insisted that the stone was a little hazy. A six-figure sale. *Hazy?* Even Em and Justin told him he was nuts to do it. The stone hadn't changed! *The woman just didn't want it anymore.*

The Metro-North train rattled past the housing projects in the Bronx. Kate sank back in her seat. She was worried for him, what he must be feeling. She closed her eyes.

She was the oldest—by six years. How many times had her father told her what a special bond that created between them? *It's our little secret, pumpkin.* They even had their own little private greeting. They had seen it in some movie and it just stuck: a one-fingered wave.

She looked a bit different from the rest of them. She was wide-eyed and pretty, kind of like Natalie Portman, everybody always said. Her hair was shoulder-length and light brown. Everyone else's was thicker and darker. And those sharp green eyes—where did those come from? *Flipped chromosomes*, Kate always explained. *You know, the dominant-recessive Y . . . how it skips a generation.*

"Pretty," her dad would tease her. *"I just can't figure out how she got to be so smart."*

Leaning against the glass, Kate thought of

how many times he had come through for her.

For all of them.

How he'd leave work early to come home and catch her soccer games in high school, once even hopping a plane a day early from the Orient when her team had made the district finals. Or drive all over the Northeast to Emily's squash tournaments—she was one of the top-ranked juniors in Westchester County—and coax her back to earth when that famous temper got the best of her after she lost a tough match.

Or how at Brown, after Kate had gotten sick, when she took up crew, he'd drive up on weekends and sit there on the shore and watch her row.

Kate always figured that her dad was such a committed family guy because, truth was, growing up, he'd never had much of one of his own. His mother, Rosa, had come over from Spain when he was a boy. His father had died there, a streetcar accident or something. Kate actually never knew that much about him. And his mother had died young as well, while he was putting himself through NYU. Everyone admired her father. At the club, in his business, their friends—that's why this didn't make any sense.

What the hell did you do, Daddy?

Suddenly Kate's head started to throb. She felt the familiar pressure digging into her eyes, the dryness in her throat, followed by the wave of fatigue.

Shit . . .

She knew that this might happen. It always came on with stress. It didn't take but a second to recognize the signs.

She dug through her bag and found her Accu-Chek—her blood monitor. She'd been diagnosed when she was seventeen, her senior year.

Diabetes. Type 1. The real deal.

Kate had gotten a little depressed at first. Her life underwent a radical change. She'd had to drop soccer. She didn't take her SATs. She had to watch her diet strictly when everyone else was going out for pizza or partying on Saturday nights.

And once she had even fallen into a hypoglycemic coma. She was cramming for a test in the school cafeteria when her fingers began to grow numb and the pen slipped out of her hand. Kate didn't know what was happening. The dizziness took over. Her body wouldn't respond. Faces started to look a little gauzy. She tried to scream—*What the hell is going on!*

Next thing she knew, she was waking up in

the hospital two days later, attached to about a dozen monitors and tubes. It had been six years now. In that time she had learned to manage things. She still had to give herself two shots a day.

Kate pressed the Accu-Chek needle into her forefinger. The digital meter read 282. Her norm was around 90. *Jesus, she was off the charts.*

She dug into her purse and came out with her kit. She always kept a spare in the fridge at the lab. She took out a syringe and the bottle of Humulin. The train car was not crowded; no reason she couldn't do this right here. She lifted the syringe and pressed it into the insulin, forcing out the air: 18 units. Kate lifted her sweater. It was routine for her. Twice a day for the past six years.

She pressed the needle into the soft part of her belly underneath her rib cage. She gently squeezed.

Those initial worries about what it meant to live with diabetes all seemed like a long time ago now. She had gotten into Brown. She had changed her focus, started thinking about biology. And she started rowing there. Just for exercise at first. Then it created a new sense of discipline in her life. In her junior year—though she was only five feet four and barely 115 pounds—she had placed second in the All-Ivy single sculls.

That's what their little wave was about. The sign between them. *Em's got that temper,* her Dad would always wink and tell her, *but you're the one with the real fight inside.*

Kate took a swig of water from a bottle and felt her strength start to return.

The train was approaching Larchmont. It started to slow into the redbrick station.

Kate stuffed her kit back in her bag. She pulled herself up, looped her satchel around her shoulder, and waited at the doors.

She never forgot. Not a single day. Not for an instant:

When she opened her eyes in the hospital after two days in the coma, her father's had been the first face she saw.

Ben will fix this, Kate knew. Like he always did. He'd handle it. Whatever the hell he had done. She was sure.

Now, her mother . . . She sighed, spotting the silver Lexus waiting in the turnabout as the train pulled into the station.

That was a totally different deal.

CHAPTER SIX

It was a long, difficult drive back to Westchester that afternoon for Raab, in the back of the black Lincoln limo his lawyer, Mel Kipstein, had arranged.

An hour before, he'd been brought in front of Judge Muriel Saperstein in the United States courthouse at Foley Square for arraignment, the most humiliating moment of his life.

The frosty government lawyer who'd been in on his interrogation referred to him as a "criminal kingpin" who was the architect of an illicit scheme by which Colombian drug lords were able to divert money out of the country. That he had knowingly profited from this enterprise for years. That he had ties to known drug traffickers.

No, Raab had to hold himself back from shouting, *that's not how it was at all.*

Every time he heard the judge read off a

charge, it cut through him like a serrated blade.

Money laundering. Aiding and abetting a criminal enterprise. Conspiracy to defraud the U.S. government.

After some negotiation, during which Raab grew alarmed he might not even be freed, bail was set at $2 million.

"I see you own a fancy home in Westchester, Mr. Raab?" The judged peered over her glasses.

"Yes, Your Honor." Benjamin shrugged. "I guess."

She scribbled something on an official-looking document. "Not anymore, I'm afraid."

An hour later he and Mel were heading up Interstate 95 toward Westchester. All he told Sharon was that he was okay and that he'd explain everything when he got home.

Mel thought they definitely had some wiggle room. He figured there was a reasonable case for entrapment. Up to now he had represented Raab on matters like contract disputes, the office lease, and setting up a trust for his kids. Just two weeks before, the two of them had come in second in the Member/Guest golf tourney at Century.

"The law says you had to assist them, *knowingly*, Ben. This Concerga never declared to you what he intended to do with the gold, did he?"

Raab shook his head. "No."

"He never explicitly told you the money he was giving you was derived from illicit means?"

Raab shook his head again. He took a long gulp from a bottle of water.

"So if you didn't know, you didn't know, right, Ben? What you're telling me is good. The RICO statutes say you have to conspire with 'knowing' or 'intent.' You can't be a participant, still less aid or abet, if you didn't know."

It somehow sounded good when Mel said it. He could almost believe it himself. He had made some critical mistakes of judgment. That was what he had to get across. He had acted blindly, stupidly—out of greed. But he never knew whom he was dealing with or what they were doing with the gold. Tomorrow morning they had a follow-up meeting with the government that would likely determine the next twenty years of his life.

"But this last thing, Ben, this Berroa guy . . . this complicates matters. It's bad. I mean, they have your voice on tape. Discussing the same arrangements with an FBI agent." Mel looked at him closely. "Look, this is important, Ben. We've been friends a lot of years. Is there anything you're not telling me that could have an impact on this case? Anything the government might know? Now's the time."

Raab stared Mel in the eye. Mel had been his friend for more than ten years. *"No."*

"Well, one thing's lucky." The lawyer looked relieved and jotted a few notes on his pad. "You're lucky you're not the one they really want here. Otherwise there'd be nothing to discuss." Mel kept his gaze on him awhile, then just shook his head. "What the hell were you possibly thinking, Ben?"

Raab dropped his head back and closed his eyes. Twenty years of his life, gone . . . "I don't know."

What he *did* know was that the hardest part was yet to come. That would take place when he arrived home. When he walked in the door and had to explain to his family, who had trusted and respected him, how the smoothly climbing arc that had been their lives the past two decades had basically been blown from the sky. How everything they counted on and took for granted was gone.

He'd always been the rock, the provider. He always talked about pride and family. His handshake was his bond. Now everything was about to change.

Raab felt his stomach churn. What would they think of him? How would they understand?

The car pulled off the thruway at Exit 16, traveled north along Palmer into the town of

Larchmont. These were the streets, stores, and markets he saw every day.

By tomorrow this would all be public. It would be in the papers. It would be all over the club, the local shops, Em and Justin's school.

Raab's stomach started to grind.

One day they'll understand, he told himself. *One day, they will have to see me the same way.* As a husband and a provider. As a father. As the person he'd always been. *And forgive me.*

He had been a coach to Emily. He had given Kate her insulin shots when she was ill. He had been a good husband to Sharon. All these years.

That was no lie.

The limo turned down Larchmont Avenue, heading toward the water. Raab tensed. The houses grew familiar. These were the people he knew. People his kids went to school with.

On Sea Wall the Lincoln turned right, and then it was only a short block with the Sound directly in front of them, to the large fieldstone pillars, and then on to the spacious Tudor house at the end of the landscaped drive.

Raab let out a measured breath.

He knew he had let them down—their faith, their trust. But there was no turning back now. And he knew that what happened today would not be the end of it.

When the truth came out, he would let them down a whole lot more.

"You want me to come in with you?" Mel asked, squeezing Raab's arm as the car pulled into the pebbled driveway.

"No." Raab shook his head.

It was only a house. What's important is the people in it. Whatever he'd had to do, his family hadn't been a lie.

"This I have to do alone."

CHAPTER SEVEN

Kate was in the kitchen with her mother and Em when the black limo turned down the drive.

"It's Dad!" Emily shouted, still in her squash clothes. She made a beeline for the front door.

Kate saw her mother's hesitation. It was as if she couldn't move, or was afraid to. As if she were afraid what opening that door would reveal.

"It's going to be okay." Kate took her arm and led her to the door. "Whatever it is, you know, Dad'll make it okay."

Sharon nodded.

They watched him climb out of the car, accompanied by Mel Kipstein, whom Kate knew from the club. Emily bolted down the flagstone steps and straight into her father's arms. "Daddy!"

Raab just stood there for a moment, hugging

her, staring up at Kate and her mom over his younger daughter's shoulder as they stood on the landing. He had an ashen shadow on his face. He could barely look at them.

"Oh, Ben . . ." Sharon slowly came down the steps, tears in her eyes. They hugged. A hug aching with worry and uncertainty, deeper than Kate could remember seeing in years.

"*Pumpkin.*" Her father's face brightened as his eyes met Kate's. "I'm glad you're here."

"Of course I'm here, Daddy." Kate ran down to the driveway and put her arms around him, too. She placed her head on his shoulder. She could never remember seeing shame on her father's face before.

"And you too, champ." He reached out for Justin, who had just come up behind them, mussing his son's shaggy brown hair.

"Hey, Dad." Justin leaned against him. "*You okay?*"

"Yeah." He did his best to smile. "I am now."

Together they went inside.

For Kate, the huge stone house by the water had never really felt like home. "Home" had been the more modest, fifties ranch where she'd grown up in Harrison, a couple of towns away. With her cramped corner room covered in posters of U-2 and Gwyneth Paltrow, the marshy little pond in back, and the constant whoosh of traffic off the back deck from the Hutchinson Parkway.

But Raab had bought this place in her senior year. His dream house—with its large Palladian windows overlooking the Sound, the gargantuan kitchen with two of everything—Sub-Zeros, dishwashers—the flashy basement theater some Wall Street guy had decked out to the nines, the five-car garage.

They all took a seat in the tall, beamed living room. Kate, with her mother, in front of the fireplace. Emily plopped herself on her father's lap in the high-backed leather chair. Justin pulled up the tufted ottoman.

There was a weird, uncomfortable silence.

"So we gonna start with *your* day," Kate quipped, trying to cut the tension, "or would you like to hear about mine?"

That made her dad smile. "First, I don't want any of you to be afraid," he said. "You're going to hear some terrible things about me. The most important thing is that you understand I'm innocent. Mel says we've got a solid case."

"Of course we know you're innocent, Ben," said Sharon. "But innocent of what?"

Kate's dad let out a nervous breath and gently moved Emily to an adjacent chair.

"Money laundering. Conspiracy to commit fraud. Aiding and abetting a criminal enterprise—that enough?"

"*Conspiracy . . .*" Sharon's jaw dropped open. "Conspiracy with *whom*, Ben?"

"Basically, what they're saying"—he locked his fingers together—"is that I provided some merchandise to people who ultimately did some bad things with it."

"Merchandise?" Emily echoed, not understanding.

"Gold, honey." Ben exhaled.

"So what's wrong with that?" Kate shrugged. "You're in the trading business, aren't you? That's what you do."

"Believe me, I tried to make that point—but in this case I may have made some mistakes."

Sharon stared at him. "You provided this gold to whom, Ben? What kind of people are we talking about?"

Raab swallowed. He moved his chair a little closer to her and wrapped his fingers around her hand.

"Drug traffickers, Sharon. *Colombians.*"

Sharon let out a gasp—half laughing, half incredulous. "You must be kidding, Ben."

"Now, I didn't know who they were, and all I did was provide the gold, Sharon, you have to believe that. But there's more. I introduced them to someone. Someone who altered what I sold them. In an illegal way. Into things like tools, bookends, desk ornaments—and painted them over. So they could ship them back home."

"Home?" Sharon squinted. She looked over to Kate. "I don't understand."

"Out of the country, Sharon. Back to Colombia."

Kate's mother's hand flew to her cheek. "Oh, my God, Ben, what have you done?"

"Look, these people came to me." Raab squeezed his hand around hers. "I didn't know what they were doing or who they were. They were some export company. I did what I always do. I sold them gold."

"Then I don't understand," Kate cut in. "How can they arrest you for that?"

"Unfortunately, it's slightly more complicated, pumpkin," her father said, shifting back. "I set them up with someone, in order to accomplish what they wanted. And I also took some payments, which makes it seem like I was a party to what was going on."

"Were you?"

"Was I *what*, Sharon?"

"Were you a party to what was going on?"

"Of course not, Sharon. I just—"

"So who the hell did you introduce them to, Ben?" Sharon's voice rose, tense and alarmed.

Raab cleared his throat and looked down. "Harold Kornreich. He's been arrested, too."

"Jesus Christ, Ben, what have the two of you done?"

Kate felt her own stomach tie into a knot. Harold Kornreich was one of her dad's business buddies. They went to trade shows together. He and Audrey had come to her bat mitzvah. It was like they were two stupid white guys who had walked into a scam. Except her dad wasn't exactly stupid. And he had taken money—from criminals. Drug dealers. You didn't exactly have to be a constitutional scholar to see that this wasn't about to just go away.

"Now, there's no grounds to prove I knew exactly what was going on," her father said. "I'm not even sure they really want to focus on me."

"Then what do they want?" Sharon asked, her gaze troubled and wide.

"What they want is for me to roll."

"Roll . . . ?"

"Testify, Sharon. Against Harold. The Colombians, too."

"At a trial?"

"Yes." He swallowed resignedly. "At a trial."

"No!" Sharon stood up. Tears of anger and bewilderment flashed in her eyes. "That's how we get to keep our life? By turning state's evidence against one of your closest friends? You're not going to do that, are you, Ben? It would be like admitting you were guilty. Harold and Audrey are our friends. You sold these people gold. What they did with it is their business. We're going to fight this, aren't we, Ben? Isn't that right?"

"Of course we're going to fight this, Sharon. It's just that—"

"It's just that *what*, Ben?" Sharon kept her gaze on him, razor sharp.

"It's just that the payments I took from these guys all these years don't exactly make me look innocent, Sharon."

His voice had elevated, and there was something in it Kate had never heard in her dad before. That he was afraid, and not entirely blameless. That maybe he wasn't going to be able to make this come out okay. They all sat there looking at him, trying to figure out just what that meant.

"You're not going to go to jail, are you, Dad?"

It was Justin, in a voice that was halting and

tight. The question that was suddenly front and center in everyone's mind.

"Of course not, champ." His father pulled him close and stroked his bushy brown hair and looked past him. At Kate.

"No one in this family's going to jail."

CHAPTER EIGHT

Luis Prado didn't ask too many questions.

He'd been in the United States for four years now. His papers said he was here to visit a sister, but that was a lie. He had no family here.

He'd come here to do work. He was hand-picked because of the way he handled himself back home. And what he did, Luis did very well.

He did jobs for the Mercados. Dirty jobs. The kind you did because of the oath you had sworn. You didn't look into someone's face. You looked through them. You didn't ask why.

That's what had gotten him out of the slums of Carmenes. What enabled him to send money back home to his wife and child—more money than he could ever dream of there. What paid for the fancy suits he wore and the private tables at the salsa clubs—and the occasional woman he met there who looked at him with pride.

It's what separated him from the *desesperados* back home. A man with no worth. No significance. Nothing.

The driver, a cocky kid named Tomás, played with the radio in the customized Cadillac Escalade while he drove. *"Ha!"* He tapped his hands against the wheel to the steady salsa beat. "José Alberto. *El Canario*."

The kid was probably no more than twenty-one, but he had already cut his cherry and would drive through a fucking building if he had to get out the other side. He was fearless and good, if maybe a little reckless, but that was just what was needed now. Luis had worked with him before.

They drove north out of the Bronx. Through the kinds of neighborhoods they had never seen before. Places that when Luis was just a kid back home were only hidden behind high fences, with guards at the gates. Maybe, Luis thought as they passed by, if he did his jobs and played his cards right, one day he might have such a home.

They followed the route from the highway carefully. They retraced it, making sure they knew the lights, the turns. They had to be able to retrace it, fast, on the way out.

It went back a long way, Luis thought. Cousins, brothers. Whole families. They all made the same oath. *Fraternidad.* If he died for his work, so be it. It was a lifelong tie. However long or short that was.

They drove down a dark, shaded street and pulled up outside a large house. They cut the lights. Someone was walking a dog down by the water. They waited until the person was well out of sight, checking their watches.

"Let's go, *hermano.*" Tomás drummed against the wheel. "It's salsa time!"

Luis opened the satchel under his feet. His boss had been very specific about this job. Precisely what had to be done. Luis didn't care. He had never met the person. He wasn't even a name to him. All he was told was that they could do harm to the family—and that was enough.

That was everything.

Luis never thought too much about details when it came to work. In fact, only one word ran through his brain as he stepped out of the car in front of the fancy, well-lit house and drew back the TEC-9 automatic machine pistol with an extra clip.

You do the family harm, this is what you get. *Maricón.*

CHAPTER NINE

Kate decided to stay on at the house that night. Her mother was a mess and closed the door to her room. Emily and Justin just seemed shell-shocked. Kate tried her best to calm them. Dad had never let them down, not ever, had he? This time, she wasn't sure if they believed it. Around nine, Em put on her iPod and Justin went back to a video game. Kate went downstairs.

There was a light on in the den. Her father was there, a magazine on his lap, watching CNN on the oversize plasma TV.

Kate knocked, quietly. Her father looked up.

"This a good time to talk about my rent allowance?" She hung in the doorway with a crooked grin.

That brought a smile to her dad's face. "If it's you, it's always a good time, pumpkin." He turned down the volume on the TV. "Did you do your shot?"

"Yes." Kate nodded with a roll of her eyes. "I took care of my shot. I've been to college, Dad. I basically live with a doctor. I'm twenty-three."

"Okay, okay . . ." Her father sighed. "I hear ya—it's just reflex."

Kate curled up next to him on the couch. For a moment they just avoided the obvious. He asked about Greg. How things were going at the office. "With the *leusk* ophy . . ."

"*Leukoscopophy*, Dad. And it's called a *lab*. Not an office. And one day you'll be proud of me for what we're doing. You just won't ever be able to pronounce it."

He chuckled again and put the magazine aside. "I'm always proud of you, Kate."

Kate looked around the room. Their den was filled with pictures from all the trips they'd taken. There was a Northwest Indian mask on the wall they had picked up skiing in Vancouver. An African basket they'd brought back from Botswana, where they'd been on safari. This room had always been a friendly place for Kate, filled with the warmest memories. All those memories seemed threatened now.

Kate met his eyes. "You'd tell me, Daddy, wouldn't you?"

"Tell you what, sweetheart?"

She hesitated. "I don't know. If you really did something wrong?"

"I did tell you, Kate. Mel thinks we have a good shot at fighting this thing. He claims that the RICO statutes—"

"I don't mean legally, Daddy. I mean if you really did something wrong. Something we should know about."

He shifted toward her. "What are you asking, Kate?"

"I'm not sure." The words stuck in her throat. "If you *knew* . . ."

He nodded, keeping his eyes on her, and clasped his hands together. He didn't answer.

"Because it's important to me, Daddy—who you are. All this stuff, these trips, how we've always talked about family—it's not just words or pictures and mementos to me. All of us need to believe in something right now—to get through this—and the thing I choose to believe in is *you*. Because it's what I've always believed in." Kate shook her head. "I don't really want to start looking for someone else right now."

Ben smiled. "You don't have to, pumpkin."

"Because I can give Mom pep talks," Kate said, eyes glistening, "and remind Emily and Justin how you never let us down—because you haven't! But I've got to know, above everything, Dad, that the person who walked through that door tonight, who's going in there tomorrow to fight this as I know you will, is the same one I've known all my life. The person I always thought I knew."

Her father looked at her, then took her hand and massaged it, like she remembered from when she was sick.

"I am that man, pumpkin."

Kate's eyes welled up. She nodded.

"*C'mere* . . ." He pulled her close, and Kate rested her head against him. It made her feel the way she always did in his arms. Safe. Special. A thousand miles away from harm. She wiped the tears off her cheek and tilted her face up to him.

"Money laundering, conspiracy . . ." She shook her head. "It just doesn't fit you, Dad."

He nodded wistfully. "I'm sorry. I know."

"Now, tax felon." Kate shrugged. "Or jewel thief. That would be a different story."

Her father smiled. "I'll try to do better next time."

Suddenly she couldn't hold back. Kate squeezed his hand and felt a rush of tears streaming down her cheeks—stupid and like a little girl, but impossible to hold back. It hurt her, how her father had always been so in control—how *everything* had always been so in control—and now, she knew, she couldn't fight it, their life was about to change. No matter how he tried to pretend it would go away. This *wouldn't* go away. This was going to hang over them. This was bad.

"You know, they're talking fifteen to twenty years," her father said in a low voice as he held her. "That's federal prison, Kate. No plasma TV there. You'll be married then. With kids—maybe the same age Em is now . . ."

"You'll do what you have to do, Daddy," Kate said, squeezing him tighter. "We're behind you, whatever that is."

There was a shuffling of feet. Sharon looked in at the door. She was in her bathrobe, holding a cup of tea. She stared at Ben a little blankly. "I'm going to bed."

That was when they heard the click of a car door being opened out front. Footsteps coming up the drive.

"Who's that?" Kate's mother turned.

Her father exhaled. "Probably the fucking *New York Times*."

Suddenly the windows exploded in gunfire.

CHAPTER TEN

There was an ear-shattering barrage—glass splintering everywhere, bullets shrieking over their heads, flashing in the night.

Raab hurled himself on top of Kate. For a second, Sharon just stood there, paralyzed, until he reached over and grabbed her by the robe, dragging her onto the floor, and pressed his body tightly over both of them.

"Stay down! Stay down!" he screamed.

"Jesus Christ, Ben, what's going on?"

The noise was terrifying—deafening. Bullets ricocheted everywhere, thudding into the cabinets and walls. The large Palladian window was gone. The house alarm was blaring. Everyone was screaming, faces pressed into the floor. The noise was so frightening and seemed so close, *directly over them,* Kate had the terrifying sense whoever was shooting had climbed into the room.

She was certain she was about to die.

Then suddenly she heard voices. Yelling. The same paralyzing thought occurred to everyone at once:

The kids. Upstairs.

Kate's father arched up and shouted above the frenzy, *"Em, Justin, don't come down! Get on the floor!"*

The barrage continued. Maybe twenty, thirty seconds, but it seemed like an eternity to Kate, huddled with her hands over her ears, her heart pounding out of control.

"Hold on, hold on," Kate's father kept repeating, blanketing them. She heard screaming, crying. She didn't even know if it was hers. The window was wide open. Bullets were still flying in every direction. Kate just prayed: *Whoever you are, whatever you want, please, God, please, just don't come inside.*

And then there was silence. As quickly as it had begun.

Kate heard footsteps retreating, an engine starting up, and a vehicle lurching away.

For a long time, they just clung to the floor. Too afraid to even look up. The silence was just as terrifying as the attack. Sharon was whimpering. Kate was too frozen to speak. There was a steady pounding very close by, loud, above the shrieking of the alarm.

Gradually, almost joyously, Kate realized that it was the sound of her own heart.

"They're gone. They're gone." Her father finally exhaled, rolling off of them. "Sharon, Kate, are you all right?"

"I think so," Kate's mother muttered. Kate just nodded. She couldn't believe it. There were bullet holes everywhere. Shattered glass all over the floor. The place looked like a war zone.

"Oh, my God, Ben, what the hell is going on?"

Then they heard voices coming down the stairs. *"Mom . . . Dad . . . ?"*

Justin and Emily. They ran into the study. "Oh, thank God . . ." Sharon literally leaped up, throwing her arms around them, smothering them with kisses. Then Kate, too. Everyone was crying, sobbing, hugging each other in tearful relief. "Thank God you're all all right."

Slowly the panic began to recede, and in its place was the horrifying sight of what had happened. Sharon looked around at the devastation of their once-beautiful home. Everything was shattered. They were lucky to be alive.

Her eyes came back to her husband. There was no longer terror in them. There was something else—*accusation*.

"What the hell have you done to us, Ben?"

CHAPTER ELEVEN

"The purpose of this meeting"—James Nardozzi, the U.S. Attorney, stared across the table, focusing on Mel—"is for you and your client to fully understand the seriousness of the charges facing him. And to determine a path of action that would be in his best interest. As well as the best interest of his family."

The conference room in the U.S. Attorney's office at Foley Square in Lower Manhattan was glass-paneled and narrow, its white walls decorated with photos of George W. Bush and the attorney general. Booth and Ruiz were seated across from Mel and Raab. There was a stenographer at the far end of the table, who looked like a prim schoolteacher, taking everything down. Raab's family was sequestered at the house, which was now cordoned off and being guarded by the FBI.

"First, Mr. Raab believes he has done nothing wrong," Mel was quick to reply.

"*Nothing wrong?*" The U.S. Attorney ruffled his brow as if he hadn't heard correctly.

"Yes. He denies ever knowingly being part of any scheme to launder money or defraud the U.S. government. He's never once concealed any monies he's made from these transactions. He's even up-to-date in his taxes on them. Whatever business took place between Mr. Kornreich and Mr. Concerga was totally without my client's consent."

Special Agent Booth looked back at Mel, surprised. "Your client denies knowing that Paz Export Enterprises was a company set up to receive altered merchandise intended to launder money for the Mercado drug cartel? And that his actions did not serve to aid and abet these felonies when he introduced Paz to Argot Manufacturing?"

Raab stared nervously at Booth and Ruiz. Mel nodded at him.

"Yes."

The U.S. Attorney sighed impatiently, as if this were wasting his time.

"What my client does admit to," Mel explained, "is that he may have been foolish, if not even a bit misguided, not to suspect that something was afoot given the regular and generally lucrative result of Mr. Concerga's business. But the mere acceptance of payment doesn't constitute knowledge of who the end user was or what the finished product was being utilized for."

Special Agent Booth scratched his head for a second and nodded patiently. "As Mr. Nardozzi explained, Mr. Raab, what we're trying to do is give you a chance to keep your family together—before we go at this another way."

"The RICO statutes very specifically state," Mel said, "that a suspect must willfully and knowingly contrive—"

"Mr. Kipstein," Agent Ruiz cut Raab's lawyer off in midsentence, "we know what the RICO statutes state. The man we introduced your client to yesterday is a special agent of the FBI. Agent Esposito identified himself as a business acquaintance of Luis Trujillo. Your client offered to do business with him in the same manner he assisted in the altering of gold for Paz. That's money laundering, Mr. Kipstein. And conspiracy to commit fraud."

"You set my client up," Mel was quick to charge. "You lured him into an illicit act. You put his life, and the life of his family, in danger. That's entrapment. It's more than entrapment. It's reckless endangerment in my view!"

Booth leaned back. "All I can say is, maybe your view's a little cloudy over there, Counselor." He had a face like someone concealing a winning poker hand.

Booth nodded to Ruiz, who reached inside his folder and came out with a cassette. "We have his voice on tape, Mr. Kipstein. Your client has made six visits to Colombia in the past eight years. Do you want me to play what was said?" He slid the tape across the table. "Or can we just get down to the business we came here for today, which is saving your client's life?"

"Be my guest," Mel Kipstein said.

The agent shrugged and reached forward for the recorder.

Raab put his hand on his lawyer's arm. "Mel . . ."

The lawyer stared at him.

Raab always knew that one day this would happen. Even when he pretended every day that it would never come. That it would go on forever.

They had his relationship to Argot, the monies he'd received. They had his voice on tape. The RICO statutes only needed to establish a pattern of racketeering. Just the knowledge alone of such activity would be enough to get a conviction. Under the kingpin statute, they could put him away for twenty years.

He knew. He always knew. He just wasn't prepared to feel so empty inside. He wasn't prepared to have it hurt so much.

"What is it you want from me?" He nodded dully.

"You know what we want from you, Mr. Raab," Booth replied. "We want you to testify. We want Trujillo. We want your friend. You tell us everything you know about Paz and Argot. We'll see what Mr. Nardozzi is willing to do."

They laid out in a very matter-of-fact way to Raab how they were going to seize his assets. The house. The bank accounts. The cars. They wanted him to turn on everyone—including his friend—otherwise they'd toss him in jail.

"Of course, if that bothers you, we could just do nothing." Ruiz shrugged with a gloating smile. "Let you hang out on the street. Go about your business. Tell me, Mr. Raab, after what happened last night, how long do you think you'd last like that?"

Raab pushed away from the table. "*All I did was buy the gold!*" He glared at them. "I didn't steal anything. I didn't hurt anybody. I put two people together. All I did was what a thousand people would have done."

"Look," Mel said, his voice betraying a tone of desperation, "my client's a well-respected member of the business and social community. He's never been implicated in any crime before. Surely, even if his actions inadvertently assisted in the commission of a crime, it's a stretch at best, these charges. He has no information you're seeking. He's not even the person you really want. That ought to count for something."

"It does count for something, Mr. Kipstein," Agent Booth replied. "It accounts for why we're talking to you, Mr. Raab, and not to Harold Kornreich."

Raab stared at him and touched Mel's shoulder. It was over. No more. He suddenly saw all the consequences crashing in on him like the girders of a building caving in.

"You're cutting out my heart, you know." He stared at Booth. "My life, my family. You've killed it. It's all gone."

The FBI man crossed his legs and looked at Raab. "Frankly, Mr. Raab, considering last night, I think you've got even bigger things to worry about than that."

CHAPTER TWELVE

"We're talking about the matter of your personal safety," Agent Ruiz cut in.

"My safety . . ." Raab suddenly turned white, flashing back to the events of the previous night.

"Yeah, and that of your family, Mr. Raab." The agent nodded.

"I think it's time we explain a few things." Booth opened a file. "There's a war going on right now, Mr. Raab. A war of control—between factions of the Colombian drug cartels. Between those operating in this country and those back home in South America. You've heard of Oscar Mercado—"

"Of course I've heard of Oscar Mercado." Raab blanched. Everyone had.

Ruiz pushed a black-and-white photo across the table. The face was gaunt and hardened, the hair long, the eyes callous and empty. The chin was covered in a thick goatee. It brought to mind images of murdered judges and families who got in their way.

"Mercado's been thought to be in hiding in the United States or Mexico now for several years," Agent Booth started to explain. "No one knows. The people you were doing business with are part of the finance arm of his organization. These people are cold-blooded killers, Mr. Raab, and they protect to the death what they think of as theirs. In the past few years, their organization's been rocked by some key defections from within. The family patriarch has died. There's a war for control going on. They're not going to let some 'white-collar, Jewish, business-school type' who's been living high off their proceeds for several years take down the rest of it in a trial."

"You've seen what these people do, Mr. Raab," Ruiz put in. "They don't just go after you, like in those Mafia movies. This is *fraternidad*, Mr. Raab. Mercado's brotherhood. They kill your family. Your wife, your lovely kids. They'll kill the fucking dog if it barks. You heard in the news about that whole family that was murdered in Bensonhurst last month? They left a six-month-old kid in a baby chair with a bullet through its head. Are you prepared for that? Is

77

your wife prepared for that? Your *kids*? Let me ask you, Mr. Raab: Are you prepared not to have an easy night's sleep for the rest of your life?"

Raab turned toward Mel, an ache widening in his gut. "We can fight this, right? We'll take our chances in court."

Booth's tone intensified. "You're not hearing us, Mr. Raab. You're in danger. Your whole family's in danger. Just by your being here."

"And even if you choose to fight this," Ruiz added, coyly, "they're never really going to be entirely sure just what you might say, are they, Mr. Raab? Are you prepared to take that chance?"

The ache in Raab's gut intensified, accompanied by a wave of nausea.

"You're in bed with them, Mr. Raab," the Hispanic agent chuckled. "I'm surprised you never thought about this stuff when you were driving around town in that fancy Ferrari of yours up there."

Raab felt as if his insides were slowly sliding off a cliff. He was finished. No point in keeping up his defense. He had to do what had to be done now. He couldn't stop the ball from rolling. From rolling over him. Twenty years of his life ripped away . . .

He looked forlornly at Mel.

"You have to take care of your family, Ben," the lawyer advised, grasping his arm.

Raab closed his eyes and let out a painful breath. "I can give you Concerga," he said to Booth when they opened again. "Trujillo, too. But I need you to protect my family."

Booth nodded, glancing toward Ruiz and the U.S. Attorney with a triumphant stare.

"In return for your testimony," Nardozzi said, "we can arrange for you to receive protective custody and move you and your family to a secure place. We can work it out so you'll get to keep a percentage of your assets, so you can live in a manner not dissimilar to how you live now. You'll serve about ten months someplace—until the trial. After that, you and your family will just disappear."

"Disappear?" Raab gaped at him. "You mean like the Witness Protection Program? That's for mobsters, criminals . . ."

"The WITSEC Program has all kinds of people in it," Booth corrected him. "The one thing they've got in common is a fear of reprisal as a result of their testimony. You'll be safe there. And, more important, so will your family. It's never been penetrated if you live by the rules. You can even pick an area of the country you want to live in."

"It's your only bet, Mr. Raab," Ruiz urged. "Your life's not worth a dime, on the street or in jail, whether you challenge these indictments or not. You dug this hole for yourself the day you took up with these people. Since then you've just been transferring the dirt."

How are we going to deal with this? Raab thought, the agent's words hitting him like hollow-point slugs. Sharon and the kids? Their life—everything they knew, counted on, gone! What could he possibly say to make them understand?

"When?" Raab nodded, defeated, eyes glazed. "When does all this begin?"

Nardozzi drew out some papers and slid them across the table in front of Raab. An official-looking sheet headed "U.S. Department of Justice. Form 5-K. Cooperating Witness Agreement." He flicked the cap of a ballpoint pen.

"*Today*, Mr. Raab. As soon as you sign."

CHAPTER THIRTEEN

Everyone was gathered at the house. Kate and Sharon were trimming some hydrangeas in the kitchen, trying to keep their nerves at bay, when a dark blue sedan accompanied by a black Jeep turned into the drive.

Ben had called an hour earlier. He told them he had something very important to discuss. He wouldn't say how the meeting with the FBI had gone. No one had left the house all day. The kids hadn't gone to school. Cops and FBI agents had been all around their house constantly.

A man and a woman dressed in suits stepped out of the sedan, then Raab. The Jeep pulled around in the circle and blocked the head of the drive.

"I don't have a good feeling about this." Sharon put down her shears.

Kate nodded back, holding her breath. This time neither did she.

Her father stepped into the house and took off his coat, ashen. He gave Kate a halfhearted wink, then Sharon a stiff hug.

"Who are those people, Ben?"

He merely shrugged. "We've got some things to talk over as a family, Sharon."

They sat around the dining room table, which didn't exactly make anyone feel relaxed, because they never sat in the dining room. Ben asked for a glass of water. He could barely look any of them in the eyes. A day before, they'd been thinking about Em's SATs and planning their winter trip. Kate had never felt such tension in the house.

Sharon looked at him, uneasily. "Ben, I think you're scaring everyone a bit."

He nodded. "There was something I didn't quite go into last night," he said. "There was someone else who came to me at the office, who I introduced to Harold as well. Someone who was looking for the same arrangement as the guy I told you about, from Paz. Convert some cash into gold. Get it out of the country . . ."

Sharon shook her head. "Who?"

He shrugged. "I don't know. It doesn't matter anyway. Maybe he proposed a few things I shouldn't have agreed to." He took a sip of water. "Maybe they got some things I said on tape."

"On *tape* . . . ?" Sharon's eyes widened. "What kinds of things are you talking about, Ben?"

"I don't know . . ." He stared ahead blankly, still avoiding everybody's gaze. "Nothing very specific. But just enough that, combined with the payments I received, it really complicates things. It makes it all look pretty bad."

"*Bad* . . . ?" Sharon was growing alarmed. Kate, too. They'd been shot at the night before! Just the fact that the conversations had been recorded was insane.

"*What are you saying, Ben?*"

He cleared his throat. "This other guy . . ." He finally looked up, pallid. "He was FBI, Sharon."

It was like a dead weight had crashed into the center of the room. At first no one spoke, only looked in horror.

"*Oh my God, Ben, what have you done?*"

He started to unravel it in front of them, in a low, cracking monotone. How all the money in the past few years—the money that paid for the house, their trips, the cars—was all dirty. Drug money. How he knew it but just kept doing it. Getting deeper. He couldn't pull out. Now they had him. They had his voice on tape offering the same arrangements to an undercover agent.

They had the monies he'd received, the fact that he'd set up the connection.

Kate couldn't believe what she was hearing. Her father was going to jail.

"We can fight this, can't we?" her mother said. "I mean, Mel's a good lawyer. My friend Maryanne, at the club, she knows someone who's defended people for securities fraud. Those Logotech people. He got them a deal."

"No, we can't fight this, Sharon." Ben shook his head. "This isn't securities fraud. They have me dead to rights. I had to cut a deal. I may have to go to jail for a while."

"Jail!"

He nodded. "Then I'll have to testify. But that's not even it. It's deeper than that. A lot deeper."

"Deeper?" Sharon stood up. She still had her apron on. "What could be deeper than that, Ben? We were almost killed! My husband just told me he's going to jail! *Deeper* . . . ? You plead. You pay a fine. You give back whatever you took unfairly. What the hell do these people want from you, Ben—*your life* . . . ?"

Raab jumped up. "You're not seeing it, Sharon." He went over to the window. "This isn't a bad stock trade. These are Colombians, Sharon! I can hurt them. You saw what they did last night. These are bad people. Killers!

They're never going to let me go to trial."

He threw back the curtains. Two agents were leaning on the Jeep at the head of the driveway. A police car blocked the entrance up by the pillars. "These people, Sharon ... they're not here to drive me home. They're federal agents. They're here to protect us. That's exactly what these bastards want from me." His eyes filled with tears and his voice rose to a harried pitch.

"They want my life!"

CHAPTER FOURTEEN

Sharon sank back into her chair, her glassy gaze remote and uncomprehending. A heavy silence settled over the room.

Kate stared at her dad. He looked different to her suddenly. She saw it now. There was no hiding it anymore. *He knew.* Every night when he walked through the door. Every wonderful trip they took together. Even when he held her last night, and promised her he would never go to jail . . .

He was lying.

He knew.

"What are you saying, Dad?" Justin gaped. "These people want to kill you?"

"You saw it, Just! You saw it last night. I can unravel part of their organization. I can expose them in a trial. These are dangerous people, son." He sat back down. "The FBI . . . they don't think we can go back to a regular life."

"*We . . . ?*" Emily leaped up, straining to understand. "You mean all of us? We're *all* in danger?"

"You saw what happened last night, honey. I don't see how any of us can take that chance."

"So by 'a regular life,' you're saying *what*, Dad? That these guards'll be with us when we go to school for a while? Or into town? That we're basically, like, going to be prisoners . . . ?"

"No, that's not what I mean." Raab sat, shaking his head. "I'm afraid it's a whole lot more than that, Em."

There was a pause, as if an earthquake had shaken the roof and they were sitting there watching it about to collapse. Except it wasn't the roof but their lives that were suddenly imploding. Everyone stared at him, trying to figure out just what that meant.

"We're going to have to move away, Ben," Sharon uttered somberly. "Aren't we?"

It wasn't even a question. A glaze of tears filled her eyes. "We're going to have to hide, like criminals. Those people out there, that's what they're here for, isn't it, Ben? They're going to take us from our home."

Kate's father pressed his lips flat and nodded. "I think so, Shar."

Tears ran down her face freely now.

"Take us *where*, Dad?" Emily shouted in frustration. "You mean like somewhere else around here? Another school, nearby?" This was her life that was suddenly being ripped from under her. School, friends. Her squash. Everything she knew.

"I don't think so, Em. And I'm afraid you won't be able to let anyone know where you are."

"Move away!" She turned to her mother, then Kate, waiting for someone to say this was all some kind of joke. "When?"

"Soon." Her father shrugged. "Tomorrow, the day after . . ."

"This is fucking crazy!" Emily screamed. "Oh, my God!"

It was as though he'd come home and told them that all the people they knew, all the things they did, had been wiped out in some terrible accident. Except it was more like they were the ones wiped out. Everyone they knew. Their history. Their life up to this point would be blank, dead.

Left behind.

"I'm not going anywhere!" Emily shouted. "I'm staying. *You* go. *You're* the one who did this to us. *What the hell have you done, Daddy . . . ?*"

She tore out of the dining room, footsteps

pounding on the stairs. The door to her room slammed.

"She's right." Kate stared at her father. "What *have* you done, Daddy?"

It was one thing to see him like this. Not the strong, respected person she always thought he was but someone who was weak, beaten. She could deal with that. People cheat on their wife or lose their bearings, steal from their company. Some even go to jail.

But this . . . That he had put them all at risk. Made them all targets. All the people he supposedly loved. Kate couldn't believe it. Her family was being torn apart in front of her eyes.

"What about Ruthie, Ben?" Sharon looked at him glassily. Her mother. "We can't just leave her. She's not well."

Raab just shrugged helplessly. "I'm sorry, Shar . . ."

"I don't understand," Justin said. "Why can't we just live here? Why can't they just protect us? This is our house."

"Our house . . ." His father blew out a breath. "It won't belong to us anymore. The government's going to take it. I may have to go to prison until the trial. They think they can get my sentence commuted to time served. Then, afterward, I'll join you—"

"Join us . . . ?" Kate's mother gasped. Her eyes stretched wide, and there was a trembling, unforgiving look in them. "Join us *exactly where*, Ben?"

He shook his head. His face was blank. "I don't know, Shar."

CHAPTER FIFTEEN

Upstairs, Emily was freaking out. Kate tried her best to calm her. Her sister was lying spread-eagled on her bed, punching the mattress in tears.

She had her tournaments, her coach, her eastern ranking. This was the season all her friends were having their sweet sixteens. She was taking the SATs next Saturday.

"This is our home, Kate. How can we just uproot our lives and leave?"

"I know, Em . . ."

Kate lay next to her and gave her sister a hug, like when they were kids and shared their favorite music. Em had her ceiling painted sky blue, with a canopy of Day-Glo stars that illuminated when you turned off the lights.

Kate looked up at them. "You remember when we were at the old house and gold was in the dumps? We didn't go anywhere that year, and Dad was having a hard time. I was at the high school but you were at Tamblin. He kept you there, Em. Even when it was hard for him. He did it so you could keep playing squash."

"That doesn't make it okay, Kate." Emily glared, wiping away tears. "What he's done. You're gone. You're out of here. What are *we* supposed to say to people? My daddy's a drug dealer. He's in jail. We have to take off now for a few years. See you in college. *This is our life, Kate* . . ."

"And it doesn't erase it, Em . . . I know. It just . . ."

Em sat up and stared at her. "It just *what*, Kate?"

"You're right." Kate squeezed her hand. "It doesn't make it okay."

Justin was at his desk at the computer, leaning back with his feet up, like someone in a trance, playing a video game. Kate asked how he was doing. He just looked blankly at her and muttered back, in his usual way, "I'm okay."

She went down to her old room at the far end of the hallway.

They pretty much kept it just as it had been when she lived there. Sometimes she still slept over on weekends or holidays. Kate stared up at the red bookshelves which still had a lot of her old textbooks and folders. The walls were plastered with her old posters. Bono of U-2. Brandi Chastain—the famous soccer shot of her on her knees when the U.S. team won the Olympic gold. Kate was always into Brandi more than Mia Hamm. Leonardo DiCaprio and Jeremy Bloom, the mogul snowboarder. It always felt warm coming back here.

But not tonight. Em was right. *It didn't make it okay*.

Kate rolled onto her bed and took out her cell. She hit the speed dial and checked the time. She needed someone now. Thank God, he picked up.

"Greg?"

They had met at Beth Shalom, her family's Sephardic temple in the city. He just walked right up to her, at the kiddush after Rosh Hashanah services. She'd noticed him across the sanctuary.

Greg was great. He was a sort of Wandering Jew himself, from Mexico City. He didn't have family here. He'd been in his last year of medical school at Columbia when they met. Now he was a second-year resident in children's orthopedics. He was tall, thin, lanky, and he reminded her a bit of Ashton Kutcher with his mop of thick, brown hair. They'd basically been living together for the past year in her Lower East Side apartment. Now that they were getting serious, the big question was where he would end up in practice. What would happen to them if he had to leave New York?

"*Kate!* God, I've been really worried. You've been leaving these cryptic messages. Is everything all right up there?"

"No," Kate said. She held back the tears. "Everything's not all right, Greg."

"Is it Ben? Tell me what's happened? Is he okay? Is there anything I can do?"

"No, it's not medical, Greg. I can't go into it. I'll tell you soon, I promise. There's just something I need to know."

"What, pooch?" That was what he called her. His pet. He seemed very worried about her. She could hear it in his voice.

Kate sniffed back the tears and asked, "Do you love me, Greg?"

There was a pause. She knew she'd surprised him. Like some stupid kid. "I know we say it all the time. But now it's important to me. I just need to hear it, Greg . . ."

"Of course I love you, Kate. You know that."

"I know," Kate said. "I don't mean just that way . . . What I mean is, I can trust you, Greg, can't I? I mean, with everything? With *me* . . . ?"

"Kate, are you all right?"

"Yeah, I'm all right. I just need to hear you say it, Greg. I know it sounds weird."

This time he didn't hesitate. "You can trust me, Kate. I promise you, you can. Just tell me what the hell's going on up there. Let me come up. Maybe I can help."

"Thanks, but you can't. I just needed to hear that, Greg. Everything's okay now."

She had made up her mind.

"I love you, too."

CHAPTER SIXTEEN

Kate found him on the back porch, sitting in an Adirondack chair in the chilly late-September air, overlooking the Sound.

She already felt that something was different about him. His fingers were locked in front of his face, and he was staring out onto the water, a glass of bourbon on the chair arm beside him.

He didn't even turn.

Kate sat on the swinging bench across from him. Finally he looked at her, a brooding darkness in his eyes.

"Who are you, Daddy?"

"Kate . . ." He turned and reached for her hand.

"No, I need to hear it from you, Daddy. Because all of a sudden, I don't know. All of a sudden, I'm trying to figure out which part of you—which part of all *this*—isn't some kind of crazy lie. All that preaching about what made us strong, our family . . . *How could you, Dad?*"

"I'm your father, Kate," he said, hunching deeper in the chair. "That's not a lie."

"No." She shook her head. "My father was this honest, stand-up man. He taught us how to be strong and make a difference. He didn't look in my eye and tell me to trust him one day and then the next say that everything about his life is a lie. *You knew, Daddy.* You knew what you were doing all along. You knew every goddamn day you came home to us. Every day of our lives . . ."

He nodded. "What isn't a lie is that I love you, pumpkin."

"Don't call me that!" Kate said. "You don't get to call me that ever again. That's gone. That's the price you pay for this. Look around you, Dad—look at the hurt you've caused."

Her father flinched. He suddenly looked small to Kate, weakened.

"You can't just build this wall down the center of your life and say, 'On this side I'm a good person—a good father—but on the other side I'm a liar and a thief.' I know you're sorry, Dad. I'm sure this hurts. I wish I could stand behind you, but I don't know if I'll ever be able to look at you quite the same way."

"I'm afraid you're going to have to, Kate. We're all going to need one another more than ever now, to get through this."

"Well, that's the thing." Kate shook her head. "I won't be going with you, Daddy. I'm staying here."

He turned—his pupils fixed and widening. Alarmed. "You have to, Kate. You could be in danger. I know how angry you are. But if I testify, anyone who might possibly lead back to me—"

"No," she stopped him, *"I don't.* I don't have to, Daddy. I'm over twenty-one. I have my life here. My work. Greg. Maybe Em and Justin, you can drag them along, and somehow I hope to God you can repair the hurt you've caused. But I won't be going. Don't you see, you've ruined lives, Daddy. And not just your own. People you love. You've robbed them of someone they loved and looked up to. I'm sorry, Dad, I won't let you ruin mine, too."

He stared at her, stunned at what he was hearing. Then he looked down. "If you don't," he said, "you know it might be a very long time before you can see any of us again."

"I know," Kate said. "And it's breaking my heart, Daddy. About as much as it's breaking my heart to look at you now."

He sucked in a breath and reached out a hand toward her, as if looking for some kind of forgiveness.

"All I did was buy the gold," he said. "I've never even seen a bag of cocaine."

"No, you don't get to think that, Dad," Kate said angrily. She took his hand, but his fingers had changed from the ones that she felt yesterday—now foreign and unfamiliar and cold.

"Look around you, Dad. This was our family. You've done a whole lot more than that."

CHAPTER SEVENTEEN

The following afternoon two people from the U.S. Marshals Service showed up at the house.

One was a tall, heavyset man with salt-and-pepper hair, named Phil Cavetti. The other, a pleasant, attractive woman of about forty named Margaret Seymour, whom they all immediately liked, said she'd be their case handler. She told them to call her "Maggie."

They were from WITSEC. The Witness Protection Program.

At first Kate assumed they were merely there to explain the program to everybody. What lay ahead. But after talking to them for a few minutes, it became clear what was actually going on.

They were here to take her family into custody today.

They told everyone to pack a single suitcase.

The rest, they said, including the furniture and personal belongings, would come along in a few weeks. *Come along where?*

Justin stuffed his iPod and his Sony PlayStation into a knapsack. Em mechanically collected her squash racquets and goggles, a poster of Third Eye Blind, and some snapshots of her closest friends.

Sharon was a wreck. She couldn't believe the parts of her life she couldn't take, that she was having to leave behind. Her mother. Her family albums. Her wedding china. All her precious things.

Their lives.

Kate tried her best to help. "Take these," Sharon said, pressing folders filled with old photos into Kate's hands. "They're of my mother and father, and their families . . ." Sharon picked up a small vase that contained the ashes of their old schnauzer, Fritz. She looked at Kate, her composure starting to fracture. *How can I just leave these behind?*

When their bags were packed, everyone came down to the living room. Ben was in a blazer and an open plaid shirt, not saying much to anyone. Sharon was dressed in jeans and a blazer, her hair pulled back. Like she was headed on a trip or something. They all sat down silently.

Phil Cavetti started to lay out what would take place.

"Your husband will be delivered to the U.S. Attorney later today," he said to Sharon. "He'll begin serving a prison sentence in a secure location until the trial. That could be eight, ten months. Under his agreement, he will have to be a witness at additional trials as they come up.

"The rest of you will be in protective custody until a final location is determined. Under no circumstance can you divulge to anyone where that location is." He looked at Em and Justin. "That means not even an e-mail to your best friend. Or a text message. This is only for your own protection—do you understand?"

They nodded tentatively. "Not even to Kate?" Em looked over at her sister.

"Not even to Kate, I'm afraid." Phil Cavetti shook his head. "Once you're settled, we can arrange a few calls and you'll be able to e-mail through a WITSEC clearing site. A couple of times a year, we can arrange visits with family at a neutral location under our supervision."

"A couple of times a year," Sharon gasped, taking hold of Kate's hand.

"That's it. You'll be given new identities. New drivers' licenses, Social Security numbers. As far as anyone will be concerned, all this did not exist. You understand that this is only for your own protection? Your father is doing something that will make him very unpopular with the people he's testifying against. And you've already seen firsthand what these people will do. Agent Seymour and I have handled several similar cases. Even people within the Mercado family itself. If you follow the rules, you'll be okay. We've never had a case that was detected yet."

"I know how scary this must all seem," Margaret Seymour said. She had a little mole on the right side of her mouth and a hint of a Southern drawl. "But it won't be so bad, when you find a home. I've handled many relocations like yours. Families in similar situations. I'm sort of a cock-eyed specialist in the Mercados, you might even say. You'll have more than most families do. Enough money to live comfortably. Maybe not in the exact lifestyle you've been used to, but we'll do our best to pick a comfortable place." She smiled at Emily, who was clearly having a hard time. "You ever been to California, hon? Or the Northwest coast?"

"I play squash, Agent Seymour." Em shrugged. "I have a ranking."

"Maggie, they call me. And I promise you'll continue to do that, hon. We'll work all that out. You'll go to school, college. Just like you would've here. People adapt. You'll learn to make the best of it. Most important, you'll be together. Of course"—she glanced at Kate—"it'd be best if *all* of you went along."

"No, it's been decided, I'm staying," Kate said, tightening the grip on her mother's hand.

"Then you have to keep a very low profile," Phil Cavetti insisted. "It would be helpful if you changed addresses. Made sure the phone and electric bills are not in your name."

Kate nodded.

"We'll go over how you handle things after your parents leave."

"Will we ever be able to come back?" Em asked hesitantly.

"No one ever says *never*"—Margaret Seymour smiled—"but most families end up growing comfortable in their new places. Plant roots. The Mercados have a long memory, I'm afraid. I think it's best you look at this as a new phase in your life. This will be who you are now. You'll get used to it. I swear on a stack of squash racquets . . . Anything else?"

"So this is it." Sharon drew in a breath. Her eyes darted around, on the edge of tears. "Our house. Our friends. Our life. Everything we built."

"No." Kate shook her head. She took her mother's hand and pressed it firmly against her own heart. "*This* is everything, Mom. *This* is what you built. Don't ever forget that. Our name is Raab, Mom. Kate and Justin and Emily Raab. No one can ever take that away."

"Oh, honey, I'm gonna miss you so very, very much." Her mother gave Kate a deep, long hug. Kate felt tears, Sharon's tears, on her shoulder. Emily came up. They both embraced her.

"I'm a little scared," Em announced. Tough as nails on the squash court, but now just a sixteen-year-old girl about to be separated from everything familiar in her life.

"I'm scared, too, babe," answered Kate, tightening her arms around her sister. "You have to be strong," she whispered in her ear. "*You're the fighter now.*"

"So it's all agreed, then," her father interjected. He had barely said a word through the whole proceeding. Phil Cavetti nodded to a young WITSEC agent by the door. He came over and respectfully took Raab by the arm.

"Okay." Sharon wiped her eyes, taking a last, long look around. "I don't want to say any more. It's just a place. There'll be others. Let's just go."

Kate suddenly realized she was saying good-bye to her family as she knew it for the last time. This wasn't a trip. They weren't coming back. She walked to the door with her arms wrapped around Em and Justin. She looked at them, her heart beating anxiously. "I don't know what to say."

"What is there to say?" Her mother smiled and wiped the tears from Kate's cheek. "I have something for you, darling." She took out a small brown jewelry box from her blazer and pressed it into Kate's hand.

Kate opened the lid. There was a delicate gold chain inside with a pendant on it. It was a half sun made of hammered gold with a diamond set in. The edges were jagged, as if someone had split it in two. It seemed Aztec—or Incan, maybe.

"It holds secrets, Kate." Sharon smiled and placed it around Kate's neck. "There's a story behind it. One day I'll tell it to you. One day you'll fit the pieces together, okay?"

Kate nodded, fighting back tears.

Then suddenly she turned and faced her dad.

"I transferred some money into your account," he said stiffly. "Mel will handle it. It ought to hold you for a while."

"I'll be okay." Kate nodded. She wasn't sure quite what to feel.

"I know you'll be okay, Kate." Then he pulled her into his arms. He squeezed her, and Kate didn't fight it. She didn't want to. Her head came to rest against his shoulder. "You're still my daughter," he told her. "No matter what you may feel. That doesn't change."

"I know, Daddy." Kate sniffed, and hugged him back.

They pulled apart. Kate's cheeks were wet with tears. She looked into his hooded brown eyes one last time.

"You be good, pumpkin. Watch your blood levels. I know you're twenty-three. But, hey, if I'm not here to remind you, who will?"

Kate nodded and smiled. "You be good, too, Daddy."

A federal agent took him by the arm. They led him outside toward a black Jeep with a light on the top. He kissed Sharon. He hugged Justin and Em. Then he and the agent climbed into the car. A misty drizzle started to fall.

Suddenly the pressure in Kate felt like it was about to burst. "I could still come." She turned to her mother. "Just until Dad gets out . . ."

"No." Margaret Seymour shook her head. "There's no halfway here, Kate. You come, you come for good. You don't get to leave."

Sharon took hold of her daughter and smiled, ever so slightly. "Live your life, Kate. That's what I want for you. *Please* . . ."

Kate haltingly nodded back. Then it all started to fall apart, the composure she'd struggled to hold on to.

The agents took them out to a U.S. Marshals Explorer that had quietly appeared. Their bags were already in the back. They got in. Kate ran up and placed her palm on the wet window. *"I love you all . . ."*

"I love you, too," her mother mouthed, spreading her hand over Kate's on the opposite side of the glass.

The Explorer started to pull away. Kate watched, frozen, the tears flowing freely now. It was taking everything she had not to lunge and rip the door open and throw herself inside. She couldn't help the thought that maybe she was seeing them all for the last time.

"We'll see each other soon!" she called after them.

Everybody spun around through the darkened glass and waved. The Explorer came to a stop at the end of the driveway. Then it turned at the stone pillars. The brake lights flashed— and they were gone.

Kate stood there with her hand raised in the deepening rain.

Then two agents climbed into the front seats of the Jeep. The engine started up. Kate could see her father's face through the gray-tinted glass. Suddenly a stab of panic sliced through her ribs.

The government vehicle began to pull away.

Kate took a few steps after it. *"Dad!"*

Her heart was pounding now. She couldn't let him leave like this. Whatever he'd done. She wanted him to know. He needed to know. She did love him. *She did.* She started running after the vehicle.

"Daddy, stop, please . . . !"

The Jeep came to a halt near the end of the driveway. Kate took one or two more steps. The rear window slowly rolled down.

She saw his face. They looked at each other, the rain intensifying. He winked. There was a sadness on his face—a wordless resignation. She felt like there was something she had to say.

Then the vehicle started to move again.

Kate did the one thing she could think of, as the window began to roll up and only his eyes were visible. The one thing she knew he would understand as the vehicle pulled away.

She gave him a one-fingered wave.

CHAPTER EIGHTEEN

Greg pulled his car up in front of the stone pillars on Beach Shore Road. An unmarked car from the U.S. Marshals office sat blocking the driveway. It was three days since Kate's family had been taken into protective custody.

A young agent stepped out of the car and checked their IDs, looking at Kate closely. Then, with a friendly nod, he waved them through.

Kate stared at the quiet, closed-up house as they approached down the long, pebbled drive. "This is totally weird, Greg," she said. "This is my home."

"I know." Greg nodded, reaching across the seat and squeezing her hand.

Kate had no idea where her family was. Only that they were safe and okay and thinking of her very much, Margaret Seymour had told her.

The five-car garage was empty now. Her

father's Ferrari had already been impounded. So had the Chagall, the Dali prints, and the contents of the wine cellar, she was told. Her mother's Range Rover was parked outside in the turnabout. It would find its way to them soon.

That was all that was left.

There was a notice taped to the door. The house had been impounded. Just walking through the doors, into the two-story vestibule, elicited the eeriest, loneliest sensation Kate had ever felt.

Their things were boxed and left in the front hall. Ready to go to some unknown destination.

Their possessions were there—but her family was gone.

Kate flashed back to how the place had looked the day they first moved in. "It's so big," her mother had said, gasping. "We'll fill it," her dad had said, smiling. Justin found a room with a loft on the third floor and put his dibs on it. They all went out back and peered at the water. "It's like a castle, Dad," Em had said, amazed. "It's really ours?"

Now it was just filled with this stark, brooding emptiness. As though everyone had died.

"You okay?" Greg squeezed her hand again as they stood in the vestibule.

"Yeah, I'm all right," Kate lied.

She went up to the second floor while Greg checked around downstairs. She remembered the sounds of the place. Footsteps pounding up the stairs. Emily shrieking about her hair. Dad watching CNN in the den on the big screen. The scents of Mom's flowers.

Kate looked into Emily's room. Photos were still taped to the walls. Arcade snapshots with her school friends. Her squash team from the Junior Maccabean games. They'd had to rush out so quickly. These were important.

How were these left behind?

One by one, Kate started to untape them. Then she sat down on the bed and looked up at the blue, starry ceiling.

She realized she was going to miss seeing her little sister grow up. She wasn't going to see her go to her prom. Or watch her graduate. Or see her kick ass playing number one for her school. They wouldn't even have the same last name anymore.

The tears rolled down Kate's cheeks, angry and unexplainable. Greg came bounding up the stairs. "Hey, where are you? Look at this!" he called.

He came into Em's room holding large masks of Bill Clinton and Monica Lewinsky, from some Halloween party her parents had gone to the year before. He saw Kate's face and stopped.

"Jeez, Kate." He sat down next to her and took her in his arms.

"I can't help it!" she said. "I'm just so goddamn fucking mad. He had no right to do this to us. He stole our family, Greg."

"I know . . . I know . . ." he said. "Maybe this wasn't such a good idea. You want to go?"

Kate shook her head. "We're here. Damn it. Let's do this."

She picked up Emily's pictures and before they went downstairs opened the door to her parents' bedroom. There were tons of boxes in there. Clothes, perfumes, pictures. All packed. Ready to go.

A dresser drawer was open, and Kate noticed something inside. A leather folder crammed with old stuff she'd never seen before. It must have been her father's. It was filled with old pictures and documents. Early photos of him and Sharon, when he was at NYU and she was a freshman at Cornell. Some gemological certificates. A photo of his mother, Rosa. Letters . . . *How could he just leave them behind?*

She bundled the folder up and tossed in Em's pictures. These were all Kate had.

They went downstairs and stood in the high-ceilinged vestibule one last time.

"You ready?" Greg asked eventually. Kate nodded.

"You want to take these?" He grinned, holding out the Bill and Monica masks.

"Nah, my father hated Clinton. That was just his dumb idea of a joke."

He tossed them in a trash bucket by the door. Kate turned around one last time.

"I don't know what to feel," she said. "I'm going to walk out this door and leave my entire past." A wave of sadness came over her. "I don't have a family anymore."

"Yes you do," Greg said, and pulled her toward him. "You have *me*. Let's get married, Kate."

"Right." She sniffed. "You know how to hit a girl when she's down. Screw the big wedding, right?"

"No, I'm serious," he said. "We love each other. In eighteen months I'll be practicing. I don't care if it's just you and me. Let's do this, Kate—get married!"

She stared at him, struck silent, with glistening eyes.

"I'm your family now."

PART TWO

CHAPTER NINETEEN

FOURTEEN MONTHS LATER . . .

"Hey, Fergus . . . c'mon, boy, let's go!"

It was a crisp autumn morning as Kate jogged through the entrance of Tompkins Square Park with Fergus, the six-month-old Labradoodle she and Greg had adopted. He was chasing a squirrel on his run-leash a short distance behind.

The terrible events of the past year seemed a long way away.

She was Kate Herrera now. She and Greg had gotten married eight months earlier at City Hall. They lived in a loft on the seventh floor of a converted warehouse building over on Seventh Street, just a few blocks away. Greg was finishing his last year of residency now.

Kate ran with Fergus pretty much every morning before she headed to work. And she also rowed early on two other mornings, Wednesdays and Saturdays, up at the Peter Jay Sharp Boathouse on the Harlem River. She was still working at the lab. In another year she'd have her master's. After that, she didn't know. Greg had applications out. It all came down to the question of where he would end up practicing. In the past year, they'd had to pull away from a lot of their old friends.

Kate still had no idea where her family was. Somewhere out west . . . that was all she knew. She got e-mails and letters every couple of weeks, the occasional phone call routed through a neutral WITSEC site. Em was playing squash again and starting to think about college. And Justin was having trouble adjusting to a new school, new friends. But it was her mom she was worried about. Hiding out in this new place, not exactly making friends, was taking its toll. Since he'd been released, Kate had heard that things had gotten pretty tense between Mom and Dad.

Kate had seen her father only once. Just before the trial. The WITSEC people had arranged it—secretly. They didn't want her to be seen attending the proceedings. Only a few weeks before, one of the key government witnesses, a bookkeeper from Argot—a forty-year-old woman with two kids—had been shot dead, right on Sixth Avenue.

At rush hour. It had made all the papers and news broadcasts and stirred up a whole new round of fear. That's why they'd gotten the dog, they joked. But of course it wasn't funny. It was scary as shit.

And anyway, all Fergus would ever do was lick you to death if anyone ever tried anything.

"C'mon, buddy!" Kate pulled Fergus over to a bench. A street mime was performing on the path, going through his routine. Something was always going on here.

In the end, Concerga, the Colombian guy from Paz, the one everybody wanted, had fled the country before trial. The other, Trujillo, was released, because with the key witness gone, the government could not make its case. Harold Kornreich was convicted. Dad's friend. That's why her family has been ripped apart. Her father put in jail. Dad's golfing buddy . . . he was in a federal prison now, serving twenty years.

Kate glanced at the time. It was already after eight. She had to be at the lab by nine-thirty. She had to get going. She watched the performer a minute more, breaking off a piece of a PowerBar to boost her sugar level. Fergus seemed amused as well.

"He is good, yes?"

The voice came from the bench across from them, startling Kate. A man with a trim, graying beard, in a rumpled corduroy jacket and a flat golfing hat. A newspaper sat on his lap. Kate had seen him in the park a few times before.

"I am not sure I know this breed." He smiled and gestured toward Fergus. When he leaned forward and motioned the dog over, Fergus, who didn't have a wary bone in his body, happily obliged.

"It's called a Labradoodle," Kate answered. "It's a cross between a golden Lab and a poodle."

The man cupped Fergus's face. "All these new things . . . Something else to be hopelessly out of touch with. I thought it was merely the Internet." He smiled.

Kate smiled, too. She thought she detected some kind of accent. Anyway, Fergus seemed to be enjoying the attention.

"I've seen you here from time to time," he said. "My name is Barretto. Chaim, now that we're old friends."

"I'm Kate," Kate replied. The WITSEC people had warned her to always be cautious and never reveal her last name. But this guy . . . She felt a little foolish keeping her distance. He was harmless. "I think you already know Fergus."

"A pleasure to meet you, Kate." The man bowed politely. He took Fergus's paw. "And you, too, my friend."

They went back to watching the mime for a moment, and then he said something to her that caught her completely off guard.

"You're a diabetic, Miss Kate, are you not?"

Kate looked at him. She felt herself grab hold of Fergus's leash a bit more tightly. A tingle of nerves coursed down her spine.

"Please, don't be alarmed." The man tried to smile. "I didn't mean to be forward. It's just that I've seen you from time to time and noticed you checking yourself after you run. Occasionally you'll take out a piece of something sweet. I didn't mean to frighten you. My wife, she was diabetic, that's all."

Kate relaxed and felt a little ashamed. It riled her that she had to react this way, so guarded toward people she didn't know. The guy was just reaching out, that's all. And just this once, it actually felt nice to open up to someone.

"How is she," Kate asked, "your wife?"

"Thank you," the man said fondly, "but she's been gone a long time."

"I'm sorry," Kate said, meeting his twinkling eyes.

The street performer finished. Everyone gave him a polite round of applause. Kate stood up and checked her watch. "I'm afraid I've got to get going, Mr. Barretto. Maybe I'll bump into you again."

"I hope so." The old man doffed his cap. Then, for the second time, he said something that made her insides clutch.

"And *buenos días* to you, too, Fergus."

Kate did her best to smile, starting to back away, her heart quickening. Cavetti's voice was never far from her thoughts: *"If something ever seems suspicious, Kate, just get out of there . . ."*

She reined in Fergus's leash. "Come on, big guy, we've got to get home."

Kate headed toward the entrance to the park, telling herself not to look back. But as she approached the Avenue C gate, she glanced around.

The man had put his glasses on and gone back to reading his newspaper.

You can't go through life being nervous of everyone, she admonished herself. *He's older than your father, Kate!*

CHAPTER TWENTY

The incident in the park stayed with Kate a couple of days. It made her feel embarrassed, even a little angry. She never mentioned it to Greg.

But two days later it was the bolt to their apartment door that started to get her scared.

She was rushing home after work with her arms full of groceries. She heard the phone ringing and Fergus barking inside. Greg was at the hospital. Kate jammed her key into the lock and twisted, balancing the groceries on her knee.

The door wouldn't open. The dead bolt was shut.

Kate felt a flash of alarm ripple through her.

The dead bolt was never shut.

They never locked it.

It was one of those heavy steel contraptions, like they used on warehouse doors. It was always such a headache to open. And it kept getting stuck. The trial was long over. The place was alarmed. The lease and the phone were both in Greg's name.

Kate fumbled for the dead-bolt key, warily pushing open the door.

Something wasn't right . . .

Kate knew it as soon as she stepped in.

"Greg . . . ?" she called. But she knew that Greg wasn't there. Fergus wagged his way up to her. Kate scanned around. Everything seemed in place. The apartment had high ceilings and tall, arched windows looking east over Avenue C. The mess was still there—magazines, pillows, a water bottle, the TV remote on the couch—just as she'd left it this morning.

It was weird, and a little creepy. She knew it didn't make sense. She petted Fergus. Everything seemed the same.

She just couldn't put away the feeling that someone had been inside.

Then, the very next day, she and Tina were having coffee in the research unit's cafeteria.

They'd been working together for a year now, and they had pretty much become best friends. Sisters. In fact, since Tina had dyed her hair lighter, people thought they were even starting to look a little alike.

Tina was telling Kate about this new project Packer had given her. "Injecting this isotrophic solution into the nucleic material. It basically disperses the surface fluid and . . ."

Suddenly Kate felt her attention drawn to something across the room.

This guy, at the far end of the cafeteria, at a table by himself. He had short, wiry hair, sideburns, a dark mustache. Hispanic features. Kate had the sensation she'd seen him somewhere before. She just couldn't place where . . . Every once in a while now, she noticed his gaze through the crowd glancing toward her.

She tried to stay with Tina, but she kept glancing up at the guy, who once or twice met her eyes. It made her uneasy. But she had to admit she'd been feeling uneasy a lot lately . . . since that female witness was killed on Sixth Avenue.

When she looked back again, the guy was gone.

"Earth to Kate. Hello . . ." Tina snapped her fingers. "I know this is boring. But are you still with me?"

"Sorry," Kate said. "Isotrophic solution . . ." She looked around.

Then she saw the man again.

This time he had gotten up. He was threading

his way through the tables. *Toward her.* He had on a dark raincoat, which fell open, as if he was going for something. Kate felt a stab of alarm.

"Kate." Tina waved a hand in front of her face. "What's going on?"

This is crazy, she told herself. But her heart wasn't listening. It was bouncing off her ribs. *It's a crowded place. Nothing can happen here. He was coming right up to her.*

She felt the blood drain from her face. "Tina . . ."

It was a pager he was going for. The Latino man came directly up to her, stopped in front of her table. She almost jumped out of her chair.

"You work for Packer, don't you?"

"What?"

"It's Kate, isn't it?" The Latino guy broke into a smile. "I was up in your office about a month ago. I work for Thermagen. You remember? I sell you the Dioxitribe."

"Yeah." Kate smiled, relieved. "It's Kate . . ."

This was getting out of hand.

Later Kate was in the cramped computer room they called the library, copying over the results notes onto a CD. There was a knock. She turned around and saw Tina at the door. Looking puzzled and a bit concerned.

"You want to tell me what was going on back there?"

"You mean downstairs?" Kate shrugged guiltily.

"No. Italy. Junior year. Yes, of course downstairs. What's going on, Kate? Some random guy comes up to you and you pretty much lose it—right in the cafeteria. You've been a little off all week. Lymphoblastic—the other day you filed it under cyclosporic. Is everything okay?"

"I'm not sure." Kate wheeled her chair away from the computer. She took a breath. "I'm feeling a little weird. I don't know, like I'm imagining things. You know, related to my dad."

"Your dad?" Tina pushed herself up onto the counter. She didn't have to have that explained to her. "Why now?"

"I don't know. Something triggered it the other day." She told Tina about the guy in the park with Fergus. "Maybe it's just the trial being over and the fact that he's out now. It's like I'm imagining things, Teen. I feel a little like I'm going nuts . . ."

"You're not nuts, Kate. You lost your family. Anyone would understand that. So what does the good *doctor* have to say?"

"Greg? He says I'm just jumpy. And maybe he's right. I mean, the other day I pretty well had myself convinced someone had toyed with our locks and broken into our apartment. Even Fergus was staring at me a little strangely."

"I've heard they're doing good work in acute schizophrenic paranoia at the medical center. Maybe Packer can get you a discount," said Tina, holding back a smile.

"Thanks." Kate scrunched her face in mock appreciation. "Maybe I'm just missing my family, Tina. It's been over a year now."

"I know what it is," Tina said.

Kate looked at her friend. "What?"

"*Laborafuckingphobia*," Tina said.

"Huh?"

"Laborafuckingphobia. Basically, you're spending too much of your time in this goddamn place."

"Right." Kate laughed. "Thank God we caught it early. Symptoms?"

"Look in the mirror, honey. But fortunately I know the cure. You gotta get the hell out of here, Kate. Go home. Have a nice, romantic night with your honey. I'll finish up tonight."

"I'm sure you're right." Kate sighed, wheeling her chair back over to her workstation. "But I just have a little more work to do tonight."

"I mean it." Tina grabbed her arm. "Remember, I trump you. I'm a year closer to my Ph.D. Just get yourself home, Kate. You're not crazy. You're missing your family. Who wouldn't be? Everyone knows what you've been through."

Kate smiled. Maybe Tina was right. Maybe that was all she needed. Clear her head, curl up in bed with some Chinese food and some stupid Adam Sandler movie on pay-per-view. Do something romantic. Greg had even mentioned that he had the night off tonight.

"It wouldn't exactly be torture to get out of here for a night."

"Damn right. So do it, girl, before I renege. I'll close up the place."

Kate stood up and gave her friend a hug. "You're a doll. Thanks."

"I know. And, Kate . . ."

Kate turned at the door. "Yeah?"

Tina winked. "Try your best *not* to have a meltdown if the wrong guy sits next to you on the bus home."

CHAPTER TWENTY-ONE

When Kate got home, there were candles lit all around the loft. The stereo was playing. Something soothing and romantic—Norah Jones.

Greg slid out to meet her, wearing his cheesy tuxedo T-shirt with a tie around his neck. "Signora Kate . . ." Fergus wagged his way up, a necktie wrapped around his collar, too.

Kate eyed Greg suspiciously. "Tina got to you, right?"

"Not *me*." Greg winked, gesturing with his chin toward Fergus. "*Him*."

Kate giggled, removing her jacket. "Okay, Casanova, what is it you have in mind?"

Greg led her over to the folding card table they had found at a thrift shop for five bucks, which he had centered in front of the windows. The Williamsburg Bridge was lit up beautifully.

There was a flickering candle on the table and a bottle of wine.

"I waz about to pour ze 1990 Mazis-Chambertin," Greg said in a silly, Clouseau-like accent, more his native Spanish than French, "but eenstead zere is its distant cousin, ze Two-Buck Chuck." He poured. "All a third-year resident can afford."

"Vintage 2006. July. Nice!" Kate giggled. Greg draped a paper napkin across her lap. "And to go with it . . . ?"

"To go *with* it"—Greg made a flourish toward the kitchen—"our chef's signature dish . . . the Beef in Green Curry and the Shrimp Pad Thai, served, as always, in their ceremonial tureens."

Kate spotted a couple of take-out containers from their favorite local Thai restaurant still on a tray, chopsticks to the side.

She laughed approvingly. "Is that all?"

"'*Is that all?*'" Greg sniffed derisively. "And for later, to make your romantic dream date complete . . ." From behind his back, he produced a DVD case.

Jack Black. *School of Rock.*

"Perfect!" Kate couldn't help but laugh. Truth was, she could use something totally dumb and mindless tonight. Maybe Tina was right. This was what she needed after all.

"Mademoiselle is impressed?" Greg asked, pouring a little more wine.

"Very impressed." Kate winked. "It's just that maybe I have my own idea."

"And what eez dat?" Greg asked, bringing his wineglass together with hers for a toast.

"*Bedroom*. Say, two minutes? I'm just going to freshen up and make myself smell great."

Greg scratched his chin and dropped the silly accent. "I can live with that."

Kate jumped up, giving him a teasing kiss on the lips. Then she hurried into the bathroom, removing her T-shirt and kicking off her jeans.

She hopped in the shower, her pores reviving as the warm spray splashed on her face. With Greg's insane hours and all the stress of the past year, they'd become like some old married couple. They'd forgotten what it was like to just have fun. Kate let the water soak her hair and run down her body and lathered herself in a sexy lavender-scented soap she'd found at Sephora.

Suddenly the shower door opened. Greg hopped in, an impish grin on his face. "Sorry, couldn't wait."

Kate's eyes twinkled mischievously. "So . . . what took you so long?"

They kissed, the hot spray beating down on

them. Greg pulled her close to him, and every cell in her body seemed to spring alive.

"You smell fantastic," he sighed, his chin nuzzling against her shoulders, while his hands massaged the tightness of her buttocks, her breasts.

"And you smell like the ER." Kate grinned. "Or is that the chili sauce speaking?"

He shrugged apologetically. "Lidocaine."

"Oh." She widened her eyes, feeling him press warmly up against her. "But I see you've brought along the pad Thai."

They laughed, and Greg turned her around, easing her back gently as he guided himself into her.

"Good plan, Kate."

He always knew the way to make her forget everything. She knew how lucky she was. They rocked a few moments, his hands on her thighs. The feel of him inside her made her body fill with warmth, her heart quicken. Kate let out a gasp, her breath intensifying. Then faster and harder as the spray splashed over them and they slapped against each other's thighs. Their rhythm started to build, and she tightened inside. Greg was panting, too. The rush was beautiful. Kate closed her eyes. A few moments later, he was pressed up against her in the warm spray and her heart beat feverishly, her body both freed and coiled.

"Sorry about dinner," he teased.

"No sweat." Kate nestled her head on his shoulder and sighed. "This'll have to do."

Later they did have dinner. In bed. Right out of the containers.

They watched the Jack Black movie and laughed out loud. Kate rested her head crosswise on Greg's chest. Fergus was curled up at the foot of their bed in his basket. She hadn't felt so relaxed in a long time.

"More wine *maintenant, s'il vous plaît*," Kate said, tipping her empty glass.

"Your turn." He shook his head. "I've been slaving in the kitchen all day."

"My turn?" She kicked him playfully. "It's *my* night."

"Oh, like you didn't already get enough?"

"Okay." Kate gave in. She threw on her nightshirt. "See if I come back with anything for you."

The phone rang.

"Fuck." Greg sighed loudly. They'd learned to hate the sound of the phone at unexpected times. It was usually the hospital, calling for him to come in.

Kate fumbled for the phone. The number on

the screen wasn't familiar. At least it wasn't the hospital. "Hello," she answered.

"Kate, this is Tom O'Hearn. Tina's father."

"Hi!" She wondered why he was calling so late at night. His voice sounded weary and strained.

"Kate, something terrible has happened . . ."

Kate looked anxiously at Greg, a tremor of nerves rippling down her spine. *"What?"*

"Tina's been shot, Kate. She's in the OR now. It's bad. They don't know if she's going to pull through."

CHAPTER TWENTY-TWO

They rushed there as fast as they could, throwing on sweatpants and pullovers, catching a taxi up to the Jacobi Medical Center in the Bronx, about thirty minutes away.

The whole way up, Greg squeezed her hand. Over the Triborough Bridge and onto the Bronx River Parkway. It didn't make sense. How could Tina have been shot? Kate had just left her. Her father said she was in the OR now. *Pull through,* Kate kept repeating to herself, trying to control her nerves. *C'mon, Tina, you've got to make it through.*

The cab pulled into the emergency entrance. Greg knew precisely where to go. They ran up the stairs to the Trauma Center ER on the fourth floor.

Kate spotted Tom and Ellen O'Hearn, Tina's parents, huddled on a bench outside the operating room. They jumped up as soon as they saw her and hugged her. She introduced Greg. The O'Hearns' anxious faces reflected the same deep-set worry that Kate knew was on her own.

"How is she?" Kate asked.

Tina was still in surgery. She had been shot in the back of the head. Just outside the lab, as she was leaving. Right on the street. Things didn't look so good. She'd lost a lot of blood, but she was holding on.

"It's bad, Kate." Tina's father just shook his head. "She's fighting. There's been a lot of tissue damage. The doctors say they just don't know."

Greg squeezed Tom's arm and said he would try to get an update from someone inside.

"Who could have done this?" Kate asked numbly, taking a seat next to Ellen on the bench. "How did this happen?"

"Apparently it was just as she left the lab." Tom shrugged, helpless. "Right out on the street. On Morris Avenue. The police were here earlier. Some people spotted the person running away. They think it might be gang-related."

"Gang-related?" Kate's eyes went wide. "What the hell does Tina have to do with gangs?"

"Some kind of initiation rite, they said. These animals supposedly prove themselves by doing some random killing. They said it was like he was waiting for someone on the street as she came out of the lab. She had just called us, Kate. A few minutes before. She was in the wrong place at the wrong time."

Kate reached over and hugged him. But what started out as only a throbbing in the pit of her stomach grew into something far more fearsome.

Right on the street. Outside the lab. Kate understood exactly what that meant.

"How long has she been in there?" she asked.

"Going on two hours now. They said it was a small-caliber gun. Fired from behind. That's the only reason she's still alive."

"Tina's strong." Kate squeezed Tom's hand and gave Tina's mother's arm a tug. "She'll pull through."

Please pull through.

Greg came back out a while later and said they were still in surgery. All they could do was wait. And that's what they did. For over two hours. Kate sat on the floor with her back pressed against the wall. The fast-forming truth was really starting to scare her. It was *she* who should have been there on that street. She gripped Greg's hand.

Finally, after 1:00 A.M., the surgeon came out.

"She's alive," he said, taking off his surgical cap. "That's the good news. The bullet entered through the occipital lobe and lodged in the right frontal. We're not able to get to it yet. There's been a lot of swelling. I'm afraid she's lost a lot of blood. It's a very tricky procedure. I wish I could tell you more right now, but we just don't know."

Ellen clung to her husband. "Oh, Tom . . ."

"She's fighting," the doctor said. "Her life signs are stable. We have her on a respirator. We're going to treat her as best we can for now and see how the swelling goes down. All I can honestly tell you now is, it's touch and go."

"Oh, Jesus, God," Ellen O'Hearn gasped, placing her head against her husband's chest.

Tom stroked his wife's hair. "So all we can do is wait? *How long?*"

"Twenty-four hours, forty-eight. I wish I could give you more. The best I can tell you is, she's alive."

Kate held on to Greg. Tina's mother started to sob.

Tom nodded. "Assuming she pulls through"—he swallowed tightly—"she'll be all right, won't she?" The meaning on his face was clear. Brain damage. Paralysis.

"We'll get to that when it's time to get to it." The doctor squeezed his shoulder. "Right now we're just hoping she survives."

Hoping she survives . . .

Kate sank back, her head crashing and empty at the same time. She wanted to cry. She leaned against Greg. In the hollow of her heart, the questions had disappeared. A horrible new fear had started to emerge.

Not so much a fear as a certainty.

It was *she* who always closed up the lab. *She* who should have come out that door. The police had said as much. *It was as if they were waiting for her . . .*

She looked at Tom and Ellen and wanted to tell them. *This was no gang killing.*

But they were right about one thing: Tina *was* in the wrong place at the wrong time.

With all the certainty in her heart, Kate knew— that bullet had been meant for her.

CHAPTER TWENTY-THREE

Emily Geller pushed through the doors of her high school, spotting the familiar Volvo SUV waiting at the end of the long line.

He hadn't even pulled the car up to her.

Weirdo. Emily shook her head. But Dad had been acting a little weird since he'd been back with them. He wasn't the same person she'd always known—interested and funny and full of life—who always drove her around to squash tournaments and pushed her if she hadn't finished her homework. Or got pissed at her when the cell-phone bills came in sky-high.

Maybe something had happened to him while he was away. (They'd all decided not to call it prison.) Now her dad always seemed distracted and remote. If you told him something that happened at school or how you kicked someone's ass on the squash court, he only nodded back with this glassy, half-pleased look in his eyes, like he wasn't even there.

Nothing was the way it was before.

Emily didn't like it out here. She missed her friends, her coaches. Most of all, she missed Kate. They didn't do things the same way now—as a family. One more year and she'd be out, Emily kept telling herself—in college. The first thing she would do was take back her name.

"Dad?" Emily rapped on the passenger window.

He was staring vacantly ahead, like he was deep in thought.

"Calling Dad?"

He finally acknowledged her, unlocking the passenger door. "Em . . ."

She threw her heavy knapsack into the back-seat. "Did you remember my squash bag?"

"Of course." He nodded. But he had to turn and check to make sure it was there.

"Yeah, right," Emily snorted, climbing into the front. "Mom probably put it there."

It was the one thing they could still do together. He seemed to love to watch her play. Of course, they didn't have a school team where they were now, and the competition wasn't the same. But there was a club about fifteen minutes away that had some pros she could train with.

It was a risk, but she was pushing to get to the nationals in the spring, under a different name.

They pulled out of the school lot and drove down the main road of the suburban town they lived in. In a minute they were on the highway.

"I'm hitting with this guy Brad Danoulis today," Emily told him. He was this cocky kid who got in early at Bowdoin and who played for a private school a couple of towns away. "He's always bragging that the guys can whip the girls. You wanna watch?"

"Course I do, tiger," her father said, distracted. He was dressed in a jacket and a plaid dress shirt, as if he was going somewhere. He *never* went anywhere anymore. "I just have something I have to do. Then I'll be back."

"Try not to be late, Dad, okay?" Emily said sternly. "I have a chem quiz and this take-home on *The Crucible*. Anyway, you want to watch me kick this guy's butt."

"Don't worry. Look up. I'll be in my spot. I'll be there."

They pulled off the highway and into the business park where the North Bay Squash Club was located. There were a few cars parked in front of the aluminum-sided building. Emily reached over and grabbed her bag. "Next month there's this regional in San Francisco. I need to enter

145

there. I need a West Coast ranking. We could go. You and me. Like we used to?"

"We could do that." Her father nodded. "We used to have a lot of fun, didn't we, tiger?"

"We *all* had fun," Emily answered, a little acidly. She reached behind and yanked her squash bag out of the back. "Any last words of advice?"

"Just this." He looked at her a little cock-eyed. "Always remember who you are, Em. You're Emily Raab."

She tilted her head at him. Everything he did now was weird. "Guess I was thinking more like, 'Keep pressing his backhand, Em.'"

"That too, tiger." He smiled.

As Emily pulled open the door to the squash club, he shot her a wink, and just for a flash it seemed to have a little of the old Dad in it. The one Emily hadn't seen for a long time.

"Kick his ass, babe."

Emily grinned back. "I will."

Inside, Brad was already waiting on the court, crisply smacking the ball. He had on a T-shirt that read CABO ROCKS.

Emily went into the locker room, put her hair in a ponytail, and changed into her shorts. She came out and stepped onto the court. "Hey."

"Hey." Brad nodded. He tried this show-off, behind-the-back "boast" to get her the ball.

Emily rolled her eyes at him, a little skeptically. "You ever even been to Cabo?"

"Yeah. Christmas last year. It was cool. You?"

She started cracking forehands. *"Twice."*

They played three games. Brad took a lead on her in the first. He had a wicked cross-court kill and was fast. No slouch. But Emily came back. She tied him at eight, and they alternated game points until she pulled out a win with a perfectly executed corner kill. Brad looked annoyed and bounced his racquet off the floor. He acted like it was a fluke. "Let's go again."

She took him the next game, too, 9–6. That was when Brad started walking gingerly on his ankle, as though he had an injury.

"So you gonna play for Bowdoin?" Emily asked him, knowing that Bowdoin was Division I in squash and that he didn't stand a chance. By the third game, she was sailing. She took it 9–4.

Cleaned his clock.

"Nice match." Brad shook her hand limply. "You're good. Next time I won't hold back."

"Thanks." Emily rolled her eyes. "My wrist will probably have healed by then."

She sat on the bench with a towel over her head and gulped down some bottled water. That's when it first occurred to her. She looked up at the balcony.

Where the hell is Dad?

He hadn't come back for her match. He wasn't sitting where he usually watched her matches. She pressed her lips together in frustration. A little anger, too. It was already after five. She had asked him to be back.

Where the hell is he?

Emily went outside and looked for the Volvo. No sign. Then she went back inside and settled in watching two seniors battle it out for almost another half an hour, doing her math, checking the door, until she was so pissed she couldn't stand it anymore. She took out her cell and punched in her home number.

"We're not at home . . ." The answering machine came on. This was starting to get annoying. Someone should be there. Where was everybody? She checked the clock. It was going on six. She had work to do. She'd told him that. Emily listened to the message and waited impatiently for the beep.

"Mom, it's me. I'm still at the club. *Dad never showed.*"

CHAPTER TWENTY-FOUR

Twenty-four hours passed. No change.

No change in Tina's condition the next day either.

The surgeons still couldn't get anywhere near the bullet. Her brain scans were steady, but the swelling around the wound was massive, the intracranial pressure high, the tissue damage unknown. All they could do was wait for it to recede. They just didn't know if she'd pull through.

Kate spent most of those next days at the hospital with Ellen and Tom. She told the police how Tina had closed up for her that night. How she wasn't into drugs or anything illegal. That she was the last person on earth to have a connection to any kind of gang.

The cops claimed they had leads. A man in a red bandanna was seen jumping into a white van down the street from the building and heading up Morris Avenue. Red bandannas were the trademark of the Bloods. It was how they cut their bones, the detective said. Shooting an innocent victim, right on the street. An informer in a rival gang had put the word out that that's what was going down.

A gang initiation rite. Her friend was lying in a coma. How Kate would have liked to believe that, too.

That second night she and Greg got back to their apartment after 2:00 A.M. Neither of them could sleep. Or even think about sleep. All they could think about was Tina. They just sat on the couch, shell-shocked and stunned.

One day it had to come out, Kate knew. What would she say? Tom and Ellen had the right to know.

"I've got to contact Phil Cavetti, Greg," Kate said. "The WITSEC people have to know."

Kate understood that once she made that call, everything in their lives would change. They'd have to move. That was for sure. Maybe change their names. Greg was almost finished with his residency. He couldn't simply leave. They were just starting out their lives.

Was this going to be hanging over their heads forever?

"The police say they have leads," Greg said, trying his best to be calm and logical. "What if they're right—and this is just some tragic co-incidence?"

"This wasn't about some gang." Kate shook her head. "We both know that!"

This was killing her. Her *best friend* was fighting for her life, not some faceless person on the news.

"We both know that Tina was shot, Greg, because they thought it was me!"

He held her, and Kate tried her hardest to feel secure in his arms. But she knew. Cavetti and Margaret Seymour had warned her. Mercado wasn't going to let this go away. What was it they had said? That it wasn't just about revenge? It was deeper than that. They called it "insurance." Insurance that the next time someone like her father turned against *fraternidad*, this wouldn't happen again.

They finally managed to fall asleep there, in each other's arms, mostly out of sheer exhaustion.

And in the morning they agreed to wait. Only one day longer—maybe two. Just to let the police play out their leads.

But during the night, Kate woke up. She lay there, pressed against Greg, heart beating, her T-shirt drenched in clammy sweat.

They knew.

The premonitions of the past few days had been right. The police could play out all the leads they wanted, but Kate would be able to conceal it only so long.

They had found her. There would be a next time. Of that she was sure. And what would happen then? When they found her for real.

What would happen when they realized that the wrong person had been shot?

Kate stirred, freeing herself from Greg's embrace. She sat there in the dark for a moment, knees tucked tightly to her chest. She prayed her family was safe, wherever they were. From under her shirt, she pulled out the pendant her mother had given her the day she'd left. The halved golden sun. *"It holds secrets, Kate. One day I'll tell them to you."* Would they ever fit the two halves back together?

Mom, I wish I could hear those secrets from you now.

Kate got up and, in the shadows of the darkened apartment, stepped over to the front door. She reached for the heavy bolt. And drew it shut.

CHAPTER TWENTY-FIVE

"Kate." Tom O'Hearn reached over to her. "*Go home.*"

He put his arm around her on the ICU bench. "You look exhausted. Nothing's going to happen tonight. I know you want to be here. But go home and get some sleep."

Kate nodded. She knew he was right. She hadn't slept six hours in the past two days. Her blood sugar was low. She hadn't been to work. She basically hadn't been anywhere except the hospital in the days since Tina had been shot.

"I promise." He took her over to the elevator and gave her a hug. "We'll call you with any news."

"I know."

Tina had been transferred to the head trauma ward at Bellevue Hospital on Twenty-seventh Street, the best in the city. Kate went down to the lobby and stepped out onto First Avenue. It was dark, going on 6:00 P.M. She'd been there all day. Not seeing any cabs, she walked over to Second and got on the downtown bus.

Okay . . . Kate found a seat in the back and, just for a moment, closed her eyes. Tom was right, she was exhausted. She needed to sleep. She had left the apartment that morning without giving herself her insulin shot. Greg was back at work doing sixteen-hour shifts. It was unsettling. This would be the first time since Tina's shooting that she'd be back in the apartment alone.

Kate dozed a little. The bus ride went by in a flash. She woke up just in time to hop off at Ninth Street, a couple of blocks from where she lived. She'd almost slept through it.

As she stepped off the bus and started to walk along darkened Second Avenue, Kate had a sense that something was wrong.

Maybe it was the man stepping away from a building across from the bus stop, tossing a cigarette onto the sidewalk and following a short way behind. His footsteps against the pavement, keeping pace with hers. She told herself not to look back.

Kate, you're just being paranoid. This is New York. The East Village. It's crowded. This happens all the time.

She caught a glimpse of him in a storefront window. Still behind her. Hands in the pockets of his black leather jacket. He had a cap drawn over his eyes.

But she wasn't being paranoid! Not this time. Not like back in the apartment. Kate's heart started pounding. A shiver of fear ran down her spine.

Pick up your pace, she told herself. *You only live a few blocks away.*

Kate crossed the avenue heading down to Seventh. Her heart was slamming off her ribs now.

She turned onto her street. She felt the presence of the person following her a few yards behind. Up ahead there was a market she sometimes shopped in. Kate headed for it, forcing herself not to look around. She virtually ran inside.

For a second she felt safe. Kate grabbed a basket and ducked down one of the aisles, praying he wouldn't come inside. She threw a few things in she pretended she needed—milk, yogurt, whole wheat bread. But all the while she was just waiting, focused on the window. There were people here. Her heart started to calm.

She took out her purse and went to the counter. She smiled a little nervously at Ingrid, the checkout girl, pushing back a harrowing thought: *What if she's the last person to see me alive?*

Kate stepped back outside. For a moment she felt relief. *Thank God.* No sign.

Then she froze.

He was still there! Leaning against a parked car on the other side of the street, talking into a phone. Their eyes slowly drifted together. She wasn't imagining this.

Okay, Kate, what the hell do you do now?

Now she started to run. An indistinguishable pace at first, then faster, her eyes fixed on her building, the green canopy, just a few yards ahead.

The man picked up his pace behind her. A jolt of electricity ran down her spine. Kate's heart throbbed wildly.

Please, God, only a few yards more.

The last feet Kate took at a full-out run. Her fingers fumbled for her key in her bag. She jammed it into the outer door. The lock turned. Kate flung open the door, expecting the man to run up on her now. She looked back along the street. The man in the cap had crossed the street a few doors down.

Kate hurled herself inside, the outside doors clicking as the lock mercifully engaged. *It's over now. Thank God!* Kate pressed her back against the lobby wall. Her back was drenched in sweat. Her chest imploded with relief.

This has to end, she knew. *You've got to go to someone, Kate.*

But go to whom?

Her family? *Your family's gone, Kate. Face it, they're gone for good.*

Greg? As much as she loved him, what could they do, just pick up and leave? In his last year of school?

The police? *What do you tell them, Kate? That you've been lying to them, holding things back. That your best friend's in a coma with a bullet in her brain, a bullet that was meant for you?*

It's too late, too late for any of that now . . .

Kate stepped into the elevator and pressed the button for seven.

It was one of those old industrial types, clattering as it passed every floor.

All she wanted to do was get inside her apartment and bolt the fucking door.

The elevator rattled to a stop on seven. Kate clutched her key and threw open the heavy outer door.

Two men stood facing her.

Oh, God, no!

Her heart rose up in her chest. Kate backed away and tried to scream. But to what end? No one would hear her.

She knew what they were there to do.

Then one of the men stepped forward. *"Ms. Raab?"* His hands reached to steady her shoulders.

"Kate."

She looked up. Tears welled in her eyes. She recognized him. She broke down in sobs, staring at his salt-and-pepper hair.

It was Phil Cavetti. The WITSEC agent.

CHAPTER TWENTY-SIX

Kate literally hurled herself at him, her whole body paralyzed by fear.

"It's okay, Kate," he said, and wrapped her safely in his arms.

Kate nodded, pressing her face against his jacket. "I thought I was being followed. I thought—"

"I'm sorry." Cavetti held her closely. "That was probably my man. At the bus stop. We just wanted to be sure you were heading home."

Kate shut her eyes and sucked in a shaky breath, a mixture of nerves and unimaginable relief. She felt her heart rate subside. She pulled away, trying to compose herself.

"Why are you here?"

"This is James Nardozzi," Cavetti said, introducing the man with him—lean, sharp-jawed, a plain gray suit and equally plain red tie under his raincoat. "He's with the Justice Department."

"Yes." Kate nodded, slightly chagrined. "I remember you from the trial."

The lawyer smiled thinly.

"We need to ask you some questions, Kate," the WITSEC agent said. "Can we come in?"

"Of course." Her hands were still a little jittery. She had some trouble aligning the key with the lock and pulling back the bolt. Fergus was barking at the door. "It's okay, boy . . ."

She opened the door to her apartment and flicked on the lights. Kate could never remember feeling such an overwhelming sensation of relief. Thank God they were here. It was about Tina, she assumed. She wanted to tell them anyway. She couldn't go on holding it back like this anymore.

"Okay." She placed her groceries on the counter. "Shoot . . . Poor choice of words." She smiled.

Kate gradually felt back on her axis. "Go ahead. I know why you're here."

Phil Cavetti looked at her a little blankly. What he said sent her axis reeling.

"When was the last time you heard from your father, Kate?"

CHAPTER TWENTY-SEVEN

"My father . . . ?"

Kate blinked back at him, wide-eyed, and shook her head. "I haven't spoken to him since the trial. Why?"

Cavetti shot a glance to the Justice lawyer. Then he cleared his throat. "We have to show you some things, Kate." He took out a manila envelope from under his raincoat and stepped over to the kitchen counter. His peremptory tone had Kate a little scared.

"What I'm going to show you is highly confidential," he said, unfastening the clasp. "It may also be a bit distressing. You might want to sit down."

"You're making me nervous, Agent Cavetti." Kate looked at him, lowering herself onto a stool. Her heart began to quicken.

"I understand." He started to lay out a series

of graphic eight-by-ten black-and-white photos on the counter.

Crime-scene photos.

Kate held back a start, convinced she was about to see her father there. But it wasn't. All the shots were of a woman. Stripped down to her underwear. Tied to a chair. Some of the photos were full body and others were close-ups—her face, parts of her body, covered in wounds. They were gruesome. The woman's head hung to the side. There were bloodstains— her shoulders, her knees. Kate winced. She could see they came from multiple gunshot wounds. She put a wary hand on Cavetti's arm.

There were marks on both the woman's breasts, deep discolorations. The next shot was a close-up of one breast. Kate saw now what the marks were. She'd been burned. On her breasts and nipples. *Charred.* Her right nipple had been entirely removed—cut off.

"I'm sorry, Kate," Phil Cavetti said, placing a hand on her shoulder.

"Why are you showing me these?" Kate looked at him. "What do these have to do with my father?"

"Please, Kate, just a couple more." Cavetti spread out two or three more photos. The first was a stark close-up of the left side of the victim's face. It was totally swollen and discolored, bruised from the eye to the cheek. Whoever she had been was barely recognizable.

Kate pushed back a surge of bile in her gut. This was sickening, horrible. *What kind of monster would do this?*

"The wounds you're seeing"—Cavetti finally laid down the envelope—"weren't meant to be fatal, Kate. They were meant to keep the victim alive as long as possible, to prolong her agony. There was no sexual abuse. All her belongings were in place. This woman was simply tortured."

"Tortured . . . ?" Kate felt her stomach turn.

"To extract information, we believe," the Justice lawyer put in. "To induce her to talk, Ms. Raab."

"I thought you were here about Tina." Kate stared up at them, confused.

"We know about Ms. O'Hearn," Phil Cavetti said. "And we know how that must be for you, Kate, in all regards. But please, I'm sorry, one more . . ."

The WITSEC agent removed a final photograph from the envelope and placed it on the counter in front of Kate.

It was even more disturbing. Kate averted her eyes.

It displayed the far side of the woman's face.

Her bruised and swollen eyes were rolled back under her lids. Her matted brown hair fell forward, slightly covering her face.

But not enough to conceal the dark, dime-size hole in the right side of her forehead.

"*Christ!*" Kate sucked in a sharp breath, wanting to turn away again. "*Why are you showing me these?* Why are you asking about my father?"

But then something stopped her. Her eyes grew wide, transfixed.

Kate went back to the photo. *She saw something.* She slowly picked it up and stared.

"Oh, my God ..." Kate gasped, the blood draining from her face.

I know her.

At first she couldn't see it—the poor woman's wounds were so disfiguring, but suddenly the features—the mole on the side of her mouth— came clear.

Kate turned back to Phil Cavetti, a cramp of revulsion gripping her abdomen.

The woman in the photo was Margaret Seymour.

CHAPTER TWENTY-EIGHT

"Oh, good Lord, no . . ." Kate shut her eyes, nausea overcoming her. "This can't be true. It's horrible . . ."

Margaret Seymour had been attractive and pleasant. She had reached out to Em in order to make her transition as easy as possible. The whole family's. They all liked her. *No . . . good God.*

"Who did this?" Kate shook her head, repulsed. *"Why?"*

"We don't know." Phil Cavetti got up and went over to the sink and poured her a glass of water. "This happened Thursday, last week. In a warehouse park outside of Chicago. All we do know is that Agent Seymour went there to meet someone—related to a case. I know how troubling it is."

Kate gulped down a mouthful of cooling water, unable to stop shaking her head.

Cavetti squeezed her arm. "Like we said, we're thinking this wasn't designed to kill her at first but to get her to talk. To divulge something."

"I don't understand . . ."

"The whereabouts of a reassignment, Ms. Raab," the Justice lawyer interjected. "Someone in the program."

Suddenly she understood. A tremor of alarm gripped her. "Why are you showing me all this, Agent Cavetti?"

"Kate, we found something in Agent Seymour's car." The WITSEC agent paused. He took out something new from the envelope.

This time it wasn't a photograph but a single sheet of notepaper, blank, like from a small perforated notepad, contained in a plastic bag.

Kate looked back at him, confused.

"The car was gone over, Kate, from front to back, by whoever did this, no doubt, to make sure it was clean. This sheet was still attached to a notepad on the dashboard. Something had been written on the page above it—and removed."

"It's blank." Kate shrugged. But as she looked closer, she could see the faint outline of someone's writing.

"Here, under UV light"—Cavetti took out one more photo—"you can see it enhanced."

Kate held the new photo. Something *had* been scrawled there. Five letters came to life. In Margaret Seymour's hand.

M-I-D-A-S.

"Midas?" Kate looked blank. "I'm not understanding. How does all this relate to me?"

Cavetti stared at her. "MIDAS is the code name we gave to your family, Kate."

It had the force of a fist, hitting her squarely in the abdomen, squeezing the oxygen out of her lungs.

First Tina, outside the lab. Then Margaret Seymour, her family's case agent. Now they were asking if she'd heard from her father.

"What's going on, Agent Cavetti?" Kate stood up. "My family! They could be in danger. Have you notified them? Have you spoken with my father?"

"That's why we're here." The WITSEC man paused, staring into her eyes. "I'm afraid your father is missing, Kate."

CHAPTER TWENTY-NINE

"Missing . . . ?" The word fell numbly from Kate's lips. *"Missing since when?"*

"He dropped your sister off at a squash club last week, then disappeared," Cavetti said, tapping the photographs back into a stack and setting them down. "We don't know where he is. You're certain he hasn't been in touch?"

"Of course I'm certain!" A wave of anguish swept over Kate. Her father was missing. His case agent had been brutally murdered.

"My mother! My brother and sister! Are they all right?"

"They're safe, Kate." Cavetti raised his palm in a cautioning way. "They're under guard."

Kate looked back at him, trying to figure out just what that meant. "Under guard!"

She slid off the stool, touching a hand to her face. Her worst fears had now come true. They had tried to get to *her*. They had killed Margaret Seymour. Now they might have found her family. Kate stepped over to the couch and lowered herself onto the armrest. She knew one thing: Her father, whatever he had done, loved his family. If he was missing, something had happened. He would never just leave.

"Is my father dead, Agent Cavetti?"

He shook his head. "The truth is, we don't know. We're going to assign a protective agent to you, Kate. Maybe somehow he's okay. Maybe he'll try to contact you. You may even be a target yourself."

"I already was," Kate said. Then she looked up with a start. "You said you knew about Tina."

At first Cavetti didn't respond. He just glanced a bit uncomfortably in the direction of Nardozzi.

Kate stood up and stared at them. "You knew about Tina, and you never even contacted me. You—"

"Kate, we know how you must have felt with that, but the police . . ."

In a daze she tried to connect the timelines in her mind. Tina was three days ago, Margaret Seymour, so they said, last Thursday. Her father . . . How could her father be missing since then? Why wouldn't they have warned her?

"I want to talk to my family," she said to Cavetti. "I want to make sure they're all right."

"I'm sorry, Kate. That isn't possible. They're in protective custody now."

"What do you mean, they're in protective custody?"

"Kate," Cavetti said, helplessly, "the people running the Mercado operation would do anything to retaliate against your father. They may already have. The agency's been penetrated. Until we know what's happened, the worst thing we can do is compromise their security. This is the way it has to be."

Kate glared back. "Are you saying they're prisoners? That I'm a prisoner, too?"

"No one knows what Agent Seymour might have divulged, Kate," Nardozzi said quietly. "Or to *whom*."

It was as if a car had slammed into her head-on, a body blow of doubt and uncertainty, and she was reeling. Her father was missing. Margaret Seymour was dead. The rest of them were being kept from her. Kate looked at Cavetti. This was the person her family had bet their lives on. And he was lying to her. She knew it. He was holding something back.

"I want to talk to my family." Kate met his eyes. "My father may be dead. I have that right."

"I know you do," Cavetti said. "But you just have to trust us, Kate . . . *They're okay.*"

CHAPTER THIRTY

They attached a protective agent to watch over her.

The short, mustached guy in the baseball cap who had followed her off the bus turned out to be an FBI agent named Ruiz.

Maybe this was for the best, Kate told herself. With everything that was going on, with what had happened to Tina. Greg was back at work and wouldn't be home until later. Truth was, Kate would sleep a little easier knowing that someone was there.

But she couldn't sleep. Not knowing what had happened to her father. Whether he was dead or alive. She thought of her mom and Em and Justin. Wherever the hell they were. If they were even all right. How panicked they must be. *God, I'd give anything to hear their voices.* One thing Kate knew—whatever her father had done, whoever he was, he would never just leave them.

Her mouth felt like cotton. She needed something to drink. She felt a tingling sensation in her fingers and toes. This kind of stress, it wasn't good for her. Kate pulled the Accu-Chek out of her purse and took a blood reading: 315. Goddamn it, she had spiked. That was bad.

She knew she'd been slacking off lately. She hadn't run or rowed since last week. All she'd had to eat today was a few bites of a salad she'd picked up in the hospital cafeteria.

She pulled out a syringe from the kitchen cabinet, took the vial of Humulin from the fridge, and gave herself her shot.

C'mon, Kate, you have to take care of yourself, or it won't matter who the hell finds you.

She brought her dog close and petted his floppy ears. "Right, Fergus?"

Kate made herself something to eat, a little tuna out of the can, mayo, ketchup, sweet relish, a chopped-up egg. Dad's famous recipe. She took the bowl over to the computer on the desk by the window. She clicked on Yahoo! She knew that it was futile, but she'd give anything just to see a message from Em or Mom.

Nothing.

Kate punched up Sharon's e-mail ID.

Yogagirl123. It didn't go to her directly. Her messages were forwarded through some sort of clearing Web site at WITSEC, so she always had to be a little careful about what she said. This time she just started to write, copying Em and Justin.

Mom . . . guys. I'm worried about you. I don't even know if you will ever get this. I know Dad is missing. I'm so scared that something terrible has happened.

There's something I need to tell you, something that happened here, but most of all I just want to hear your voices. They said you are in protective custody. If you get this, please get the okay to call me.

I love you all. I pray that Daddy is all right and that you are, too. My heart is with you guys. Write me, call me, just let me know. I can't tell you how much I want to hear your voices.

K.

Kate clicked "send" and watched the message disappear. She realized she was sending an e-mail to no one. She called Greg and got his recording and hung up without leaving a message. She had never felt this alone in her life.

She curled up with Fergus on the bed with the TV on.

Around 2:00 A.M., Greg woke her from a light sleep. A rerun of *ER* was on.

"I'm glad you're here," Kate murmured, feeling for his hand.

"I stopped in on Tina," he said. "They had to do a procedure. To relieve pressure in the brain. They drained some fluid and scraped away a little of the dead tissue."

Kate raised up, alarmed. "Is she okay?"

"She's fighting, Kate." Greg climbed in next to her, still in his clothes. "You know Tina—she'll string this out forever just to make us sweat," he said, trying to sound upbeat. "I'm really sorry, baby. About Ben. About your family. I'm sorry I couldn't be here for you."

Kate nodded, anguish on her face. "I saw the pictures, Greg. Of what happened to that woman agent in Chicago. It was horrible. They have no idea where he is. I was thinking, if they did that to her to get to him, what if . . ."

"Don't think *if*, Kate." He pulled her toward him, nestling in beside her. "Don't go there. You don't know."

"He wouldn't just leave, Greg. Not like that. Whatever you might want to say about him, he wouldn't just disappear."

"I know . . ." Greg said, gently stroking her hair. They lay there for a while, Kate pressed against him tightly. Then he chuckled. "So I met Ruiz."

Kate did her best to smile. "You're the one who always said you wanted a doorman building."

He stroked her cheek. "I know you're scared, Kate. I wish I could just take us away somewhere. I wish I could just shield you from all this. Protect you."

"Like Superman," Kate said and squeezed him. "Superhombre . . ."

Greg lifted her chin with his finger. "I know you're going through a lot. All this. Tina. But here's one thing you *can* count on, pooch: *I* won't leave. I'm here, Kate. I'm not going anywhere. I promise."

She rested her head against him and closed her eyes. For the moment she felt safe. Far away from it all. That feeling was the one thing she was able to cling to right now.

She nodded softly against him. "I know."

CHAPTER THIRTY-ONE

The phone rang. Kate groggily opened her eyes.

It was light. Almost eleven. She must've been exhausted. She never slept this late. Greg was already gone. The phone rang a second time. Kate fumbled for the receiver. "Hullo ... ?"

"Kate? Hon ... ?"

The voice jolted through her like a shot of pure adrenaline. *"Mom!* Is that *you*?"

"Yes, it's me. How are you, honey? They won't let me talk a long time. I just wanted to let you know we're all right."

"Oh, God, I was so worried, Mom! I know about Dad. I know he's missing. The WITSEC people were here."

"They told me," her mother said. "He's been missing since last Wednesday. No one's heard from him, Kate. We don't know where he is."

"Oh, God, Mom." Kate shut her eyes, flashing

to those horrible pictures of the night before. "Mom, I don't know what you know, but Margaret Seymour is dead. Cavetti was here. They showed me pictures of her. They think it was Mercado's people. Trying to extract information, maybe about Dad. It was gruesome, Mom. They tortured her. You have to be careful. They may know where you are."

"We're okay, Kate. They have us under round-the-clock guard. It's just that we've had no word about your father."

"What are they telling you?" Kate asked nervously, pushing back the fear that her father might truly be dead.

"They're not telling me anything, honey. I don't know what to think."

"Me either. How's Em? And Justin?"

"They're okay, Kate," her mom replied. "We're trying to keep things as normal as we can. Em's got a tourney this week. She's doing well. And Justin's Justin. He's almost six feet now."

"God, I'd like to hear their voices."

"I can't, Kate. There's a WITSEC person here. They're telling me I have to hang up now."

"Mom . . . something else has happened you should know about. Something bad. Tina O'Hearn's been shot."

"Oh, Lord," her mother gasped. *"Shot?"*

"On the street, just outside the lab. The police think it's some kind of gang-related thing, but listen, Mom, I don't believe that. She was closing up for me that night. I think they thought it was me."

"Kate, you have to stay out of sight. You have to let these people protect you."

"They are, Mom, they're here. It's just that—"

"How is she, honey?" Sharon asked. "Is she dead?"

"No, but it's bad. She's hanging on, but they've had to do a couple of surgeries. They just don't know. Mom, I really need to see you guys."

"I wish we could do that, Kate. I really do. There are some things I've been holding back for a long time now that you need to know. But, Kate—"

A male voice cut in on the line, instructing them that they had to hang up now.

"Mom!"

"Kate, stay safe. Do what they tell you. They're making me go now. I love you, sweetie."

Kate jumped up, cradling the phone with both hands. *"Mom!"* Tears filled her eyes. "Tell Justin and Em I love them. Tell them I miss them. That I want to see you soon."

"We miss you, too, Kate."

The line clicked off. Kate just sat there, letting the receiver fall in her lap. At least they were safe. That was the best news she could possibly have.

Then something occurred to her. Something important. Something Sharon had said that now, rolling it around in her brain, didn't seem right.

Margaret Seymour. Cavetti had said that she'd been killed outside Chicago. Last Thursday. To gain information.

Thursday . . .

So how could her killer have used what he learned to find Kate's father? He had disappeared the night before.

CHAPTER THIRTY-TWO

"Is my father dead, Agent Cavetti?"

Kate pushed through the doors of his office in the Javits Building at Federal Plaza and looked the WITSEC agent solidly in the eyes.

There were two other people there: Nardozzi, the angular Justice lawyer, and a tall, balding man with light red hair who remained in the corner. He was introduced as Special Agent Booth from the FBI.

"We just don't know, Kate." Cavetti met her eyes in turn.

"I think you do. My apartment was broken into last week. A bolt on the door that we never use was closed. At first I was worried someone might be after me. But then it occurred to me when all this started happening . . ."

Kate gazed at him accusingly. "Are my phones bugged, Agent Cavetti?"

"Kate." The WITSEC man stood up and came around the desk. "You know that our agency has been compromised. One of our agents has been brutally murdered. Someone was trying to gain information from her. We know it was related to your father's case."

"But it turns out my father disappeared on Wednesday—isn't that right, Agent Cavetti?" Kate demanded. "Margaret Seymour wasn't killed until the following day. So I'm asking you again: *Is my father dead?*"

"*Ms. Raab* . . ." Nardozzi cleared his throat.

"Herrera." Kate glared sharply. "You're the ones who wanted me to change my name. It's Herrera."

"Ms. *Herrera*." The lawyer stood up. "You should know that there are over forty-five hundred people currently protected in the Witness Protection Program. Many are ordinary people who simply wanted to do the right thing in the face of reprisal. Whistle-blowers, witnesses. Others are some of the best-known figures in organized crime. People who have brought down crime families. Helped create numerous convictions. Names that would be highly recognizable if they were divulged."

"You're still not answering my question," Kate insisted.

"There are *others*"—the Justice Department prosecutor didn't respond—"with whom the government has, at times, struck deals privately, who have helped us on a number of investigative fronts. The reliability of this protection"— he nodded for her to take a seat—"to offer a secure life to those who put themselves at risk for their testimony has become the backbone of the federal justice system as we know it today. It is why organized crime has been dealt a major blow in the past two decades. It is why major drug commerce has been significantly reduced. It may also very well be the reason this country has not been attacked again since 9/11."

"Why are you telling me all this?" Kate sank into a chair across from them.

"Because, Ms. Herrera"—the FBI agent in the corner stepped forward—"your father purchased a cell phone a couple of weeks ago, under your brother's name. That's Justin, isn't it?"

Surprised, Kate nodded, almost reflexively.

"There was no activity on it at first. That changed last Thursday. That was the day *after* your father disappeared. A call was placed to Chicago."

Kate felt the slightest spark of hopefulness catch fire.

"The number that was called, Ms. Herrera," the FBI man said, tossing a file on the table in front of her, "was Margaret Seymour's secure line."

Kate blinked. "I'm not understanding." *What were they trying to say, that her father was alive?*

"Kate, a man matching your father's description boarded a plane Wednesday night from a city that will remain nameless, heading for Minneapolis," Phil Cavetti said, laying out some pages for her to see. "The ticket was made out to a Kenneth John Skinner, an insurance broker in Cranbury, New Jersey, who had reported his driver's license stolen over two years ago. We ran your father's likeness by various car rental agencies at the Minneapolis airport. A car was rented at the Budget office there, to the same Kenneth John Skinner, and returned there two days later by the same man. According to their records, the reading on the odometer was eight hundred and twenty miles."

"Okay . . ." Kate nodded, unsure what to feel.

"Eight hundred and twenty miles, I'm pretty sure you'll find, is the approximate driving distance from Minneapolis to Chicago and back."

Kate stared. For a second there was a flicker of joy in her blood. They were saying that her father was alive!

Then it was crushed by their stony silence.

"There was a directional request input into the car's GPS system, Kate. It was programmed for the Barrow Industrial Park, in Schaumburg, Illinois, a few miles outside of town."

"Okay . . ." Kate's heart was beating faster now.

Cavetti pushed a photo across to her. One of Margaret Seymour's death-scene photos. "A vacant warehouse in the Barrow Industrial Park is where Margaret Seymour was murdered, Kate."

Kate's heart stopped. All of a sudden it came clear to her what they were thinking.

"No!"

"You already know your father went missing the day before Agent Seymour was killed. We believe it was your father Agent Seymour was going to meet."

"No!" Kate shook her head. She picked up Margaret Seymour's photo. She felt sick to her stomach. "What are you saying?" Her limbs began to feel a little weak.

"That license was stolen over two years ago, Kate. There were credit cards issued in the same name. I think you have to realize that whoever did this has been planning things for a very long time."

"This is crazy!" Kate stood up, glaring back at them.

They didn't think someone killed Margaret Seymour to find out where her father was.

They thought *he* killed her. *That he murdered his own case agent.*

"So as to your question"—Phil Cavetti leaned back—"of whether your father is dead or alive, I'm afraid it's a whole lot deeper than that, Kate."

CHAPTER THIRTY-THREE

"No!" Kate's voice rose, her head shook with incredulity. "You're wrong! Whatever he's done, my father's no killer." Her eyes fastened on the horrible crime photo. The image of Margaret Seymour's empty expression almost made her retch. *"Not that!"*

"She was headed there to meet him, Kate," Cavetti said. "He ran away from your family. That much we know."

"I don't care!" Her face flushed with frustration. It was impossible. Too horrible to even contemplate. "You steamrolled my father into a conviction. You took away his life. You don't even have proof he's still alive."

She picked up the file. She wanted to throw it against the wall. Her head was swimming. She tried to focus on the facts.

Someone did purchase a cell phone in her

brother's name. She couldn't deny that. Someone had boarded a plane for Minneapolis the night her father disappeared. Someone had placed that call to Margaret Seymour. And rented a car. The GPS led to the murder site. Margaret Seymour's scribbled note.

MIDAS.

Why . . . ?

"Why would he want to kill her?" Kate shouted back. "What possible reason would he have to kill the one person who was trying to keep him safe?"

"Maybe she knew something he didn't want her to divulge," Booth, the FBI man, answered, shrugging. "Or cover up something she'd found."

"But you would know that." She spun to Cavetti. "You were Margaret Seymour's senior officer. That would be part of his file. Goddamn it, this is my father we're talking about!"

"Whatever it was, we know he went to meet her, Kate." The WITSEC agent just stared at her. "The rest—you connect the dots."

Kate sank back down. "Maybe he made a foolish choice or two that's made him look bad. I don't know why he tried to contact Margaret Seymour. Maybe someone was after him. Maybe *she* contacted *him. But those pictures . . .*" She shook her head, her eyes horrified and wide. "What they did . . . That's not my father. He's no killer. You know him, Agent Cavetti! How could you possibly think it was him?"

Suddenly Kate felt a sickening realization.

The bolt. To her apartment.

She looked back at Cavetti. "That's why you didn't warn me, wasn't it? After Tina was shot. *It was you.* You broke into the apartment. You were using me, to find my father. You wanted to know if he contacted me."

Cavetti stared at her without apology. "Kate, you have no idea what's at stake in this case."

"Then tell me, Agent Cavetti!" Kate stood up again. "Tell me what's at stake, and I'll tell you. My father may be dead. Or worse"—she pointed to the photo—"he may have done *that*. And I have a friend who's fighting for her life with a bullet in her brain that may have been meant for me.

"That's what's at stake, Agent Cavetti, for *me*. Whatever it is for you, I hope it's worth all that!"

Kate grabbed her bag, stepping over to the door.

"He'll try to contact you, Ms. Herrera," the FBI man said. "There'll be a missing-persons alert out for him. But you realize we're talking more than that."

"I saw those pictures, Agent Cavetti." Kate shook her head in anger. "And that's not him. It's not my father—no matter where the dots lead. He testified for you. He went to jail. You're the one who's supposed to be protecting *us*, so protect us, Cavetti. You're so sure my father's alive—find him!

"Find him." Kate opened the door. "Or I promise I will."

CHAPTER THIRTY-FOUR

Stroke . . .

Kate reached forward, powering her legs into the drive.

Stroke . . . Every five beats. In perfectly timed rhythm. Her muscles straining.

Then glide . . .

The Peinert X25 racing shell sped gracefully through the waters of the Harlem River. The early-morning sun glinted off the apartment buildings along the shore. Kate feathered the blades, sliding forward, shifting into her recovery. Her stroke was fluid and compact.

Drive . . .

She was taking it out on the river: All her anger. Her doubt. She rowed twice a week like clockwork, before work. In the cold and the rain. Under the railroad trestles, past Baker Field to the Hudson River. Two miles. She needed to do it—to fight off her diabetes. But today she just needed it for her peace of mind.

Stroke . . . .

Kate focused on her rhythm. Zen-like, two breaths to every stroke. Her heart rate climbing to 130. The spray kicked in her face. Her neoprene top clung to her. She trained her gaze on her wake, like perfectly carved ski edges in the snow.

Stroke . . .

She didn't believe them. The WITSEC agents. How could she? They couldn't even prove if her father was dead or alive.

She had grown up with him. He had given her his love—whatever he'd done. He always came out to watch her row. He always rooted her on. He helped her come through her illness. He taught her to fight.

She had to believe someone, right?

The WITSEC people were protecting something. Basically they had used her—to get to him. *"You don't know what's at stake in this case."*

The pain started to intensify in her chest. *Yes I do.*

Kate got as far as the cliffs across from Baker Field, a little over a mile. Then she turned around and picked up her pace against the current.

Every four beats now.

Her mother, Kate thought, she knew something, too. *"There are some things I've been holding
back for a long time now that you need to know . . ."*

What? What was it she was trying to say?

It wasn't fair that Kate had to be separated
from them. Sharon and Justin and Em. It wasn't
fair that they had to go through this without her.

Two Columbia University eights were on the
river practicing, too. The Peter Jay Sharp
Boathouse, where she stored her shell, was only
a short distance ahead.

Kate leaned into the last couple hundred
meters.

She picked up her stroke, the one she had in
college, her thighs pushing into the drive, her
body sliding forward in the shell. Then the craft
cut the surface on a perfectly even keel.

Faster.

She increased to every three beats. Her legs
driving in perfect unison with her arms. Kate
felt the muscles in her back straining, her heart
rate escalating. The fire burning in her lungs.

The final fifty meters, she stepped it up to an
all-out sprint. Kate glanced behind her—the
boathouse pier was just ahead of her now. *Stroke,
stroke* . . . Kate grimaced, her lungs exploding
with the burn.

Finally she released . . . the sleek craft gliding

through the imaginary finish line. Kate dropped her oars and brought her knees up to her chest, wincing in pain. She pushed her Oakleys high on her forehead, dropping her head on her arms.

What kind of animal do they think he is?

She let her mind drift back to the image of those horrible crime-scene photos. The sight of that poor woman beaten and murdered. What could she possibly have known that he would have done that for? What reason would he have? It made no sense—regardless of the facts.

Suddenly it scared her. Her whole life scared her.

Kate pulled in her oars and let the shell drift on its own toward the boathouse pier. The voice was back—the one inside her that had defended him so strongly just a day before.

Except this time it was saying something different. A doubt she couldn't put away.

Who the hell are you, Daddy?

Who?

The watcher stood high on the shore. He sat on the hood of his car, his binoculars trained on the river. He focused on the girl.

He had followed her many times—had seen her take out her striped blue craft in the early-morning mist. Always the same time. Seven A.M.,

Wednesdays and Saturdays. The same route. *Llueva o truene*. Rain or shine.

Not so smart, chica. He chewed on a wad of tobacco leaf in his cheek. The river can be dangerous.

Bad things can happen out there to a pretty girl like you.

She was strong, the watcher thought, impressed. In a way he admired her. She always pushed herself very hard. He liked how she always took it home in the final meters like a champion. She put her heart into it. The watcher chuckled to himself. She could lick most guys.

He watched her pull up to the pier and stow her oars and hoist the sleek craft up onto the landing. She shook the sweat and the salt of the river from her hair.

Es bonita. In a way he hoped he would never have to do anything to her or cause her harm. He liked watching her. He tossed the binoculars on the seat of the Escalade, next to the TEC-9.

But if he had to, *qué lástima*. . . . He tucked a large gold cross and chain into his shirt.

She should know better than anybody. The river is a dangerous place.

CHAPTER THIRTY-FIVE

Kate remained at home that night. Greg was doing a last late-night rotation at the ER for a while. He promised he would change his schedule so he could be with her at nights. That was when Kate felt the most alone.

She tried her best to fill the time by working on her thesis, 'Trypanosoma cruzi and the Molecular Strategies of Intercellular Pathogens Interacting with Their Host Cells'. Trypanosoma were parasites that blocked the fusion of lysosomes in the plasma membrane, which aided cell repair. Pretty ponderous, Kate knew, and unreadable—unless you happened to be among the fourteen people in the world who actually were turned on by lysosomal exocytosis.

Which tonight Kate wasn't. She pushed her glasses up on her forehead and turned off the computer.

The doubts about her father kept intruding. What to believe. Whom to trust. Was he dead or alive? This was the man she had lived with her whole life—whom she respected and adored, who raised her, shaped her values, who was there for her. Now she had no idea just who that man was.

Something flashed in her mind. Kate got up and went over to the old Irish armoire they had found at a flea market and where they now kept the TV. She knelt, opening the bottom drawer. Tucked way in the back, under an old Brown sweatshirt and a stack of manuals and magazines, she found what she'd buried there.

The envelope of photos and mementos she'd found in her parents' dresser more than a year before.

Kate never quite had the heart to look through it.

She shut the drawer and took the envelope over to the couch, curling up against the cushions. She slid the contents out onto the antique trunk that acted as their coffee table.

It was a lot of old stuff she'd never seen before. Her father's things. A few snapshots of him and Sharon when they were back in college. The late sixties, straggly long hair and all. A couple of gemological certificates. The program from his NYU graduation in 1969.

Some other things that went back much further than that.

Kate had never seen any of this before.

Letters to his mother, Rosa, in an early, barely discernible scrawl. From summer camp. From some early travels. Kate realized she didn't know very much about her father's past. His early years had always been a blur.

His mother had come from Spain. Kate knew virtually nothing about her grandfather. He had died in Spain when Ben was young. A car accident or something. In Seville. There was a large Jewish community there.

Out of the pile, Kate pulled a dog-eared black-and-white snapshot of a handsome woman in a stylish hat, standing, holding the arm of a slight man in a homburg in front of a café. Maybe back in Spain.

She was sure she was staring at her grand-father.

Kate smiled. Rosa was beautiful. Dark, European-looking, and proud. All Kate knew about her was that she had a love of music and art.

And she found others. One was of Rosa on horseback in the country, wearing an old-fashioned leather riding jacket and boots, her hair in braids. And another, on a streetcar, in a city Kate didn't recognize, holding an infant whom Kate recognized as her father. She traced the familiar lines in his infant face. *Her* lines . . . It almost brought tears to her eyes, tears of joy. Why had these been hidden? They were fascinating. She was finding a family history here, a family she never knew.

Kate stared closely at the undeveloped face of the man who had raised her. Which was easier to accept, she asked herself, that he was dead somewhere, murdered for a betrayal? Or that he was *alive*? Hiding out somewhere, having abandoned his family. And having committed this terrible crime.

Kate shuffled the photos and old letters into a pile. Outside, there was a government agent in an unmarked car, protecting her. Maybe Ben had gone to meet Margaret Seymour. Maybe there was something he'd needed to talk to her about. But he didn't kill her. *Kate knew her father.* She could look at these photos and see it in his face.

She was sure.

Kate started to stuff everything back inside the envelope. As she did, one last photo from the bottom of the pile dropped out.

It was a small, faded snapshot of her father as a teenager. Like one from an old Kodak. He had his arm around the shoulder of another man Kate didn't recognize, a few years older. She couldn't help but fix on the resemblance.

They were standing in front of a large wooden gate. It looked like the entrance to a country estate, or maybe an old estancia, a ranch, mountains in the background. There was writing on the back: *Carmenes. 1967.* That would have made him about eighteen.

Carmenes . . . Where was that? *Spain?*

Kate flipped the photo back over. There was a name above the gate in the background. She tried to make it out—wooden letters, partially obscured, hard to read. She pulled it closer and squinted.

Her blood turned to ice.

She fixed on it again, sounding out the almost illegible name. *This can't be* . . . She ran over to the desk. They kept a magnifying loupe there. She pulled open the top drawer. She found the loupe and cleared off the desk, her heart racing now. She pressed the magnifier to the photo and looked into it and stared.

Not at the two men in the foreground, but breathless, in total disbelief, above them.

At the name on the gate.

An urge to vomit rose up in Kate. It shook every bone in her body. She stared closely at her father's youthful face—at the man who would one day raise her. In that moment she realized she didn't know him. She had *never* known him. Or what he might be capable of. Or what he might have done.

The name on the gate above her father was MERCADO.

PART THREE

PART THREE

CHAPTER THIRTY-SIX

Even in darkness the man behind the wheel noticed the terrain changing. The flatlands of Indiana and Ohio were well behind him now. The interstate wound through the rising valleys of the Pennsylvania hill country. Heading east.

Only a few hours more . . .

The driver flicked on the radio, fighting off fatigue. He'd been driving so many hours now he'd lost count. He pushed the speed-search through the static of late-night talk shows and country-music stations until he found an oldies station that pleased him. Creedence Clearwater Revival's "Have You Ever Seen the Rain?" was playing.

Benjamin Raab's eyes burned.

His name was Geller now, the name they'd been living under for the past year.

Or was it Skinner—what his license read? It

didn't matter. They were all names he would never go back to again. Raab always claimed, in business, that preparedness had been one of his chief skills.

And he had been preparing for what he was doing now for a long time.

Raab caught a glimpse of his face in the rearview mirror. His eyes had lost the softness and light of the past twenty years. His smile . . . He wasn't sure if he even remembered how to smile. That was all in the past now, buried in the lines of his old face.

His old life.

He knew he had done things they would never understand. That he was driven by a part of himself that he had never shared. The ugliness . . . that was all part of it. That had taken everything he had. He thought of the pain he'd caused everyone. All the falsehoods he'd had to bear. They hurt. They hurt, until he forced himself to forget. Bury it in the past. They hurt him even now.

Still, the past didn't die, did it?

Raab remembered how Kate had taken his hand that night, after everything had come out. *I just want to know that the person who walked through that door tonight is the same one I've known all my life.*

And how he'd looked back at her and answered, "I am that man."

I am that man.

A Chevy Blazer shot by him with Pennsylvania plates. It made Raab recall the game his family used to play when they drove on long trips.

"I see a *P!*" The Keystone State. He almost heard Justin shout out from the backseat, "There's an *N!*"

And Emily answer, "New Hampshire. *'Live Free or Die!'*"

A smile came to Raab's lips. How Justin and Em would fight it out, like boxers in the ring, until it was clear Justin had memorized all fifty states, and Em would accuse him of cheating and roll her eyes, saying that it was just a stupid game anyway, for babies . . .

A tremor of complete loneliness and isolation stabbed him. He missed them all very much. Still, there would be no doubt. He would do what he had to do. Maybe one day they would understand. Maybe even forgive him. He had not been the person they thought he was, but he had never lied.

Family, he had always told them. *It was always about family.*

Raab pulled up behind a truck in the left lane. An *I.* Illinois.

Land of Lincoln! he almost heard himself call out loud.

Blood washed away blood, he thought. That was the code. The law he lived by. It was who he was. There were actions that needed to be righted. He wouldn't stop until it was done.

The hunt was just beginning.

It was still about family now.

CHAPTER THIRTY-SEVEN

Kate could hardly work the following day.

She did her best to put it aside: the assault of questions brought on by her father's photo from the night before. She peered into the scope, recording the rate of stem-cell division, the phagocytic cytosis of Tristan and Isolde. But all she could see was his face in front of that gate, that chilling name.

Kate understood now that much of her life had been a terrible lie.

After staring at the photo, Kate had looked up the town of Carmenes on the Internet. It wasn't in Spain, as she'd thought. *It was in Colombia.*

Colombia. *Where the Mercados were from.*

In that instant everything in Kate's life changed. She wanted to believe in him, to think of him as he had been. But for the second time, she saw her father as someone different than the person she always thought she knew. Not as a victim but as someone with a past—a past unconnected to hers. With a terrible, powerful secret to hide. A secret that changed everything. And it scared her. Terrified her.

Her family's life had been ruined, her best friend shot. People had been killed in the protection of that lie.

What are you doing in front of that sign, Daddy?

Did the WITSEC agents know about this? Did her mother? All these years? Was everything just a lie, every story of his past, his work, the trial? Every time he put his arms around her?

She remembered her mother's voice: *"There are some things I've been holding back for a long time now that you need to know . . ."*

What things? Kate stood up from the scope. *What were you trying to tell me, Mom?*

The previous night, when Greg finally came home, he could see in her face immediately that something was wrong.

She was leafing through a stack of old e-mails and letters she had received from her mom and her brother and sister over the past year. She needed to feel close to them. Mom had let Emily go to her first concert alone. Third Eye Blind, Em's favorite group. Kate could almost feel Em's excitement. She was on cloud nine . . .

"What's wrong, Kate?"

Kate handed him the photo of her father she had found.

At first he didn't seem surprised. Or even angry. As he focused on the letters above her father's head, his eyes opened wide.

"I don't understand . . . There has to be some reason, Kate." An uncomprehending look crept onto his face.

"What reason, Greg? What sort of reason could there possibly be? That he's a liar. That he's been hiding something from us all my life. That he's actually *connected* to these awful people. How is it possible, Greg? *That he actually did those horrible things*. . . .

"I'm sorry," Kate said. "I just can't hide from this anymore. I have to know."

"You have to know *what*, Kate?" He put the photo down and sat at the table across from her. "That your father wasn't who you supposed he was? This is *our* life now—not his. I don't know what he's done, but I do know you're not going to find out by looking under a scope. This is dangerous, Kate. These people outside—we need them. I can't even think of what happened to Tina happening to you."

Greg is right, Kate knew, staring out at the lab. *The answer isn't under a scope.*

It was real and scary, and she didn't know how to go about finding it, or what she would find there when she did. Or even whom she could trust.

But she had to know. The picture changed everything.

Because the name on the gate that sickened her—Mercado—meant it was no longer just about him, her father. The name on that gate was about her, too.

About every memory, every touch she had felt. Every moment of laughter in her life.

The WITSEC agents wouldn't let Kate see her family. She had to find another way.

Greg was right, the answer wasn't under a lens.

It was right out in the open. And Kate had an idea where.

CHAPTER THIRTY-EIGHT

In the bedroom of her white clapboard house, Sharon began typing the words into her computer. *"Kate . . ."*

There were about a thousand things she wanted to say.

"First, I want to tell you how much I miss you and love you—and how very sad I am that we have put you at risk. But there are things, things I had almost forgotten myself, that I have to say. Time does that, you know. Time and hope. The hope that the past is the past—which it never is. And that the person you will become is different from the person you are now."

A cold wind blew off the bay, rattling the window. *"It's late. Justin and Em are asleep. This time of night, Kate, I feel like it's just you and me."*

Downstairs, a female agent stayed awake

through the night. There was a tracer on their phones. Across the street there was always a car.

"The kids are holding up well, I guess. They miss their father. They miss a lot of things. Their life. You. They're young, and they're confused. They have every right to be. As I'm sure you are, too.

"Your father may be dead—or not, I don't know. But I am sure I will never see him again. Whatever he's done, do not judge him too harshly. He loves you. He has always loved you. He's loved all of you. He's tried to protect you, all these years. Secrets are hard to keep. They burn a hole in the lining of your soul. It's so much easier to forget.

"So let me tell you, Kate . . . now."

Sharon wrote. She wrote it all out, all the things she felt compelled to say. The meaning of the pendant she had left with Kate. All the things Kate had to know. About her father.

She even told her where they were living.

How much she wanted to say, *The hell with it—come, Kate, come. We miss you so much. We need to be together. I don't care about the goddamned rules. Find us, honey. Come. You need to know the truth . . .*

Everything came rushing out. *"I'm sorry, Kate. For keeping things secret. That you have to feel afraid. For Tina. For keeping our family apart."*

She felt like a true mother again, for the first time in a year.

Suddenly a light flashed in the window. It always scared her. She glanced at the clock and knew it was time.

The government vehicle pulled up the long driveway. As it did every night. She heard the driver's door open, the agent step out, utter a couple of unintelligible words to his colleague. The changing of the guard.

Sharon stared at the screen. She read over what she had written. A sadness began to tug at her heart.

"Yes, baby, you should know it all." She read it over again. It was all there. She poised her finger over the "send" icon.

Then she hesitated.

"Live your life," she'd told her daughter. And she meant it with all her heart. Live your life. You don't have to know. There's hope there.

Sharon shut her eyes, as she had a hundred times over the same message she had written out a hundred nights before. She knew that Kate would never get to read it. She knew she mustn't get her involved.

"Live your life," she whispered again, aloud.

And she pressed "delete."

The letter disappeared. Sharon sat there facing

a blank screen. She typed four more words, then let her forehead sink to the table as she wiped a tear off her cheek.

The same words she wrote every night before she went to sleep.

"I love you, Mom."

CHAPTER THIRTY-NINE

It had never been entirely clear who had informed on Kate's father to the FBI. With his own admission of guilt, his voice caught on tape, it never really seemed to matter. He pled guilty; he testified against his friend; he went to jail. The FBI had never divulged the informant's identity—even during the trial.

The transcripts were all a matter of public record. Kate had never been to the courthouse or read over the records. She had never wanted to see him like that. But now she did. It was just a matter of finessing them from the judge's clerk, being a little circumspect to everyone about why she wanted them.

A few days later, the message was left on her cell phone. From Alice, Mel Kipstein's secretary. "Mr. Kipstein asked me to call, Kate. What you're looking for is in."

Kate went up to the lawyer's office, in a tall glass building on Thirty-fifth and Park. His secretary took her into a large room where several heavy black folders sat on the sleek rosewood conference table.

"Make yourself at home, Kate," Alice told her. "There's some water. If you need anything else, just call. Mr. Kipstein's in conference. Hopefully, he'll be in soon."

She closed the door.

Kate sank into a leather chair, pulling over the first bound volume. It was full of legal documents filed with the court: depositions, evidence forms, witness agreements. Kate didn't even know what she was looking for. Suddenly this idea seemed a little foolish and overwhelming. She was just praying that something was here.

She started with the opening statements. It was disturbing to see the evidence mounted against her father, to read about him as a co-conspirator and a felon. Admitting guilt, confessing his crimes, turning on his friend.

She moved ahead to the section in Folder Three where he took the stand. The prosecutor told the court how he had openly conspired to break the law. How he had taken kickbacks, payoffs. How he had passed them on to his friend Harold Kornreich. How all along he had known whom he was dealing with. On cross-examination the defense counsel tried his best to discredit him.

LAWYER: You've pretty much lied to everyone about your involvement. Haven't you, Mr. Raab?

RAAB: Yes.

LAWYER: You lied to the FBI when you were arrested. You lied to the Justice Department. You lied to your employees. You even lied to your own wife and children, isn't that right, Mr. Raab?

RAAB: Yes.

LAWYER: Speak up.

RAAB: *Yes.*

Kate's chest tightened. This whole charade . . . *He's lying to us even now!*

It hurt to read it. To see him pretending to be repentant at the same time he was betraying his friend. Maybe this wasn't such a good idea. Kate leafed through the pages, reading over his testimony. She didn't even know what the hell she was looking for.

Then something caught her eye.

One of the government's follow-up witnesses. His name was withheld but both attorneys called him by a pseudonym: Smith. He said he worked for Beecham Trading. Beecham was the name of the street they used to live on.

That was her father's firm.

Kate's pulse started to quicken as she leaned over the black-bound folder with heightened interest. Next to speak was Nardozzi, the government prosecutor.

NARDOZZI: What was your job at Beecham, Mr. Smith?
WITNESS: I handled the daily accounting. Cash disbursements, the resolution of trades.

Kate's eyes widened. *Oh, my God.*
She realized who it was!

NARDOZZI: In the course of your job, did you handle payments from Paz Enterprises?
WITNESS: Yes I did, Mr. Nardozzi. They were one of our largest customers.
NARDOZZI: What about receipts from Argot Manufacturing?
WITNESS: [*Nods*] Yes, again, sir. Payments, too.
NARDOZZI: And at any time did you

happen to grow suspicious of those receipts from Argot?

WITNESS: Yes I did, sir. Argot was a manufacturing company. Paz transshipped their product to them directly, so there was a lot of back-and-forth. I spoke to Mr. Raab about it at length. Several times. The invoices ... they just didn't seem kosher.

NARDOZZI: By not kosher, you mean they were well beyond the normal commission rate.

WITNESS: [*Softly*] Yes, Mr. Nardozzi. That—and that they were all for ordinary items, that were shipped offshore.

NARDOZZI: Offshore?

WITNESS: The Caymans, Trinidad, Mexico. But I knew they weren't ending up there. I spoke with Ben about it. Several times over the years. He kept putting me off by saying that this was just an unusual account that billed in their own way. But I knew where they were going. I knew the people we were dealing with and the kind of money that was coming in. I may be an accountant, Mr. Nardozzi [*laugh*], but I'm not a fool.

NARDOZZI: So what did you do, Mr.

Smith, about the questions you had? After you say you spoke with your boss several times and he kept putting you off?

Kate read the response. She pulled back from the transcript. A chill ran down her spine.

WITNESS: [*Long pause*] I contacted the FBI.

CHAPTER FORTY

Kate stepped forward, surprising the heavyset man as he stepped out of the office building on Thirty-third Street.

"Howard?"

Howard Kurtzman had worked for her father for twenty years. It wasn't hard to find him. Her dad's old secretary, Betsy, knew the toy company where he worked now. The accountant had always been a creature of habit. He always went out at twelve o'clock sharp for lunch.

"*Kate?*" His eyes regarded her nervously. People rushed by on the busy street. "Jeez, Kate, it's been a while. How've you been?"

Kate had always had a fondness for him. When she was growing up, he was the guy who always handled the office's day-to-day. The type who always felt he was the glue that held the place together. It was Howard who always sent

Kate her monthly allowance checks back in college. Once he even vouched for her when she went over her credit-card limit in Italy and didn't want her father to know. Howard was still overweight, had lost a little hair on top, and spoke with a bit of a wheeze. He was still wearing the same thick support shoes and fat, out-of-style tie. He always referred to Kate as "Boss's Daughter Number One."

"Congratulations," he said, adjusting his glasses. "I heard you got married, Kate."

"Thanks." She looked at him. There was something about this that Kate felt was a little sad.

"So is this a coincidence, or what?" The accountant tried to laugh. "I'm afraid the old checkbook is closed."

"Howard, I read the transcripts." Kate stepped forward.

"The transcripts . . ." He scratched his head uncomfortably. "Jeez, Kate, a whole year's gone by. *Now?*"

"Howard, I know it was you," Kate said. "I know you were the person who turned him in."

"You're wrong." He shook his head. "I was subpoenaed by the FBI."

"Howard, please . . ." Kate placed her hand on the accountant's arm. "I don't care. I know that my father did some bad things. I just want to know, why did you do it? After all those years? Did someone put you up to it? Pressure you? Howard, you were like part of the family."

"I told you." His eyes flitted around anxiously. "They subpoenaed me, Kate. I didn't have a choice."

"Maybe someone else did, then? In the business. Did someone pay you, Howard? Please, this is important." Kate realized she was sounding a little frantic. "I have to know."

Howard led her over to the curb, away from the flow of people. Kate could see he was really afraid.

"Why are you doing this, Kate? Why are you going back there now?"

"It isn't 'back there' for me, Howard. My father's missing. No one's seen him for the past week. My mother's crazy over this. We can't even find out if he's dead or alive."

"I'm sorry," he said. "But you can't be here, Kate. I have a life—"

"We have lives, too, Howard. Please, I know you know something. You can't hate him that much."

"You think I hate him?" There was a little denial in his voice, something Kate took as sadness, too. "Don't you understand, I worked for your father for twenty years."

Kate's eyes glistened. "I know."

He didn't budge. "I'm sorry. You were wrong to come here, Kate." He tried to pull himself away. "Face it, your father was a criminal, Kate. I did the right thing. I've got to go."

Kate reached out and took hold of the accountant's arm. She could barely hide her feelings. She had known Howard Kurtzman since she was a kid.

"I did the right thing, Kate. Don't you understand?" He looked like he was having a meltdown. "Go away now, please. This is *my* life now. Leave me alone, Kate, and don't come back."

CHAPTER FORTY-ONE

It was a chilly October morning. Kate was on the river again. The WITSEC agent guarding her was watching from the parking lot high above the boathouse on the shore.

Kate pushed off the pier and headed upstream, in the direction of the Hudson. Up ahead, on the cliff at the bend at Baker Field, the sun shone luminously off the huge painted Columbia C.

The currents were a little choppy that morning, and the traffic was light. Kate found herself pretty much alone out there. She started by doing five-beat strokes, just to get her rhythm. The sleek shell glided easily through the waves. Up ahead there was a launch boat in the middle of the river, in the stretch they called the Narrows, between Swindler's Cove and Baker Field.

She charted a course to stay clear of it. *Okay, Kate, push it ... Let it go ...*

She leaned forward and powered into her routine, increasing her pace to every four beats. Her neoprene wetsuit blocked out the biting wind and cold. In her rhythm Kate's mind drifted back to the day before. How fidgety Howard had been. How agitated he seemed even just at running into her. He was hiding something, Kate was sure. But he wasn't about to tell her. Someone had pressured him to go to the FBI. And she was sure her mother knew something as well. Kate was worried about her. Alone out there. She was worried about all of them. The WITSEC people weren't being straight with her.

Kate pushed against the current, powering with her legs, her seat sliding aft. She glanced behind her. She was approaching the Bend. The current was choppy, and the wind sliced into her wetsuit. She'd gone close to a mile.

That's when she caught sight of the launch boat she had noticed before. It was coming up behind her.

There were lanes out here. She had the right-of-way. At first Kate just groaned and thought, *Hey, wake up, asshole.* There was no one out there but the two of them. The boat was a couple of tons at least, and it seemed to be going fast. The wake alone could capsize her.

Kate broke her stroke, steering out of its way in the direction of the Bronx shore.

She glanced behind her again. The oncoming boat had shifted course as well—still on her! *Jesus, are these people even awake?* There were about a hundred yards between them now, the bright red hull starting to get very large. Kate jerked the oars again and glanced back around. Her heart started to beat faster.

The launch wasn't just headed in her direction.

It was on a collision course. It was bearing right down on her.

Now Kate started to get scared. She looked behind her toward the boathouse and the WITSEC guard up there who was powerless to do anything, even if he saw what was going on. The boat was speeding down on her. It could slice her fiberglass shell in two. Kate picked up her pace. *Don't they see me?* The boat was getting closer. So close she could make out two men in the cabin. One had long, dark hair in a ponytail and was staring down at her. That was when the truth struck home.

They weren't distracted at all. This wasn't an accident.

They were going to ram her.

Frantically, Kate dug at the oars, drawing the tiny shell around in the face of the oncoming craft. *Jesus!* Her eyes got wide, staring at it. *We're going to hit!* At the very last second, there was a deafening honk. The boat, its lumbering, massive hull right above her, veered. Kate screamed. There was a sickening, grating sound—her oar shattering in two. Her shell was lifted in the wake like a flimsy toy.

The boat ripped through the back of her scull. *Oh, God . . . no.*

The next thing Kate knew, she was underwater. It was murky and freezing cold, and it hit her like concrete. The river rushed into her lungs. Kate kicked, thrashing her arms in the boat's violent eddy. She felt like she was fighting for her life. She desperately tried to push her way up.

Suddenly she realized—*You can't come up here, Kate.*

These people are trying to kill you.

Every cell in her body was crying out in confusion and panic. She scissor-kicked underwater and swam, praying there was enough air in her lungs, as far as her strength would take her. She wasn't sure in which direction. When her lungs felt as if they were giving out, she clawed her way to the surface. She was disoriented for a second, gasping for precious, needed oxygen. She caught sight of the shore. *The Bronx shore.* About thirty yards away. The only person who could help her now was on the other side.

Kate spun around and spotted the launch boat circling in the vicinity of her capsized craft. Nearby she saw the pieces of her blue Peinert shell, severed in two. She saw the man with the dark, knotted hair in the stern of the boat scanning the wreckage. Slowly his gaze veered in a widening arc, moving toward the shoreline.

It landed squarely on her.

Jesus, Kate, you've got to get out of here now.

She sucked in a lungful of air and dove back underwater. For a few seconds, she swam parallel to the shore, petrified to come up. Then it got narrow and shallow and her muscles started giving out, and she swam the last, agonizing yards and pulled herself up, gulping convulsively, onto the rocky bank. She rolled over, too exhausted to even care about her safety. Her eyes drifted back to where she thought she should find the boat.

It was gone.

She saw it moving away, chugging full speed down the river. Ponytail was still in the stern, staring back.

Kate dropped her head onto the soil and coughed out a lungful of oily, fuel-smelling water. Somehow the boat had veered away—at the very last second. If it hadn't, she'd be dead.

She didn't know if they had tried to kill her or if she had just been warned. Either way, she understood what it meant.

Mercado was no longer just a name, or a threat.

It was the key to her survival now.

CHAPTER FORTY-TWO

She had already made up her mind, long before the police ever got to her.

Long before the launch, which had been stolen the day before from a boatyard on City Island, had been found abandoned on an East River pier.

Before the gash on her arm from the splintered oar had been treated and bandaged, and before Greg had rushed up to the hospital to take her home and before she broke down when she saw him, realizing just how lucky she was to be alive.

She had made up her mind back on the shore.

What she had to do.

With her lungs on fire, her fingers pressed into the wet but precious soil, with the boat that had almost cut her in two chugging away, and the unmistakable look of clarity in Ponytail's eyes.

Okay, you win, Kate seethed as the boat sped away. *You wanted me, you got me, you bastards, I'm yours.* She could no longer just stand by.

If they'd managed to find her, they could locate her family. Her mother knew something about why her father had disappeared. Why he was in that picture. The truth about their lives. They could be in danger.

Kate knew, even as Greg hugged her, what she had to do.

The WITSEC agents wouldn't help her get to them.

It was up to her to find her family now.

The doctor gave her some Valium, and Kate slept for a couple of hours back at the apartment. Before he left, Greg knelt by the bed and stroked her hair.

"There's an agent at the door, and the police are outside. Even better, Fergie's on guard."

"Good." Kate smiled sleepily and squeezed his hand.

"You've got to be careful, Kate. I love you. I can't even think about what might have happened. I'll be back early. I promise."

Nodding, her lids weighted, Kate closed her eyes.

She awoke in the middle of the afternoon. She

still felt a little woozy and shaken, but otherwise she was fine. There was a bandage wrapped around her left arm. She glanced outside the window and spotted an FBI man and a couple of police uniforms on the street below. There was also a guard stationed on her floor, outside the apartment.

It wouldn't be easy to go about this, Kate realized. She couldn't e-mail them. She couldn't call. The agents weren't about to let her out of their sight now.

Where the hell did she even begin?

In the bottom drawer of her desk was the accordion folder she kept filled with the old e-mails and correspondence she had received from them throughout the past year. Kate had never destroyed them, as she'd been instructed. These messages and cards were all she had. She'd read them over several times.

There had to be something in there. *Somewhere* . . .

She put a Bartók string quartet on the external iPod and began leafing through them. Truth was, she'd always had a few ideas. Justin once wrote that they had a dock on their property and they could get around by boat, which he thought was cool. Mom wrote that the winter wasn't too bad at all—that mostly it just rained a lot. Maybe

Northern California, Kate always surmised. Or the Northwest coast. Even if her hunches were right about that, it was still a huge amount of territory.

She didn't even know their new name.

Page by page, she pieced through the stack of correspondence. At first it was pretty much just "miss you" notes and a lot of complaints. Things weren't the same where they were. Nothing was like before. Justin was finding it hard to meet new friends. Em was mostly miffed about Dad and new squash coaches who weren't as good.

Mom just seemed depressed. *"You don't know how much we all miss you, darling."*

Then, over the year, the messages got a little brighter. As Agent Seymour had promised, they started adjusting. Mom was in a garden club. Justin found this guy who had a music studio in his basement, and they started recording stuff. Em met a few boys. She had aced her new SATs. Kate came across the note Em had written about the first concert that Mom had let her go to alone.

"3EB," Em signed.

No translation needed. *Third Eye Blind.*

Her sister had sent it back in June, practically giddy with elation. *"It was sooo ridiculous, K! So much fun!!! Stephan Jenkins was awesome!!!"* They stayed until after midnight. On a school night.

One of her girlfriends had arranged for a limo to drive them back home.

It made Kate smile to read it all over again. Then suddenly the smile receded. She focused on the band's name.

Third Eye Blind.

That was it! *Third Eye Blind.* Kate ran across the room to her desk and flicked on the computer. She Googled the band's name. A few seconds later, their Web site appeared on the screen. There was a link on the site for NEWS, and when Kate clicked on it, she found another link for the band's recent summer tour. She scrolled down. Em's e-mail was dated June 14. June 2 and 3, the band played in Los Angeles. June 6, they moved on to San Francisco.

June 9 and 10, they were in Seattle, Washington.

Em had said the concert was the week before. Kate started piecing together what she knew: *They took a limo home. They could get around by boat . . .*

It had to be either San Francisco or Seattle.

But even if she was right, how would she go about finding them? How did she narrow it down? There were millions of people in those cities. This was the proverbial needle in a haystack. And she didn't even have a name. She didn't even know what the needle looked like.

Until it dawned on her.

"Now on, where you go, I go," her new body-guard, whose name was Oliva, had told her. "When you're at work, I'm at work. When you row, I row ..."

Jesus, Kate, that's it!

She rowed. Sharon did yoga. And *Emily* ... Emily was the key!

Kate got up and went to the window. The WITSEC agent's car was parked on the street below.

She knew there was no way she could tell Greg. And that fact was already making her feel disloyal and ashamed. He would say it was way too dangerous, too crazy. If she told him, he would never, ever let her go. She couldn't bring it up.

And she'd somehow have to lose these WITSEC guards first.

Fergus wagged his way over, sensing something, and plopped his chin on her knee.

"Sorry, baby." Kate put her head down and stroked his ears. "Daddy's going to hate me. But I have to be gone for a while."

Maybe she did know what the needle looked like after all.

CHAPTER FORTY-THREE

Phil Cavetti had been inside the FBI's headquarters on Pennsylvania Avenue many times.

Just never to the tenth floor.

And flanked by his boss at the U.S. Marshals Service and an FBI liaison as the private elevator came to a stop, the rolling in his stomach reminded him he wasn't exactly thrilled that his initial visit there had been called for ten that night.

The doors opened to a security station with two armed soldiers on guard. The FBI escort nodded at them and led the group past a large bullpen of workstations, home to the Bureau's elite analysts and staff, then down a hall of glass-paneled offices bearing the names of some of the most powerful in law enforcement.

The door to the corner office was open, the only one with a light still on inside. Cavetti cleared his throat and straightened his tie. The door read DEPUTY DIRECTOR, NARCOTICS AND ORGANIZED CRIME.

He could see the dome of the U.S. Capitol lit up through the office window.

Ted Cummings was on the phone behind his glass-topped desk, his tie loose, his expression not exactly pleased. He waved Cavetti and his boss, Calvin White, to a couch across from the desk. The office was large. An American flag hung in one corner. Behind the desk, photos of the deputy director with the president and other prominent government officials, and the FBI seal. Someone else was already seated on the couch. Someone Cavetti had no trouble recognizing. He realized he was way above his pay grade. The FBI man who had walked them up stepped out and shut the door.

"Phil, you know Hal Roach," Cal White introduced him. The white-haired man leaned forward and shook Cavetti's hand.

Roach was assistant attorney general of the United States.

Way, way above his pay grade.

"All right." The deputy director clicked off his phone. He came over and sank into a leather chair and sighed, as if he wasn't exactly thrilled to be here and not at home with his wife and children—not to mention having one of the highest-ranking Justice officials in his office as well. Grunting, he tossed a file onto a coffee table in front of the couch, and the contents slid out.

They were photos of Margaret Seymour's torture and execution.

Cummings looked at White with a peremptory sigh. "Cal, I believe the subject of these photos is familiar to you? Any thoughts on just who she was working with?"

White cleared his throat, glancing toward Cavetti. "Phil . . ."

Cavetti didn't need to be reminded that what he said in the next few moments could determine the rest of his career.

"Frank Gefferelli, Corky Chiodo," he said, "part of the Corelli family. Ramón Quintero, from the Corrados. Jeffrey Atkins, you may remember he was a whistle-blowing attorney in the Aafco fraud?"

The deputy director shut his eyes and nodded disgustedly.

Cavetti wet his lips and held his breath, then exhaled. "Bachelor Number One."

He used the code name. The one everybody that high up in law enforcement knew. If the initial names had caused the temperature to rise, Cavetti knew, this one would blow the fucking generator.

A stunned silence fell over the room. Everyone stared at him. Cummings's eyes shifted to White's in exasperation, then over to the assistant attorney general.

"Bachelor Number One." The deputy director nodded gravely. "*Cute.*"

For a second, everyone seemed to ponder the implications of having the identity of the most important narcotics informant in U.S. custody divulged. Someone who for years had been aiding convictions against the Mercado family. Because he had spent the car ride over pondering the very same question, Cavetti flashed instead to the Northern Peninsula of Michigan, where he knew, most likely, he would be finishing out his career.

"Gentlemen." The assistant attorney general leaned forward. "I think we've all put in enough time in this game to recognize what a *total fucking disaster* looks like when it hits you in the face. Do you know what the implications would be if those were the whereabouts Agent Seymour happened to divulge?"

"We're not entirely sure Agent Seymour's murder was actually connected to this." Cal White, the head of the U.S. Marshals Service, was clearly trying to posture.

"And I'm not Shaquille O'Neal." The FBI director glowered. "But you're here—"

"Yes." The head of the WITSEC Program nodded glumly. "We're here."

"So I think the three of us have to make a commitment," the deputy director said. "This breach ends right here. This other missing guy, this 'MIDAS' figure"—he glanced at a sheet of paper—"who you think had some play in this, Benjamin Raab—just where the hell is *he*?"

"He's gone," Cavetti admitted, his boss helplessly looking on. "He's in what we call the Blue Zone. Disappeared. We have his family under watch now."

"The Blue Zone." The deputy director's gaze seemed to burn right through him. "That's what? WITSEC-speak for you basically have no fucking idea?" He looked around the room, angry, then sighed. "Okay, so much for Bachelor Number *Two*, what about Bachelor Number One? I assume you have him under wraps and moved?"

"That's why we're here." Calvin White grew pale and cleared his throat. "He's in the Blue Zone, too."

CHAPTER FORTY-FOUR

U.S. Marshal Freddie Oliva had been a WITSEC agent for six years. He'd grown up in the Bronx, where his father worked as a switchman for the MTA. He'd gone to John Jay College of Criminology, received a degree in prelaw, and maybe he'd go for the bar one day, but right now there was a kid on the way and bills to take care of, and this was a whole lot closer to the action than sitting in some room with an audio plug in his ear listening to Homeland Security chatter.

Deputy Marshal Oliva liked working for the feds. Most of these dudes, they were pretty much FBI wannabes who couldn't make it into the program at Quantico. He had it all over them. Sometimes he did guard duty at the courts or had to accompany some Mafia honcho on the trip to trial. Or to a new location. He got to talk to these goombahs, got to know some pretty well. Maybe one day he'd write a book.

What Freddie didn't like one bit was baby-sitting duty. An intern could sit here and observe that pooch taking a pee. But after what happened on the river, he'd be all over this chick like grease on bacon. Anyway, it'd be done soon enough. That dude Raab would make a mistake, show up somewhere. They'd nab him and pull her protection. He'd be back to his regular job.

"*Oliva,*" a voice suddenly crackled in his earphone, "*the subject's coming down the elevator now.*"

Subject . . . He snorted cynically and rolled his eyes. The "subject" wasn't some crazy-assed hit man they were hiding for trial. Or some twenty-to-lifer who blew jail and was on the run.

Subject was a twenty-three-year-old biologist with a dog who had to pee.

"Got it," he grunted back. Oliva cracked the car door and stretched his muscles. He could use a little exercise. Sitting in this car all day was making him stiff as a goddamned board.

A few moments later, the building door opened and the "subject" stepped out, with Fido, who had his eyeballs fixed on the curb.

Oliva couldn't believe he actually got paid for this job.

"Don't you ever call it a day?" Kate Raab came up to him, the dog pulling her along on his leash.

"You go, I go." Oliva winked. "You know that, mama. That's the drill now."

"And does the drill include going poop?" Kate stared at him. She had on nice-fitting jeans and a quilted jacket, a knapsack over her back, and Freddie found himself thinking that if he had ever had a biology teacher who looked like this, he would've spent a lot more time in the lab than on the ball field. She held out a plastic bag. "Here, Oliva, it'll make you feel useful."

He grinned. "I'm feeling useful just fine." He liked a client with a sense of humor.

Fergus came up to him wagging his tail. Oliva figured these past couple of days he had every move the pooch made down pat. First a little sniff around the pole. Then his ass would wiggle at the curb. Then squat—*Bingo!* Oliva leaned on the car, observing. *Shit, Freddie, the girl's not wrong. You gotta get yourself some new work about now.*

Kate let the dog pull her farther down the block. Oliva put his hands in the pocket of his leather jacket against the chill, checking his gun, and followed a short way behind. When they got in front of the little bodega she sometimes shopped in, Kate turned back.

"You mind if I go in and grab some toothpaste, Oliva? Or you want to call Cavetti and check if you have to come in and help me with that, too?"

"No, I figure you can handle that." Freddie put up his palms as if surrendering. He knew how women got mad, and he didn't need to make her mad at him. "Five minutes. You know the—"

"Yeah." Kate rolled her eyes. "I know the drill."

She dragged Fergus along and stepped inside. They knew her and didn't seem to mind her bringing him in there with her. She strapped him up inside the entrance and scrunched her face sourly at him.

Okay, okay. Only doing my job.

Oliva went back to the car and leaned on the hood, an eye on the market. A call buzzed in on the radio. Jenkins. His replacement. He'd be there at six. Oliva checked his watch. Twenty of. None too soon. He was set to go home, collect his three hours' time and a half, pop a beer. Little woman had his favorite meal going tonight. Snapper Veracruz. Maybe there was a Knicks game, too.

His attention shifted to a couple of kids wearing basketball jerseys coming his way down the street. One was trying to dribble past the other. One of them wasn't half bad. Freddie was thinking how back on Baychester Avenue, where he grew up, he used to handle a ball pretty well himself.

He took another glance down the street at the market. *Man, she must be checking out every brand in the store.* Several minutes went by. He didn't want to make the girl too mad. He had to see her tomorrow. And the day after that. But somewhere it started to creep in on Freddie that a boatload of time had gone by. Long enough to buy a dental practice, let alone a tube of toothpaste. An empty feeling suddenly gnawed at his stomach.

Something wasn't right.

Oliva pushed off the hood and barked into the radio. "Finch, I'm heading up the block to that market. I don't like what's going on."

He pushed through the door. The first thing he saw relieved him. Fergus was sitting there, his leash wrapped around the newspaper rack. Kate couldn't be far behind.

Then he noticed the piece of paper folded into Fergus's collar. As he opened it, every cell in Oliva's body went limp.

"Oliva," the note read, *"make sure Fergie gets a pee on the way home. My husband should be back around six."*

Oliva balled up the paper. *"Sonovabitch!"*

He bolted over the checkout counter, running frantically up and down the aisles. *No fucking sign.*

There was a doorway leading out back, behind the meat section. Oliva pushed his way through. It led to an alley that fed onto Eighth Street, a whole other block. The alley was empty. A kid in an apron was stacking crates and boxes.

"Where the hell did she go?" Oliva shouted at him.

The kid pulled out his iPod earpiece. "Where'd *who* go, man?"

Freddie Oliva closed his eyes. How was he going to explain this? Someone was trying to kill this girl. Her father may have murdered a fellow agent. He slammed his palm against the brick wall.

Kate Raab was gone.

CHAPTER FORTY-FIVE

Luis Prado pulled his black Escalade to a stop halfway down the street from the blue-shingled house in tree-lined Orchard Park, New York, outside of Buffalo. He cut the lights.

It was quiet here, Luis reflected. Kids, *familias* . . . basketball hoops over the garages. Not bent, rusted ones on dirt fields like where he grew up. Nothing bad would ever happen here. *Right?*

He reached for his binoculars and through the night-vision lenses spotted two slumping shapes in the unmarked Ford parked directly across from the blue-shingled house.

The one behind the wheel looked half asleep. The other was smoking a cigarette, probably contemplating just how unlucky he'd been to have drawn this assignment. Luis scanned the block. No vans or delivery vehicles, the usual stakeout bases where more agents might hide.

Other than the *federales* in the Taurus, he didn't see anyone else around.

A laundry truck turned onto the street. It pulled to a stop in front of a neighboring house. A deliveryman hopped out and dropped a bundle on the front stoop. He rang the bell.

Luis Prado understood that the next time he came back here, it would be messy. Just like with that pretty federal agent back in Chicago. That one had been cruel. She'd been very well trained, and it had taken all his acquired skills and stomach. But in the end it had been helpful. In the end they'd gotten the things they needed to know. It had brought him here.

Luis's attention was grabbed by the garage door opening. A woman stepped out—middle-aged, pleasant-looking, gray hair tied in a bun. She had a dog on the leash, a white Lab. He seemed to be chipper, nice. She placed a trash bag in one of the garbage bins, let the dog do his thing. One of the agents in the Ford got out and walked a short distance up the driveway. The two chatted for a moment, the woman staying in the safety of the garage. Luis looked closely. He didn't see anyone else inside.

The laundry truck lumbered down the street, passing him.

The two in the Taurus wouldn't prove to be

much of a problem. He'd dealt with this before.

Fraternidad esto destino. Luis sighed. It was fated. The choice had already been made. He would wait, watch, until he saw his target. He covered the Sig nine-millimeter on the seat across from him with a newspaper.

Next time he'd be doing his thing.

CHAPTER FORTY-SIX

Two days later Kate's taxi pulled up in front of the stuccoed, Spanish-style building tucked behind the Arby's in a strip mall in Mill Valley, California, across the bay from San Francisco.

"This it, ma'am?" the driver asked, checking the yellow stuck-on numbers over the building's glass doors.

Kate tried to read the sign. This was the fourth location she'd been to that day. She was starting to get a little jet-lagged and discouraged, starting to think maybe her brainstorm wasn't such a flash of brilliance after all, but just some crazy wild-goose chase that would land her in a lot of trouble later on.

"Yes, this is it." She cracked open the door.

The name over the entrance read GOLDEN GATE SQUASH.

Kate had decided to start out with the Bay

Area. She knew she couldn't rent a car—that was traceable, so she stuck with cabs. Yesterday she'd driven down to Palo Alto and San Jose. Earlier today to the Athletic Club downtown, then across the Bay Bridge to a sports-plex in Berkeley. No one had recognized Em's picture. Not at any of these clubs. San Francisco was only one city. Kate had three more to go, following the band's tour. And a lot more clubs.

She'd headed straight to the airport after eluding Oliva. The little escapade with Fergus was the only thing in the past few weeks that had given her a reason to smile. What wasn't nearly so amusing was the note she'd left for Greg, how she'd had to run out and not be honest with him. She scribbled, *I know it's going to be hard for you to understand this, Greg, but I've got to find something out, no matter how we try to pretend it will go away—and I couldn't let you talk me out of it and tell me how foolish this is, which I knew you would try to do. It is foolish—it is crazy. Just know that I'm safe and that I love you, and that I'll think of you every day. Please try not to worry. I'll call you when I get there. Wherever that is. I love you, but this is something I have to do.*

"And don't forget Fergus's heart pill before you go to bed!!!"

It was tough, hiding things from him. Kate felt disloyal. He was her husband, her closest friend. They were supposed to share everything. She trusted him more than anyone in her life. She knew she should at least call. Last night at the hotel, she'd picked up the phone to call him to let him know she was safe and had gotten as far as punching in his number. Then she put the phone down. Something held her back. Kate didn't know what.

Maybe he wouldn't understand. And she didn't want to hear it. Maybe she just had to keep this part of her life separate.

Kate opened the door to the squash club. Immediately she heard the sharp, *thwacking* sound of the ball slamming against the hardwood walls. There were several white-walled courts with clear glass fronts. A couple were in play. Two sweating men, who had obviously just finished up and had towels draped over their necks, were downing fluids, going over their game. Kate walked up to an athletic-looking, red-haired man in a squash shirt, standing behind the front desk.

"Excuse me, I'm trying to locate someone. You mind taking a look?"

"Not at all."

She handed him Emily's photo, one taken last

year at the junior Maccabean Games. "She's my sister. I think she plays out here."

The redheaded pro took a long look. He shook his head. "Sorry, I'm afraid I've never seen her before." He had an English accent and smiled at her, somewhat apologetically.

"You're sure?" Kate pressed. "Her name's Emily. She's seventeen. She's a ranked player back east. She's just moved out here with my dad. I know she plays somewhere in town. I just want to surprise her."

The squash pro shrugged again, handing Kate back the photo. "I run the junior program here. If she played here, I'd definitely know her. Have you checked Berkeley yet?"

Kate exhaled in disappointment. "Yeah, I have." She folded the photo back into her bag and said, "Thanks, anyway."

On her way out, she took sort of a desperate, final look around, as if she'd missed Em the first time and she might just suddenly materialize out of nowhere. She knew that this was a long shot. Even if her hunch had been right, there were dozens of places they could be and dozens of squash programs, too. Kate felt a little foolish playing cop. She was a scientist, not an investigator.

She went back outside.

"Back to the motel?" the cabbie asked as she climbed in again. He'd driven her around all day.

"No." Kate shook her head. "*Airport*."

CHAPTER FORTY-SEVEN

Phil Cavetti took the 7:00 A.M. shuttle back to New York, heading straight from La Guardia to FBI headquarters in Lower Manhattan.

The proverbial shit was hitting the fan.

As if the fact that one of his closest colleagues had been found dead weren't enough—on top of that, one of that agent's own case subjects was implicated in the murder. Now, in another of her cases, one of the government's most valuable assets in the entire WITSEC Program, a man whose information had put dozens of criminals away, was MIA as well.

Cavetti was unable to connect the dots, other than to the point where his own career intersected with disaster. And he didn't like what he saw. Forget northern Michigan—the ice fields of North Dakota seemed a more likely prospect now. It was imperative they find Raab. Even more imperative they locate Bachelor Number One.

Now, unbelievably, Kate Raab was missing, too.

Nardozzi and Special Agent Alton Booth were waiting in the small conference room on the fourth floor of the Javits Federal Building when he arrived.

"This better be important." The prosecutor put down his cell phone, looking plenty annoyed. "I've got a junior attorney stepping in to do a cross on a Pakistani cabdriver who's accused of plotting to blow up the TKTS counter in Times Square."

Cavetti removed three folders from his brief-case. "Trust me, it is."

He tossed the reports he had prepared for the deputy director, marked "Restricted Access," onto the table. They contained the FBI report on Margaret Seymour, the subsequent disappearance of Benjamin Raab, and the incident on the Harlem River involving his daughter Kate. One or two need-to-know details had been omitted.

"So how the hell *is* Kate Raab?" Alton Booth asked, taking a chug of his coffee.

"Gone."

"*Gone?* Like in Puerto Vallarta, gone. I thought after what happened on the river you had her under guard 24/7."

"*Gone*, like in left him holding the pooch."
Cavetti closed his eyes, chagrined. "She boarded
a United flight two days ago for San Francisco.
After that, your guess is as good as mine. She
was smart enough not to rent a car at the airport.
We have our guys checking cabs."

"Cabs." Booth stared implacably at him. "You
know, this Blue Zone of yours is starting to get
a little fucking crowded for me, Phil."

Cavetti smiled. The FBI man didn't know what
was about to hit him next.

"So what's your best guess?" Nardozzi asked.
"Why would she run? And why San Francisco?
Because someone targeted her?"

"We can only surmise her father's been in
touch with her. She hasn't called in. She only
left behind this vague note. There's also the
chance she's trying to get in contact with her
family." He glanced at the FBI man. "You might
want to get someone out there. *Now.*"

Booth scribbled something on a pad and
sighed. "Gee, Phil, all this concern for the girl is
downright touching. If this witness-protection
thing doesn't work out, maybe you oughta
consider the Department of Children and
Families next time."

"I am concerned for her, Al. I am."

Nardozzi's gaze bored through him. "There's

something you're not telling us, Phil. Why the hell are we here? Why was I pulled out of court?"

"Margaret Seymour." Cavetti cleared his throat. Time to fill in the blanks. "She was the same case agent—"

"The same agent for *whom*?" Alton Booth put down his coffee and stood up.

Cavetti opened his briefcase again. This time he took out an addendum to his report, containing the need-to-know details that had been omitted. On whom Maggie Seymour was protecting. On Bachelor Number One.

He tossed it onto the table and swallowed. "I'm afraid that Blue Zone, Al, is even more crowded than you think."

CHAPTER FORTY-EIGHT

Yesterday Kate was in Portland. Today Seattle. Bellevue, actually, a stylish suburb just across Lake Washington.

She knew she was running out of options.

This morning she had driven downtown to the Seattle Athletic Club. To no avail. The same for two other squash clubs in Redmond and Kirkland. And one at the University of Washington, too.

Kate knew this one was pretty much it. A banner over the doorway read PRO SQUASH IN BELLEVUE. She had followed the band's tour. She had put together the details she'd been able to glean from her family's e-mails. But this was basically the end of the line. She had run out of cities, squash centers. If this was a dead end, too, Kate didn't know where she was going to go next.

Except home.

The club was a gray, aluminum-sided building tucked into the rear of a small business park off a commercial highway. Someone had told her the Pakistani pro there was pretty much world-renowned. The main strip had all the icons of an upscale place to live: Starbucks, Anthropologie, Linens-N-Things, Barnes & Noble. The cabbie let her off in front of the entrance, as he had four times earlier today, and waited.

Kate stepped through the doors. By now every squash club in America seemed to have the same look to her. This one had four clean, white courts, glass-enclosed, with a spectator balcony overhead. It was crowded. The balls echoed off the walls. It was the end of the day, and the courts were filled with kids. Some kind of after-school youth program going on.

Okay. She drew an anxious breath, facing a pretty young woman behind the desk, in a white piqué shirt with the club's logo embroidered on it.

One last time . . .

Kate unfolded Emily's picture. "I don't mean to bother you," she said. The young woman didn't seem bothered at all. "Do you happen to know this girl?"

As Kate handed over the photo, she was already going through her options for what she would do next. Call Cavetti. Say she was sorry for ditching his agent. For probably involving the FBI in a manhunt to find her. Then beg him to break the rules and reveal where her family was. Face Greg. That option wasn't sitting well either. Kate realized she had her share of explaining to do there, too.

The girl behind the counter nodded. "That's Emily Geller."

"What?"

"*Emily Geller,*" the girl said. "She's one of our best players. She moved here from back east."

Kate's blood surged in shock and exultation.

CHAPTER FORTY-NINE

Geller. The name went through Kate's mind, as she told the taxi to come to a stop a way down the block from the white clapboard house that backed onto the lake, off Juanita Drive in Kirkland.

Nice house, Kate thought. Even in the dark, there was something about it she liked immediately. It could be anybody's house. The family next door. Just knowing that her mom and Em and Justin were inside made her smile. *Geller.*

"This where we're going, miss?"

She thought back to the day they all saw their house in Larchmont for the first time. Mom just stood in the giant vestibule, eyes wide. "It's so big." Dad took her to the windows overlooking the Sound, beaming proudly. "We'll fill it, Sharon." Em came back in and grabbed Kate's hand. "You're not going to believe this"—her eyes excited—"it even comes with a turret."

"We'll fill it, Sharon." Then we'll leave it all behind.

"You want me to pull in?" the turbaned taxi driver turned around and asked.

"No," Kate said, unsure what to do, "just pull over here."

The taxi drew up to the curb in front of a modern cedar-and-glass house under tall evergreens, two houses down. Kate was nervous. She spotted some cars on the street. She knew there were probably WITSEC marshals all around, that they were probably alerted to her, too, and that if they found her, she'd be in cuffs in thirty seconds flat.

But the fact that her family was this close, just beyond her reach, made her know she couldn't pull back now. She hadn't seen them in over a year. Suddenly Kate wasn't sure what to do. She didn't know if there were agents inside. If their phones were bugged. Maybe she should wait for them at the squash club? Maybe she should turn around and do this another day?

"What do you want to do, miss?" the driver asked, pointing toward the meter now.

"I'm sorry. I'm not sure."

Finally she took out her cell phone. Her

fingers were trembling a little, sweaty, and she felt like she was back in her shell, grabbing hold of the oars at the start of an important race. Nervously, she punched in the number the girl had given her at the squash club. It started ringing. Her stomach was knotted. Any second she expected voices to start shouting and lights to go on.

It was Emily who picked up. "Hullo."

Kate could barely contain herself. "I was just wondering what you might say to an all-expense-paid dream date with Stephan Jenkins of Third Eye Blind?"

There was a pause. "*Kate?*"

"Yeah, Em . . ." Kate felt her eyes well up. "*It is.* It's *me,* baby . . ."

Suddenly she heard Emily break out screaming, "*It's Kate! It's Kate!*" It was like she was tearing up the stairs through the house. "*Mom, Just,* Kate's on the phone! How did you find this number? I can't believe you're calling here! What are you, totally crazy?"

Kate laughed, giddy. "I don't know . . . Maybe I am."

She heard voices in the background. Her mother and Justin surrounding the phone. Em didn't want to give it up. "God, it's been so long . . .

"There's so much I have to tell you, Kate. *Where are you?*" Emily asked.

Kate stared at the house. For a second she had to dig deeply to find her voice.

"I'm right outside."

CHAPTER FIFTY

Kate told the cabbie to turn off his lights and wait, which, assuming he was no more than an unwitting player in some tearful family reunion, he grudgingly agreed to do.

Then, couched in darkness, she ducked down a pathway her mother told her about that ran past the cedar-and-glass house. It was a local lane down to the lake, with a short pier at the end.

Kate realized she couldn't exactly ring the bell at the front door and let them all leap into her arms the way she'd always pictured. Not with these WITSEC watchdogs creeping around. For all she knew, there was some kind of manhunt going on. And at this point she wasn't quite sure if they were there to protect her family from a hit or if they were waiting for her father or her to appear. Anyway, these guys were about the last people she was inclined to trust right now.

She wasn't turning back.

A white picket fence led along the property, separating the two lots with a line of dense hedges and pines. Lights were visible from inside the neighboring house. Kate could see a woman in the kitchen wearing a striped, Adidas-style warm-up top, feeding two young kids at the island.

All of a sudden, Kate felt movement on the other side of the fence.

Footsteps crunching on the gravel driveway. The unexpected sound of a car door opening, and a light flashing on. Kate's heart came to a dead stop. She crouched as low as she could beneath the hedge line.

Her family's house had one of those free-standing garages, set back from the house. There was a car there, and someone stepping out of it. She heard the crackle of a radio above her, only a few feet away. "Kim here . . . I'm just going around to check out the front."

Kate stiffened.

She pressed herself deeper against the hedges, clinging to a branch for support. Until the branch began to give way.

Kate held there, motionless. For a second she was sure she was about to keel over. *I might as well sound a goddamned alarm.* She sucked in her breath as tightly as she could, trying to work through how she would explain herself with the lights on and the guns drawn if she was caught sneaking around someone's property.

After a while she heard the sound of the radio again, the footsteps receding up the drive. "Kim, again, I'm coming back to the house . . ."

Kate's whole body seemed to exhale in a spasm of relief. At the sound of the screen door closing, she started to scurry in a tight tuck toward the backyard. She found a gate and quietly unlatched it. The yard was large. She could make out a pool and a trampoline. Even a half-pipe for in-line skates. A goddamn amusement park. The picket fence continued along to the lake.

Now the coast was clear. Kate scurried low along the fence to the end where the property sloped down to the lake. She squeezed through an opening in the brush and was able to yank aside a wire mesh backing on the fence and pull herself through.

Now she faced the rear of her parents' yard.

The house was lit up. Floods in the tall trees faced the water. On a screened-in back porch with some Adirondack chairs, Kate spotted an agent with a radio, leaning against the wall.

She also saw the boathouse her mother had told her about, and at its base a short pier.

Her heart was pounding. *How was she going to get there?* The man in back would see her running. Surely he would hear any sudden noise. The boathouse was at least twenty yards away.

Kate crawled down the pitch line to the edge of the lake, grasping at clumps of weeds and grasses, sliding down the short embankment onto the shore. She pulled herself along the edge, her sneakers sinking into the soggy soil. *So far, so good.* She was only a few yards away. She didn't know where anyone was. Only that it was dark and that she was crazy for doing this.

Finally she made her way to the base of the pier. It was only about ten feet long, with a small powerboat moored alongside. Kate got her jeans wet maneuvering around the side, but she continued, grabbing on to a branch and pulling herself up to the boathouse, where she was concealed. The only light came from the spotlights in the trees. She'd made it. The agent on the porch had barely moved.

The door that led inside was ajar. She cracked it wider and entered the boathouse. There was an exposed bulb on the ceiling, turned off. She didn't dare turn it on. She tripped over an oar in the dark, but it didn't fall. There was a rowboat on a stand, orange life preservers stacked neatly on a shelf. Other than that, it was just dark, creepy, and musty. Cicadas buzzed.

Now she just had to wait.

Kate stepped quietly across the shed to a small window that looked out at the house. The guy was still sitting there.

Suddenly she felt a hand on her shoulder.

Kate almost jumped out of her skin, turning.

With great relief she stared into the joyous face of her mother.

CHAPTER FIFTY-ONE

"*Oh, Jesus, Mom . . .*" Kate gasped, latching onto her mother's shoulders. They took a look at each other, then melted uncontrollably into each other's arms.

"*Kate . . .*" Sharon squeezed her tightly, pressing her hair. "Oh, God, I can't believe it's you."

Kate couldn't help it. She just started to sob.

It was seeing her mother's face, at last, at the end of this impossible, nerve-racking journey. Everything simply gave out. Emily and Justin crept from the shadows then, too, Em hugging Kate giddily, trying to keep it together. Justin couldn't stop smiling.

Kate couldn't believe she was actually seeing them. They couldn't believe they were actually staring at her. Sharon pressed an index finger to her lips for everyone to keep their excitement down.

"How did you find us?" Em asked.

"It was *you*." Kate embraced her. She told them about the Third Eye Blind e-mail and how she'd tracked the tour, how she'd been to three cities in the past three days, showing Em's picture at all those squash clubs . . . never knowing if she was actually ever going to find them.

And now she was here.

"I don't care how you found us." Sharon clutched Kate closely. "I'm just so happy you did. Let me look at you." She took a step back.

Kate swept the hair out of her eyes. "You had me sneaking around the back, and then I slid into the lake. I must look like a swamp creature."

"No." Sharon shook her head, eyes beaming, even in the dim light. "You look beautiful to me."

"You all look beautiful, too." Kate grinned. They hugged one another again.

Justin had grown to almost six feet, long and lanky, his hair still bushy. Emily had filled out like a young woman. Her hair was shoulder length, with a little streak of blond running through it that Kate thought looked pretty cool—and she had two small silver hoops in her left ear.

And Mom . . . It was dark, eight o'clock at night. She didn't have a stitch of makeup on.

She was wearing a light blue Fair Isle sweater and a corduroy skirt. Kate noticed a few crow's-feet around her mouth and eyes that she couldn't remember being there before.

But her eyes were sparkling and wide. There was a warming smile on her face.

Kate hugged her. "You look great, too, Mom."

They threw a lot of questions at her. How was Tina doing? And Greg? Kate shook her head guiltily. "He doesn't even know I'm here."

Then there was a pause. They all looked at her, reality creeping back in.

"What *are* you doing here, Kate?" her mother asked numbly. "You know what a risk it is to be doing this now."

"Have you heard from Dad?" Kate asked, nodding.

"No. They're not telling us anything. We don't even know if he's alive or dead."

"I think he's alive, Mom. I found something. Something I have to show you." She didn't want to say everything, not in front of Justin and Em. "At first I thought they must be lying and covering something up. They broke into my apartment and bugged my phones."

"*Who*, Kate?" Sharon asked, mystified.

"The WITSEC people. Cavetti. The FBI. But I found this photo, from a folder full of Dad's things you left back at the house." She started to reach inside her jacket. "It changes things, Mom. It changes everything."

Her mother put a hand to her arm. "There are some things we have to talk about, Kate. But not here."

They heard some movement emanating from the house. The agent Kate had seen now stepped down from the back porch. He shone a flashlight broadly around the yard.

Pushing Kate back from the light, Sharon whispered, "You can't be here, honey. I'll meet you tomorrow. In the city. I'll call you. But right now you need to go."

"I'm not leaving," Kate said, "not now." She locked her arms around Em and Justin. "I don't know when I'll get to see everyone again."

"You have to, Kate. We'll call Cavetti. We'll let him know you tracked us down, that you're here. He'll have to let you stay a few days. In the meantime I'll come into town tomorrow. We'll go over some things."

Kate pulled Em and Justin against her, nodding reluctantly. "Okay."

"Who's out there?" one of the agents called. The beam of a flashlight came a little closer.

Sharon pushed Kate toward the boathouse door. *"You've got to go!"*

She touched her hand affectionately to Kate's face. Then her eyes lit up. Gently, she lifted something from Kate's neck.

"You're wearing your pendant."

"I never take it off," Kate said. They hugged each other one last time, and then Kate jumped off the pier and slid down the embankment to the lake.

"Tomorrow I'll tell you something about it," her mother said.

CHAPTER FIFTY-TWO

The following morning rose clear and bright. From her hotel room on the edge of downtown, Kate could see Puget Sound and the sun glinting off glass-walled skyscrapers. She cracked the window, and the caw of gulls came into her room, along with a gust of brisk sea air.

It had been a long time since Kate had risen so expectantly.

Sharon called about nine and told Kate to meet her at noon in a restaurant called Ernie's at the Pike Place Market, the most public venue she knew. Kate tried to figure out how she was going to fill the next three hours. She pulled on her Lycra tights and went for a jog along Western Avenue, stopping a few times to gaze at the colorful sailboats dotting the Sound, the dazzling skyline rising above her, and the tip of the famous Space Needle. Afterward, she stopped for a coffee and a muffin at a Starbucks that claimed it was one of the first three ever opened. Around eleven she made it back to the hotel and changed into a green quilted jacket and jeans.

It was only a short walk from her hotel to the Pike Place Market. Kate got there a little early and strolled around the crowded wharf and shops. Ernie's was a large, bustling café with outdoor seating in the center of the festive market. The square was packed with young families and tourists. Kiosks hawking cool artisan crafts, rollerbladers gliding through the buzzing crowd, street artists, jugglers, mimes.

Kate stopped at a trinket stall and bought a small polished silver heart charm she thought she'd give to her mom. It had an inscription she thought was amusing.

Sugar Girl.

As she waited, glancing at her watch, the sea, and the festive scene, something old and long buried flashed into Kate's mind.

She was in the old house. She was maybe eight or ten years old, and she had stayed home from school that day, sick. She'd been pushing her mom to go out and rent her a movie, the prospects of the long day recuperating at home seeming bleak.

"How about I *show* you a movie?" Her mother smiled.

Kate didn't know what she meant.

They spent the next few hours on the floor in the den, Kate in her pj's. From a carton of old things, Sharon pulled out a dog-eared, ancient-looking *Playbill*.

The original *West Side Story*.

"That was my favorite thing when I was about your age," her mother said. "My mom took me to see it at the Winter Garden Theatre in New York. What d'ya say I take you?"

Kate beamed. "Okay."

Her mom pushed a tape into the VCR and turned on the TV, and the two of them curled up together on the couch and watched the story of Romeo and Juliet and their families, recast as Tony and Maria, the Sharks and the Jets. At times her mother sang along, knowing every word— "When you're a Jet, you're a Jet all the way,/From your first cigarette to your last dying day"—and when they played the big dance number in the gym—"I like to be in America!"— Sharon leaped up and mimicked the steps to a tee, dancing in thrilling unison alongside the character of Anita, throwing her hands in the air and kicking up her heels. Kate remembered clearly how it made her laugh.

"Everyone I knew wanted to be Maria," her mother said, "because she was the prettiest. But I wanted to be Anita because of how she danced."

"I didn't know you could dance like that, Mommy," Kate said, astonished.

"You didn't, huh?" Her mom plopped herself back down with a weary sigh. "Believe me, there's a lot you don't know about me, honey."

They watched the rest of the movie, and Kate remembered crying as her mother sang, "There's a place for us," with the doomed Tony and Maria. Kate recalled how close it made her feel to her mom, how it became something she always remembered fondly. Maybe one day she'd have the chance to share it with her own daughter.

She smiled sweetly. *There's a lot you don't know about me . . .*

"Hon . . . ?"

Kate turned. Sharon was standing there in front of her, at the market. She had on an orange turtleneck sweater and tortoiseshell sunglasses, her thick hair pulled back with a barrette.

"*Mom!*" The two of them hugged.

They gazed at each other, now in the light of day. Her mom looked so pretty. It was so good to be there.

"You won't believe what I was just thinking

about," Kate confided, a little embarrassed, shielding her eyes from the sun.

"Tell me." Sharon smiled. She looped her arm through Kate's. "C'mon, we have a lot of things to catch up on."

CHAPTER FIFTY-THREE

They talked about a million subjects. Justin and Emily, how they were getting along. How Tina was doing. Kate's diabetes. Greg. How he was finishing up his residency and had his résumé out, but right now they didn't know where they'd end up next year.

"Maybe we'll have to come out here and live with you," Kate said with a grin.

"That would be something, wouldn't it?" Sharon smiled.

They talked a lot about Dad.

For lunch they ordered from a cute, athletic-looking waiter, with the tan of a snowboard instructor. Kate ordered the Vietnamese chicken salad and Sharon a salade Niçoise. Every once in a while, the wind kicked up. Kate kept pushing the hair out of her eyes.

Finally, in a little lull, Sharon lifted her

sunglasses. She took Kate's hand and, with a bit of a worried expression, traced the life line on her palm.

"Darling, I think you ought to tell me just why you're here."

Kate nodded. "Something happened last week, Mom, on the river . . ."

She told her mother about the boat that had almost run her down and cut her shell in two.

"Oh, good God, Kate . . ." Sharon shut her eyes, continuing to grasp Kate's hand. When she opened them, there were tears. "You don't know how sorry I am that you're involved."

"I think it's too late for that, Mom. I think it was always too late." Kate reached inside her bag for her wallet. "There's something I have to show you, Mom."

She took out the old snapshot of her father she'd found back at the house and pushed it across the table.

Sharon picked it up. Kate wasn't sure if she'd seen it before. But it didn't seem to matter. Sharon looked back up. She knew what it was. She knew what it meant. It all registered, mixed with a trace of regret, on the lines of her face.

"You found it." Sharon smiled, without even a hint of surprise.

"You know about this?" Kate asked. "What

the hell is Daddy doing there, Mom? This is in Colombia, not Spain. Look what it says on the gate, behind him." Her voice grew agitated. "*Can you read it, Mom?*"

"I know what it says," Sharon answered, averting her eyes. "I left it for you, Kate."

Kate stared back at her, stunned.

"I wrote you almost every day," her mother said, placing the photo back on the table and reaching out for Kate's hand. "You have to believe me. I tried to tell you a hundred times . . . I just could never push that key. It's been so long, I'd almost forgotten. But it doesn't help. It doesn't go away . . ."

"Forgotten *what*, Mom? I don't understand." Kate picked up the photo and held it up in front of Sharon's eyes. "This is my father, Mom! *Who the hell is he?* What is he doing in front of that sign?"

Sharon nodded and smiled, a bit resignedly. "We have a lot to make up for, honey."

"I'm here, Mom."

The wind kicked up, blowing a plastic glass off the table. Instinctively, Kate bent over to grab it.

She never heard the sound.

At least that's how she always recalled it as she played the moment back in her head a thousand times.

All of a sudden there was this sharp, searing burn on the back of Kate's shoulder—a molten iron jabbing into her flesh, the impact almost knocking her off the chair.

Kate's eyes flashed to the spot. The fabric of her jacket was torn. There was a red hole there. No pain. No panic. She knew that something horrible had happened, she just didn't know what. Blood started to ooze. It took a second for her brain to realize it.

"Jesus Christ, Mom, I think I've been shot!"

Sharon was upright, still in her chair, but somehow unresponsive to Kate's desperation. Her sunglasses were gone, her head was slightly bent and slumped forward. Her pupils were fixed and glazed.

A dark circle spread against the orange of her sweater.

"Mom!"

In that instant the haze of the moment cleared and Kate focused in disbelief on the hole in her shoulder and at the ring of blood widening on Sharon's chest. The bullet had shorn right through her. And into her mom. Kate stared in horror.

"Oh, my God, Mom, no!"

There was the sound of another *ping* coming in, a woman screaming as a glass exploded at the table next to them, the shot careening off the pavement. By that time Kate had leaped up and thrown herself in front of her mother, covering her slack, unresponsive body, shaking her by the shoulders, screaming, "Mom, Mom!" into the stonelike pallor of Sharon's face as she fell to the ground.

Shouts rang out from all directions, people grabbing kids, tables upending. *"Someone's shooting! Get down! Everyone get down!"*

But Kate just lay there. She knew that her mother was dead. She brushed the hair out of her face. She wiped away a few dots of dark red spatter from her cheek.

All she could do was hold her close.

"Oh, dear God, Mom . . ."

CHAPTER FIFTY-FOUR

The emergency vehicles drove right into the square. Lights flashing. Police pushing the crowd away. A female EMT knelt next to Kate. In a soothing voice, she tried to coax her mother out of Kate's arms.

Kate wouldn't let her go. She couldn't.

Once she let go, it would be like saying it was real.

The police pushed the crowd back to a wide, murmuring arc. Everyone was pointing up at a red building behind them. The Lapierre Hotel. That's where the shots had come from. Kate didn't look. She just kept holding her mother. *What is it you wanted to tell me, Mom?* She looked into the still, green pools of Sharon's eyes. *What is it the bastards wouldn't let you say?*

Her shoulder ached. But she could barely feel

it. A female Asian EMT was still trying to coax her mom away.

"You have to lie back, miss, please. We're here to help you. You've been shot. Just let us check you out."

Kate kept shaking her head, repeating over and over, "I'm okay . . ."

It all had the feel of some TV crime show she'd watched a hundred times. Except she was living it. It was *her* blood pressure they were taking, she they were asking to lie back, her arm now strapped with sensors. It was her mother they were trying to lift from her arms.

"We're gonna take care of her. You can let us have her now."

Finally Kate let her mother go. They placed Sharon gently on a gurney. Suddenly Kate felt very alone. And afraid. There was blood all over her sweater. Siren blasts shocked her out of her daze. That's when she felt tears running down her cheek for the first time.

It was real.

"You're gonna have to go to the hospital." The EMT knelt next to her, leaning Kate back. "She'll be going to the same place. I promise you'll see her there. What's your name?"

Kate let them ease her onto a gurney. She looked up at the blue sky. She had a flash of the same blue sky she'd seen from her hotel room.

"Kate."

Her mind started to drift. To Justin and Emily. Who would tell them? They had to know. Where would they go now? Who would take care of them now? *And Greg . . .* Kate suddenly realized she had to call him. Let him know she was okay. "I have to call my husband," she said. She tried to sit up. She wasn't sure if anyone had heard.

They started to wheel Kate toward the van. She could no longer fight. She started feeling woozy. She could no longer push back the urge to close her eyes.

Suddenly she was aware she was leaving something—something important—behind.

"Wait!" Kate reached out and grabbed the arm of one of the EMTs.

The gurney stopped. The female medical tech leaned in close.

"There's something there. A photo. It's of my father." She tried to point, but her right arm wouldn't move. And she no longer knew which direction. "I can't leave it behind. It's somewhere over there."

"Wendy, we have to go," the EMT's partner put in curtly.

"Please." Kate tried to raise herself. She squeezed the EMT's arm. "I need it. Please . . ."

291

"Give it a second, Ray," the female med tech replied.

Kate let her head fall back down. She didn't hear the sirens or the crowd, only the caw of gulls and the sounds of the harbor, which came to her sweetly. It had been a day of hope and promise. The breeze swept across Kate's face. For a second she forgot why she was there.

The female EMT knelt back down and placed something in Kate's hands. "Is this it?"

Kate ran her fingers over the photo like a blind person. It had been in her mother's hands. "Yes." There were flecks of blood on it. She looked up at the woman. "Thank you."

"Right now we've got to get you to the hospital. We have to go."

Kate felt the gurney jerk, and she was lifted. A siren blared. She could no longer fight it. There was commotion all around. Hazily, she closed her eyes.

What she saw scared her. Her father, standing beneath that gate, smiling at her.

And four words she wanted to speak. The question her mother never got to answer.

Why are you there?

PART FOUR

CHAPTER FIFTY-FIVE

The wheels of American Airlines Flight 268 landed on the runway at JFK, and the large jet skidded to a stop.

Kate stared out the window from her seat in business class, her right arm cradled in a sling. In the distance she could see the familiar control tower, along with the old saddle-shaped Saarinen terminal that now housed JetBlue.

She was home.

Two U.S. Marshals sat across the aisle. They had accompanied her from the hospital to the airport in Seattle where Kate had spent three days. Her shoulder was okay—the bullet had passed cleanly through. They had treated the wound for infection and put her on an IV sedative for shock until she was ready to make the trip back. For another week or so, she'd have to wear the sling.

But all the morphine and Valium in the world couldn't dull the real pain.

The pain of reliving the horrible scene over and over, every time she had to go through it for the investigators: Staring blankly at the hole in her shoulder as she turned toward her mom, not understanding. The sight of Sharon's head pitched slightly forward, her glassy and unresponsive stare, the ring of blood widening on her sweater. The shock taking over her system. *Mom!*

And the questions. Kate's brain was not picking through them clearly. What if she'd never gone out there? What if she'd listened to the warning on the river as Greg had begged her to? What if she'd just gone up to the house on the lake and knocked on the front door? They would've had to let her see her family. What if she hadn't bent to reach for that glass?

Her mother would still be alive.

Justin and Emily had flown home the day before. They were staying with their aunt out on Long Island. The funeral would be Thursday. Then, after that, who knew? Maybe this was it. The damage had been done. The insurance paid.

They'd found something horrible in a plastic bag along with the discarded sniper's rifle on top of the hotel where the shots had come from.

A severed tongue. A dog's tongue. This time Mercado's message was chillingly clear: *This is what we do to people who talk.*

Goddamn you, Daddy. Kate closed her eyes as the jet pulled up and docked at the Jetway. *Look what the hell you've done.*

A wheelchair was wheeled up to the door. One of the agents got Kate's bag, helped her out of her seat, and wheeled her down the Jetway. Her heart was almost bursting with anticipation.

Greg stood at the end of the hall. He was in jeans and his Rice University sweatshirt. His hair was mussed, his eyes watery, and he was shaking his head a little sadly.

"Pooch . . ."

Kate pushed up from the chair and melted into his arms. For a minute they just held each other. She was unable to look him in the face, afraid to lift her head from his shoulder.

"Oh, God, Greg." She pressed into him. "Mom's dead."

"I know, baby, I know . . ."

He slid her back into the wheelchair. She was still weak. Greg knelt and checked out the sling.

"I'm okay." The government agents were huddled around. "Tell them to go away, Greg. Please. I just want everything to go back to how it was before."

"I know." He nodded, leaning his face into hers.

"Why did they do this?" Kate asked. "What do they want from us?"

Greg brushed her cheek with his knuckles. "I don't know—but I'm not going to let them hurt you ever again. I promise. I'm going to take care of you, Kate. We'll move. We'll do whatever we have to do."

"He's cost us everything, Greg. And I don't even know if he's dead or alive."

"It doesn't matter anymore," he said. "I'm just glad you're home, Kate. And safe. We're all that matters now."

He took her chair and wheeled her through the terminal. A government car was waiting by the curb. A couple of agents hopped out as they approached. Greg eased Kate from the chair and into the backseat, and the agents climbed in front. A siren sounded as the car pulled away from the curb.

Greg smiled as they drove off. "Fergie'll be glad you're back. I think he's about fed up with my cooking by now."

Kate shook her head. "All you have to do is pour it in his bowl, Greg."

"I know. I guess I'm not sure he likes the way I pour."

Kate smiled, resting her head against Greg's shoulder. The skyline of Manhattan came into view. She was going home.

"You're right," she said, "it really doesn't matter anymore."

"What, pooch?" Greg answered.

"Nothing." Kate closed her eyes. In his arms it all seemed a million miles away. *"He's probably dead."*

CHAPTER FIFTY-SIX

Thursday was damp and drizzly and windy, the day Kate, Em, and Justin said good-bye to their mom.

The service was at Temple Beth Shalom, the Sephardic congregation on East Sixty-second Street where Kate and her family had always belonged. Only a handful of their old friends were even notified, and just a single, brief notice was placed in the *Times*, by Kate and the kids, under "Raab." At Kate's insistence. Her family had been gone for over a year. A lot of their friends in Larchmont had walked away from them. Kate wasn't even sure who would show.

The simple casket they chose was made of polished walnut. Sharon would have approved, Kate knew. Rabbi Chakin, a soft-spoken, white-haired man, had known Kate's mom and dad since the kids were young. He had bar mitz-vahed all of them. But this . . . this was something you hoped you never had to do.

Kate sat numbly in the first row. She held tightly to Greg's hand, her arm around Justin and Emily. When the cantor sang the opening hymn, her clear, plaintive voice filling the sanctuary, that was when they realized why they were here. That was when the tears started to flow. The rabbi intoned:

> "Cleanse me with hyssop, O Lord,
> Wash me, and I will be whiter than snow.
> Hide your face from our sins, and blot out all my iniquity.
> Create in me a new heart, O God,
> And a steadfast spirit, renewed."

It all seemed so horribly unfair, such a waste. Only eighteen months ago, everything had been perfect in their lives. The kids were happy and achieving. Her father was admired and successful. Their holiday cards were filled with photos from fantastic trips. Now they had to bury their mom in a hushed and secretive manner.

Now no one even knew where their father was.

Em leaned her head on Kate's shoulder, sobbing. She didn't understand. Justin stared straight ahead. Kate pulled their faces close. As much as she wanted to mourn, something else was digging inside her. An anger. Mom didn't deserve this. None of them did.

Goddamn you, Dad . . . What have you done?

At some point Kate looked around. She had this silly, childish notion that she would somehow see him, in the rear of the sanctuary. And he would rush up to them, tearfully begging forgiveness, and would undo everything that had happened with just a wink and a snap of his fingers, like he'd always done. And they could go back to just being themselves.

But no one was standing there. Instead Kate saw something just as moving.

The rows had all filled in. The place was packed with people she used to know, most of whom she hadn't seen in the longest time. Faces from their club. From her mother's yoga studio. Two of Sharon's oldest friends from college, who now lived in Baltimore and Atlanta. Classmates from Westfield, Em and Justin's old school. Gathered there. For them.

Kate felt tears stream down her cheeks.

"Look," she said to Justin and Em. "*Look!*" They turned. They had denied so much of themselves in the past year. Now this showed that they weren't alone.

Look what you robbed her of, Kate imagined saying to her dad. *This was her life. It was* hers, *even if you were willing to throw it away. Where are you? Why aren't you seeing this? Look at what you've done!*

The rabbi said a few words after the prayers. When he was finished, Kate stepped up to the bimah. She looked out at the hushed, filled pews. Greg smiled, encouragingly. It took everything she had to be up there, but someone had to speak for her mother. She looked out at the tearful, familiar faces. Grandma Ruth. Aunt Abbie, Mom's sister.

"I'm here to tell you some things about my mom," Kate said. "Sharon *Raab.*"

It felt good to say it loudly. To proclaim it. Kate sucked back a rush of tears and smiled. "And I bet none of you ever knew how Mom loved to dance ..."

She told them about *West Side Story.* And how Sharon loved to watch *Everybody Loves Raymond* reruns after the late-night news and sometimes had to sneak out to the den so it wouldn't disturb her dad. And how, when she did her first successful solo yoga headstand, she screamed at the top of her lungs from the basement for everyone to come down and see. "And there was Mom, standing on her head, going, '*See! See!*'" The mourners laughed. "We all thought the house was on fire!"

Kate told them how much her mother had been there for her when Kate got sick, how she'd constructed charts and schedules to keep her on track with her insulin. And when their life suddenly changed, "this surreal, unimaginable shift of fortune," she changed. She never lost her pride. "She held our family together. She was the only one who could do it. Thank you, Mom."

Kate said, "I know you never thought you accomplished enough, but what you didn't know was that just being there for us was enough. I'm really going to miss that smile and the twinkle in your eyes. But I know that all I'll have to do is close *my* eyes and you'll be right there by me—always. I'll hear that sweet voice telling me you love me and that everything is going to work out for the best. It always does. I am so grateful to have had your presence in my life, Mom. You were a truly amazing person to have as a guide."

At the end a single cellist played "Somewhere" from *West Side Story*. Kate, Justin, and Em followed Sharon's casket down the aisle. They stopped and wrapped their arms around people with tear-stained faces. People she might never see again. At the door Kate turned. She had a moment of perfect peace. *See, Mom, they know who you are.*

Afterward the hearse led a procession of cars to the cemetery in Westchester, where they had a family plot. On foot they followed the casket up to a small knoll overlooking the cemetery gate. Under a canopy of spruces, there was a large hole in the ground. Sharon's father was buried there. His mother. There was an empty space alongside for Kate's father. Only the family gathered around. Justin rested his head against his Aunt Abbie and started to sob. Suddenly it had hit him. Kate put her arm around Emily. The rabbi recited a final prayer.

They lowered their mother into the grave.

The rabbi handed out white lilacs. One by one, each of them stepped up and tossed a flower onto the casket. Grandma Ruth, who was eighty-eight. Aunt Abbie and her husband, Dave. Kate's cousins, Matt and Jill, who came in from college. Everyone tossed a flower in, until the blooms became indistinguishable, a quilt of white.

Kate was the last. She and Greg stood silently over the casket. She squeezed his hand. Her eyes lifted for a second, and in the distance, out on the road, she spotted Phil Cavetti and two agents waiting down by the cars. Her blood grew tight.

I won't give in, she promised. *I'm going to find out who did this, Mom.*

She tossed the final flower.

I'm going to find out what you wanted to tell me. I'm going to get these bastards. You can rest on that, Mom. I love you. I'll never forget you for a second. Good-bye.

CHAPTER FIFTY-SEVEN

Two weeks passed. Kate's shoulder slowly healed. She wasn't ready to go back to the lab. She was still too angry, the wounds inside too raw. It seemed only yesterday she had watched as her mother died in her arms.

Kate still had no idea if her father was dead or alive. Just that a new world had exploded in her face. A world she hated. It had been a year since her family had gone into hiding. Her mother was dead. Her father was missing. Every truth had been turned into a lie.

When she felt strong enough, Kate went up to Bellevue to check in on Tina.

Her friend was still in a deep coma, 9 to 10 on the Glasgow Coma Scale. She was being kept in a long-term trauma ward now. She was still connected to a respirator and receiving mannitol through an IV to relieve the brain swelling.

But there were moments of hope. Tina's brain activity had increased, and there were signs of alertness in her pupils. Occasionally she would even stir. Still, the doctors said it was no more than a fifty-fifty chance that she'd recover or be the same person she was before the shooting. The left side of her brain had suffered damage, the area that controls speech and cognition. They just didn't know.

There was one piece of good news, though. Tina's killer had been found.

Amazingly, it turned out to be a gang killing after all. A random initiation rite, just as the police had said. No link to Kate's situation whatsoever. They had the seventeen-year-old kid who did it in custody. A renegade gang member had turned him in. The evidence was ironclad. It could have been anyone on that street that night.

This took a ton of pressure off Kate's mind.

Today she stayed with Tina in the cramped private room while Tom and Ellen went to lunch. The monitors emitted their steady, re-assuring beeps, one IV for keeping the swelling down, another for nourishment and hydration. A thick breathing tube went through her mouth into her lungs. There were a few pictures taped to the walls and on the bed table, happy ones: family trips, Tina's graduation. One of her and Kate on the beach at Fire Island. The respirator marked the time with a steady *whoosh*.

It still hurt deeply to see her like this. Tina looked so frail and pallid. Kate wrapped her hand around her friend's curled, inert fist. She told her about what had happened, how she'd had to go away for a while, the narrow escape on the Harlem River, then Sharon.

"See, Teen, check it out. We both got shot. It's just that . . ."

Her voice cracked, unable to finish the sentence. *It's just that my wound will heal.*

"C'mon, Tina, I need you to get better. *Please.*"

Sitting next to her, listening to the monitors beep and the respirator contract and expand, Kate felt her mind rush back in time. What was it her mother needed to tell her? Now she'd never know. The picture . . . Kate was starting to feel that Cavetti might well be right. Maybe her father did kill that agent. Maybe he was alive. Her mother was gone. That answer had died with her. What was he doing in that photo? How deep was his connection to Mercado? How many years—?

Kate heard a soft groan. Suddenly she felt a tug on her finger. Her heart leaped up into her throat. She turned.

"*Tina.*"

Tina's eyes were still shut, the monitors beeping steadily. The tube in her mouth didn't move. It had only been one of those involuntary reflexes. Kate had seen them before. It gave them hope, falsely. Maybe she'd been squeezing Tina's hand a bit too hard.

"C'mon, Teen . . . I know you can hear me. *It's me, Kate.* I'm here. I miss you, Teen. I need you to recover. Please, Tina, I need you to come back to me."

Nothing.

Kate let go of her friend's hand.

How could she just put it away, Kate thought, the drive inside her? How could she just pretend that there wasn't something horrible behind what had happened? Go on with her life. Let them win. Never know. It always came back to the same question, and now that question needed to be answered.

Who had turned her father in? How had he first come to the attention of the FBI?

But there was one person left who still knew.

"Everyone says I should let it go," Kate said, "but if it were you, you'd want to know, wouldn't you, Teen?" Kate stroked her friend's hair. The respirator wheezed. The brain monitor beeped.

No, they don't get to win.

CHAPTER FIFTY-EIGHT

Kate knocked on the door of the dreary, seventies-contemporary house in Huntington, Long Island. It was desperately in need of a coat of paint. The heavyset man in thick glasses came to the door. As he saw her, his gaze shot past her toward the street. "You shouldn't be here, Kate."

"Howard, this is important, *please* . . ."

Howard Kurtzman glanced at her arm in the sling, and a more submissive look came over his face. He opened the screen door, letting Kate in. He took her into the living room, a dim, low-ceilinged room with dark wood furniture and faded upholstery that looked like it hadn't been re-covered in years.

"I told you in New York, I can't help you, Kate. It's not good for either of us that you're here. I'm giving you a minute, whatever it is you want. Then you can leave by the door in the garage."

"Howard, I know you know what happened. You have to talk to me."

"Howard, is someone there?" His wife, Pat, stepped out of the kitchen. When she saw Kate, she stopped dead in her tracks. Kate had met her a few times at office gatherings over the years. "*Kate* . . ." she said. She looked at the sling. Then back at Howard.

"We were both sorry to hear about Sharon," Howard said. He motioned Kate to sit, but she just leaned against the padded arm of the couch. "I have nothing but fond thoughts of your mother. She was always pleasant to me. But you see it now, don't you? These are bad people, Kate."

"You think they're just going to forget about you, Howard? You think they're just going to let you walk away, or that it ends just because you glance around the street both ways before you open the door? My mother's dead, Howard. My father, I have no idea where he is or if he's even alive. It didn't end for *him*." Kate picked up a framed picture of Howard's family—grown kids, smiling grandchildren—from the side table. "This is your family. You think you're free? Look at *me*." She thrust forward her sling. "You know something, Howard. I know you do. Someone pressured you to turn him in."

Howard adjusted his glasses. "No."

"Then you were paid . . . Please, Howard, I don't give a damn what you did. That's not why I'm here. I just need to find out about my father."

"Kate, you don't know what you're even stepping into," he said. "You're married now. Move away. Rebuild your life. Start a family—"

"*Howard*." Kate reached for his flabby, cold hand. "You don't understand. Whoever you're protecting, *they tried to kill me, too!*"

"Whoever I'm protecting . . ." Howard glanced toward his wife, then shut his eyes.

"Right after I met with you," Kate said, "on the Harlem River, where I row. Was someone watching us, Howard? Did anyone know I was asking about him? I know things now about my father. I know he wasn't exactly who I thought he was. But, please—my mother was trying to tell me something when she was killed. Why are you hiding things from me?"

"Because you don't want to know, Kate!" The accountant stared back at her. "Because it was never, ever about a bunch of painted gold paperweights or Paz Exports. We always sold them the gold. You don't understand—that was what your father did!"

314

Kate stared back at him. "What . . . ?"

Howard took off his glasses. He dabbed at his brow, his complexion pasty white.

"You have to believe me," he said. "I never, ever thought anyone would get hurt in this. Certainly not Sharon." He sank into a chair. "Or, God forbid, *you*."

"Someone did pressure you, didn't they, Howard?" Kate went over and knelt in front of him. "I promise you'll never hear from me again. But, please, you have to give me the truth."

"The truth"—the accountant smiled hollowly—"it's not at all what you think, Kate."

"Then tell me. I just buried my mother, Howard." Kate was more determined than she'd ever been. "This has to end, now."

"I told you to stay out of it, didn't I? I told you it was something you didn't want to know. This was what we did! We moved money for Colombians, Kate, your father's friends. That's how you got your house, the fancy cars. You think I was disloyal? I *loved* your father, Kate. I would have done anything for your father." He pressed his lips and nodded. "*And I did.*"

"What do you mean, you did, Howard? Who paid you to turn him in? You need to tell me, Howard? *Who?*"

When he replied, it was like some meteor

slamming into her at an unimaginable speed, one world ending in a flash and another rising from the devastation, exploding in her eyes.

"Ben." The accountant looked up, his eyes runny and wide. "Ben instructed me to go to the FBI. I *was* paid—*by your father, Kate."*

CHAPTER FIFTY-NINE

The scene came back to Kate on the long train ride back to the city. Through the steady clattering of the Long Island Rail Road car, the blur of faceless passengers, Howard's words burned like flaming wreckage in her head.

I was paid. By your father, Kate.

Paid to leak information to the FBI. To turn him in. *Why?* Why would her father want to destroy his own life, the lives of those he loved? Why would he want to be put in jail, to testify? To have to hide? How could Kate resurrect who he was, why he did this, what he was capable of, from the whole confounding puzzle of her life?

The voice came from deep inside her memory. A faraway scene she had not revisited since she was a child. Her mother's voice—desperate and confused—over the rattle of the train, making Kate shudder and flinch, even now.

"You have to choose, Ben. Now!"

Why was it coming back to her here? All she wanted to do was make sense of what Howard had told her.

Why now?

Kate saw herself in the flashback. She was maybe four or five. It was back in the old house in Harrison. She had awakened during the night. She'd heard voices. Angry voices. She crept out of bed to the landing at the top of the stairs.

It was her parents. They were arguing, and it made her jump at every word. She was a little afraid. Her parents didn't argue. *Why were they so mad?*

Kate sat down. She could make out their voices distinctly now. It all came back to her through the haze of years. Her parents were in the family room. Her mother was upset, fighting back tears. Her father was shouting. She'd never heard him like this before. She moved closer to the railing. It was clear now, in the train.

"Stay out of it!" her father shouted. "It doesn't concern you. It's none of your business, Sharon."

"Then whose business is it, Ben?" Kate could hear the tears in her mother's voice. "Tell me, *whose*?"

What were they talking about? Had she done something wrong?

Kate held on to the banister. She quietly slid down the stairs, one at a time. Their voices grew louder. And there was bitterness in them. She could see glimpses of them in the family room. Her father was in a white dress shirt with his tie undone. His face was younger. Her mother was pregnant. *With Emily, of course.* Kate didn't know what was going on. Only that she'd never heard her parents argue like this before.

"You don't tell me, Sharon. You don't get to tell me that!"

Her mother, sniffling, reached for him. "Please, Ben, you'll wake up Kate!"

He threw her off. *"I don't really care."*

Kate sat on the staircase, trembling. She couldn't remember any more words. Only pieces, coming to her like images in a photographic flicker book. There was something totally different and foreign about him, about his eyes. This wasn't her father. Her father wasn't like this. He was soft and kind.

Her mother, standing up in front of him. *"We're* your family, Ben, not *them."* She shook her head, just inches away from him. *"You have to choose, Ben. Now!"*

Then her father did something, something Kate never saw him do again. Why was it coming back to her now? She turned her face away, just as she had done on the staircase maybe twenty years before. Before she buried it—the violence in his eyes, what he did—in the lifetime of happier memories that she thought were real.

He hit her mother in the face.

He wanted this.

That's what Kate suddenly understood. Stepping off the train. Climbing up through Penn Station and onto the street. In a complete daze.

Her father wanted this.

That's what Howard told her. He wanted to be exposed—his longtime dealings with the Mercados brought into the light. To testify against his friend. To go to jail. To put the family he supposedly loved above everything else at risk. *Why?* He'd engineered his comfortable, picture-perfect life to self-destruct.

And he was capable of it. That's what scared Kate the most. That's why the flashback on the train was so chilling. However buried this memory was, she had seen it in him before.

Kate walked against the crowd down to Fourteenth Street. She headed east, all the way to the Lower East Side.

Did the WITSEC people know any of this? About the photo she'd found, his past connection to Mercado? Did they know who he really was? What he was capable of? Those awful photos of Margaret Seymour. Had Mercado's people ever really wanted to kill him after all?

Do they know he brought his own life crashing down?

Her cell phone rang. Kate saw that it was Greg calling. She didn't answer. She just kept walking. She didn't know what she could say.

All of a sudden, the whole of her life had to be rethought. Why would her father have wanted to harm Margaret Seymour? What information could he possibly have needed from her? Why would her father want to bring this on himself? How could he have wanted to hurt them all? Sharon, Emily, Justin. Kate herself.

It was like the coda from some discordant, symphonic finale crashing in Kate's head.

All along, this was his plan.

Greg was on the couch watching a soccer match when she arrived back at the apartment.

"Where you been?" He spun around. "I tried to reach you."

Kate sat across from him and told him about her meeting with Howard. She shook her head in disbelief and felt numb, uncomprehending.

"Dad set it up," she said. "He set the whole thing up. He paid Howard a quarter of a million dollars to go to the FBI. He said he was closing the business and turning himself in. Howard needed the money. He had a son who was in bankruptcy. There never was any sting by the FBI. It was all my father. He did it himself."

Greg sat up, his expression both incredulous and worried. "It doesn't make sense."

"I know. Why would he want to hurt us like this? Why would he want to bring this on himself? It was like it was all part of some kind of plan. I don't know what to fucking believe anymore. My mom is dead. We're hiding out like animals. I'm starting to think they're right, the FBI. That he did kill that agent. I loved my father, Greg. He was everything to me. But I know now . . . he came home every goddamn night my entire life and he lied to us. Who the hell *was* my father, Greg?"

Greg came over and sat beside her. He cupped her face in his hands. "Why are you doing this, Kate?"

She shook her head, glassy-eyed. "Doing what?"

"Putting yourself right back in the middle of all this again. Sharon's dead, baby. You're just lucky as hell you weren't killed yourself. These people are animals, Kate. They tried to kill you, too."

"Because I have to know!" Kate shouted, pulling away. "Don't you understand? I have to know why my mother died, Greg. What she was trying to tell me . . . ?

"No one ever went to jail, Greg. Not Concerga, not Trujillo. None of the people my father testified against. No one except Harold, his stupid friend. They all got away—everyone the government really wanted. Doesn't that seem strange to you? Then he just disappears after a couple of months and that woman agent ends up being horribly killed. He lied to us, Greg. For what? Wouldn't *you* want to know?"

Greg put his arm around her shoulders and held her close. "We can't just keep living with this hanging over our heads our whole lives. All that's going to happen is you'll get yourself killed. Please, Kate, let's get back to our lives."

"I can't . . ."

"And I can't go there with you, Kate. Not like this. Not forever." He lifted her face. "I tried to reach you a while ago. I have some news."

"What?"

"New York–Presbyterian called. They offered me the position." His face widened into a proud grin. *"I got in!"*

As an attending. In children's orthopedics. The Morgan Stanley Children's Hospital was one of the best programs in the city. This was great news. A few months before, Kate would have leaped for joy. But now she just put her hand on his cheek and smiled. Now she wasn't sure.

"We can stay in New York. We can start a life. I love you, baby, but I can't do this every day and think of you putting yourself in danger. We have to set this aside. If we stay, we have to face the future. *Both of us*, *Kate*. They want to know if I'm taking it. Are we going to stay or leave, honey? Are we going to go forward and live our lives? It's up to you, Kate. But I have to give them an answer soon."

CHAPTER SIXTY

The laundry truck turned down the sleepy street for its last stop around 8:00 P.M. It braked in front of the blue-shingled ranch, blocking the navy Taurus parked on the curb. One last delivery to make.

With some shirts draped over his finger, Luis Prado climbed out of the cab.

The street was dark, illuminated by a single streetlamp. People were in their homes, cleaning up after dinner, watching *American Idol* on TV, chatting online.

Luis had already killed the young driver with a single shot to the head, stuffing his body in a pile of dirty linens and laundry bags in the back of the truck. He nodded with a wave to the two figures hunched in the Taurus as if he'd seen them before, heading up the walk toward the neighboring house. Then, as he came even with the Taurus, he drew his silenced Sig nine-millimeter from behind the hanging shirts.

The first shot splintered the passenger window with a muffled thud and hit the agent closer to Luis in the forehead, just as he exhaled a plume of smoke, leaving a round, black burn between the agent's eyes. He keeled silently into his partner, whose face became a contorted mask of alarm, groping inside his jacket for his weapon, reaching for the radio with some garbled, final cry.

Luis squeezed the trigger two more times—the nine-millimeter bullets crashing squarely into the agent's chest, spitting blotches of red over the windshield, immobilizing him with a gurgling groan. Luis yanked open the door and placed a final round in the agent's forehead, removing any doubt.

He glanced around. The street was clear. The laundry truck was blocking anyone's view. Luis took the shirts and headed up the steps to the blue-shingled house. Concealing his gun behind them, he rang the bell at the door.

"Who's there?" someone called from inside. A woman.

"Cleaning, *señora.*"

The window shade nearest the door was drawn back, and Luis spotted a blonde woman in a tan suit peering out at the white truck. "Next house!" she called, pointing to the left.

Luis grinned like he didn't understand, holding up the shirts.

The front-door lock turned. "Wrong house," the government bodyguard said again, barely cracking the door ajar.

Luis rammed his shoulder into the door, smashing it open, sending the blonde agent reeling onto the floor with a startled cry, frantically fumbling for her gun. He squeezed two silenced slugs into the white of her blouse, her hands involuntarily pushing out to stop them.

"Sorry, *hija*," Luis muttered, shutting the door. "I'm afraid it's right."

A dog came out of the kitchen, the white Lab he'd seen a few days before. Luis dropped it with a shot into its neck. The dog whimpered and fell silent on the floor.

Luis knew he had to work fast. Any second, someone walking by might spot the bloody agents in the Taurus. He didn't know how many people were in the house.

He went into the living room. Empty. He lifted a phone off the hook. No one on the line.

"Pam," a woman called from inside the kitchen. Luis followed the voice. "Pam, did you tell them it's the next house?"

Luis stood facing the lady he'd seen emptying the trash a few days before. She was at the stove in a pink robe making a cup of tea. She dropped the cup onto the floor, ceramic shattering, as her eyes fell on the gun. The gas burner was left aflame.

"Where is he, *señora*?"

The woman blinked, taken by surprise, not sure what was happening. "Chowder? Here, boy! What did you do to Chowder?" she called, louder, backing close to the fridge.

"Don't play with me, mama. I axed you where he is. Your fucking dog is dead. Don't make me ax you again."

"*Who?* What happened to Agent Birnmeyer?" The woman recoiled, staring into Luis's dark, formidable eyes.

Luis came over and cocked the hammer, forcing the Sig hard into the woman's cheek. "No one here's gonna help you, lady. You understand? So you tell me now. I don't have much time."

The woman's eyes shone with helplessness and fear. Luis had seen the look many times, her brain imagining what she could say, despite knowing that in the very next moments she might die.

"I don't know what you want from me." She

shook her head. "Where is *who*? I don't know—who do you want?"

She looked down the short barrel of Luis's gun.

"Oh, yes you do. I have no time to fuck with you, lady." He clicked back the hammer. "You know what I'm here for. You tell me, you live. You don't, when the police find you, they be mopping you off this floor. So where is he, mama? Where is your huzban?"

"My husband?" she asked. "My husband's not here, I swear."

"Is he upstairs, you fuckin' gray-haired bitch?" Luis pushed the gun into her cheek. "'Cause he is, he's about to hear your brains splatter all over this floor."

"No. *I swear* . . . I swear, he's not here. I beg you. He's been gone. For a couple of weeks."

"Where?" Luis demanded. He pulled her back by the hair and jammed the barrel into her eye.

"Please don't hurt me," the woman begged, shaking in his grasp. "Please, I don't know where he is . . . These agents, I don't even know why they're here. Why are you doing this? I don't know anything. Please, I swear . . ."

"Okay, lady." Luis nodded. He relaxed his grip. He took the gun out of her face. She was sobbing. "Okay."

He released the hammer, and the gun went out of firing mode. "Who said anything about hurting you, mama? I just want you to think. Maybe he called, maybe he told you something . . ."

She sniffled back mucus and tears and shook her head.

The burner was still on. Flaming. Luis felt the heat close to his hand. "Is okay," he said, softer. "Maybe it's something you forgot. We just wanna talk with him anyway. Just talk. You understand?"

He winked. The woman nodded, terrified, hesitantly against his shirt, smearing tears. Her breaths were frantic and short. "Calm down." Luis patted her hair.

"What I think is, maybe we just go at this from a different way."

He took hold of the woman's slender wrist. Her hand was shaking. "You know what I mean, mama?" He turned her palm over and ran his finger along one of the lines. Then he brought it closer to the burning flame.

It took a second for her to understand.

"No! God help me. Please . . . no!"

Suddenly she tried to pull herself back. Luis didn't let go. Instead he drew her closer to the flame. The woman's eyes grew in panic now, bulging out of their sockets.

"Maybe you remember now. Time to tell me where he is, mama."

A few minutes later, Luis Prado climbed back into the cab of the laundry truck. He turned the key in the ignition and threw it in gear, glancing one more time at the crumpled bodies in the government Taurus. He pulled away from the quiet street. No one came after him. The whole thing had lasted only minutes. All it took was a little prodding. He'd gotten what he came for.

Then he put her out of her pain.

A few blocks down the hill, Luis pulled the truck into the parking lot of a closed water-treatment facility. Quickly, in the back of the cab, Luis changed out of his clothes. He carefully wiped down the steering wheel and the handle on the driver's door. He threw the soiled clothes in back, on top of the linens covering the delivery driver's body. He stepped out and hurried across the lot in the darkness.

Another car was parked there. A rented SUV. Luis climbed into the waiting car.

"So . . . ?" the driver inquired as Luis shut the door.

"He wasn't there." Luis shrugged. "He's in New York. Hasn't been here in weeks."

"New York." The driver seemed surprised. He

adjusted his blazer. He had a troubled look on his face, as if he'd hoped it wouldn't come to this.

"That's what his wife told me before she died. Must be losing my touch. Wasn't able to find out where."

"It doesn't matter . . ." The thin, dark-haired driver turned. He put the car in reverse, backing out of the deserted lot. "I know where."

CHAPTER SIXTY-ONE

Fergus dragged Kate on the leash as they headed into the park.

She'd thought about it all night. What Greg had said. Not only about his offer, which she knew he had to accept. But about going forward. Trying to put the past behind her. And what had she decided?

Yesterday afternoon she'd called Packer. She said she was ready to go back to the lab for the first time. Her shoulder was still pretty stiff. She'd had the sling off for a couple of days, and there were weeks of physiotherapy ahead of her. But she could still help out. It would be good to get her mind off things. She hadn't been able to run or row in weeks, and with all the stress from Sharon's death, and what Howard had told her, her blood sugars were off the charts. But Greg was right. This was slowly killing her. They had to face the future, get back to something approximating a normal life.

"C'mon, boy." Kate tugged Fergus. "Just a short one this morning. Mommy's going to be late."

She had to lead Fergus carefully with only her left hand. She jogged with him on a loose leash for most of the run. After just a block or two, she grew winded. *Jesus, Kate, that's bad.* She dropped the leash and let Fergus run after a squirrel. She sat down, took out a PowerBar, bit off a square, and waited for her strength to return. It would be good to get back to her routine.

A man with slicked-back dark hair, wearing a black leather jacket and sunglasses, took a seat on the bench across from her.

Kate stared edgily at him. *Okay . . .*

For a second she tried not to be aware. But the warning bells started going off. Something didn't seem right. Kate looked around for Fergus. She'd had this sort of feeling before.

The man looked over, catching her gaze. Kate's pulse quickened. Where the hell was Fergus? It was time to go.

As she got up, she heard a voice from behind her. "Kate."

Kate spun around, her heart lurching. Then,

as she saw who it was, she exhaled in a nervous sigh of relief. *Thank God . . .*

It was Barretto, the bearded man she'd met here before. She knew she must've looked like a ghost.

"I didn't mean to startle you." He smiled. Dressed as always in his rumpled corduroy jacket and familiar golfing cap. He was always so reserved and polite. "I haven't seen you in a while. Do you mind if I sit down?"

"I actually have to run," Kate said, her eyes darting across the path toward the man on the bench. The old man seemed to take notice of it.

"At least let me say hi to my old friend," he said, speaking of Fergus, but she got the feeling he was trying to make her feel at ease. "Just for a short while."

"Sure." Kate felt herself relax. "Okay."

Generally they talked about her job and her family. Fergus always seemed to like him. But this time it was a little strange. It almost seemed like he was waiting for her.

"You're hurt," he said, concerned. He sat beside her, a respectful distance away.

A mother with two children walked by. Fergus trotted up. He greeted Barretto like an old friend. "Fergus!" The old man smiled, patting the dog's snout. "It's been a while."

"It's nothing," Kate said. "I'm afraid I'm late for work. I haven't been there in some time . . ."

"I know." The old man looked at her. He put his hand on the dog. "I was sorry to hear what happened to your mother, Kate."

Kate recoiled, her eyes widening sharply, as if she hadn't heard correctly.

How could he possibly have known? She hadn't seen him in weeks. She'd never revealed her real name. Even if he'd read the death notice in the papers, that wouldn't connect her to her mom.

"How could you possibly know about that?"

Then the man did something that surprised Kate. He nodded across the pathway to the man sitting on the bench. The other man stood and dutifully stepped away. Kate's heart started to pick up. She didn't know what was happening, but she knew this wasn't right. She looped the leash around Fergus, starting to rise. Her gaze darted around toward the park entrance.

For a cop. For a passerby.

"Who are you?" she asked him warily.

"Please." The man reached out and put his palm on her arm. "*Stay.*"

"*Who are you?*" Kate asked again, her voice almost accusing.

"Don't be afraid," the bearded man said. His

blue eyes shone with a sudden importance Kate hadn't noticed before. His voice was soft, but what he said cut through her like a saw hacking through bone.

"I am Oscar Mercado, Kate," the man replied.

CHAPTER SIXTY-TWO

Every cell in Kate's body slammed to a halt.

Oscar Mercado was the cold-blooded killer who had murdered her mother right in front of her eyes. The chief of the Mercado crime family. He had probably killed her father, too. She didn't know what to do. His henchman was standing only a few feet away. She had to get out of there. She latched onto Fergus, tightly. She stared into the old man's icy blue eyes. A cry of panic was paralyzed deep in her throat.

"Kate, *please*." He gently reached across to her but let his hand fall to the bench. "You have nothing to fear from me. I promise you. On the contrary, it is I who should be alarmed. It's *I* who has something to fear from *you*."

Kate rose.

A revulsion that was almost uncontrollable surged up in her chest, and she wanted to kill this man—this man who had murdered her mother. Who was behind the attempt to kill her on the river. His cartel, his *fraternidad*, was responsible for everything bad that had befallen her family.

"Your father—" the old man started to explain.

"My father *what*?" Kate glared at him. "My father's dead. You—"

"*No, Kate.*" Mercado shook his head, unthreatening. His blue pupils shone like opals in his sagging eyes. "Your father is not dead. *He is alive.* In fact, it is your father who is hunting *me*."

"*What?* I don't believe you." Her own eyes filled up with rage. "You're lying."

She balled up her fists as if to strike him, but something held her back. He just sat there. He didn't make a single move to defend himself against her rage. In his face she saw the destruction of everything she once trusted and loved. But suddenly she felt no fear, just uncertainty and anger. His words echoed inside her.

"What do you mean *he's* hunting *you*?"

"It's why he arranged for his company to be raided, Kate. Why he orchestrated his own arrest. It's why he had himself placed in the government's Witness Protection Program . . . I think you know these things, don't you, Kate?"

She locked on his gaze, unable to let go. "What

the hell are you saying? That my father destroyed his life, destroyed *our lives*, just to get himself placed inside the program?"

"Not to be protected by it, Kate." The man smiled. "In order to infiltrate it."

Infiltrate? It made no sense. But there was something about what he was saying that she felt was close to the truth. "*Why?* Why are you telling me this? You say my father's alive. Why should I believe you? You murdered my mother. I was there! Why should I believe anything you say?"

"Because your father and I both had the same case agent, Kate. Margaret Seymour. Because we were part of the same WITSEC section that specializes in drug-related informants." He reached out and touched her arm. This time she did not stop him.

"For twenty years"—he looked up at her—"I've been in the program, too."

Kate stared at him. This animal, whose very name was synonymous with violence and death. Whom her father had gone to trial in order to bring down. His eyes were soft and blue and clear.

"*No.*" She jerked her arm away. He was a killer, a hunted criminal. "*You're Mercado.* The FBI said it was you who wanted to kill him. You're just trying to use me, to find him."

"Kate . . ." He shook his head. "The FBI claims many things in order to keep my cover. I haven't been running the Mercado drug cartel all these years. I've been informing on them. I've been inside the witness program. The cartel wants me dead, Kate, just as you believe they want to kill your father. Margaret Seymour was my case agent. She knew my whereabouts, my identity. That's why your father disappeared. To *find* me, Kate. To hunt me down, for turning on them. And I can prove this to you. I can prove this as sure as I am standing before you, *Kate Raab*."

The sound of him saying her name was like a punch deep into her solar plexus. How did he know this? How did he know about her mother? She had never divulged it. She scanned his face, the sharp cheekbones, the rounded chin hidden under his beard, the purpose and lucidity in his blue eyes.

Oh, my God . . .

Suddenly she saw it. It was like a riptide of shock sweeping through her body. She stared at him, transfixed, breathless, barely able to speak.

"I know you. You're the person with him in the photograph. The two of you, standing under a gate . . ."

"In Carmenes." The man brightened and nodded.

Kate drew a breath. "Who *are* you? How do you know all this? How do you know my father?"

The old man's eyes gleamed. "Benjamin Raab is my brother, Kate."

CHAPTER SIXTY-THREE

Kate's knees buckled. She had to grab hold of the back of the bench quickly to keep from falling.

Her eyes locked on this man's face, examining his sharp cheekbones, his curved mouth, the familiar lines of her father on the man's chin. Suddenly all fear of him disappeared, and she was left with only the realization that what he was saying was true.

"*How?* How are you his brother?" She shook her head in astonishment.

"Kate . . . sit." Mercado reached for her, and she sat down.

"Why? Why now? After all these years?"

"An old man has just died, Kate," he said. "In Colombia, in the place you already know, Carmenes. That man was my father, Kate. Your grandfather."

"No." Kate shook her head again. "My grandfather's dead. He died years ago. In Spain."

"No, your father's father has always been alive, Kate," Mercado said. "These past twenty years, he's been my protector."

Kate blinked, not understanding. "Your protector?"

"I'll tell you," Mercado said, softly placing his hand back on her arm. "You realize now you no longer have anything to fear from me. There is a lot that has been kept from you. With the old man's passing, everything has changed. All these years he kept at bay those who would come after me. But now the old commitments are off."

"What commitments? What are you talking about?"

"You've heard of *fraternidad*?" Oscar Mercado asked.

Kate nodded warily.

"I know this word only brings fear to you, but for us it is a tie of honor. It is an obligation that is stronger than love, Kate. Can you understand that? Stronger even than the love a father may feel for his daughter."

Her gaze drilled on him. What on earth was he saying to her? "No."

Mercado moistened his lips. "Your father has been handling money for years for the brother-

hood. This was his job, Kate. His duty. *Su deber.*
But there was a score he had to settle, more
urgent and more real than even the comfortable
life he had built for himself. Even after twenty
years. Even after *you*, Kate—and Emily and
Justin. I understand this score. In his place I
would do the same. It's about blood, Kate. It is
stronger than love. The score was *me.*"

"*You?*"

"It's I who's turned on them, Kate. He would
do *anything*, anything in his power, to right this
wrong."

"You're saying . . . he's alive?" Kate asked haltingly. "That he was part of this *fraternidad*, this
family."

"He is very much alive. In fact, it's possible
he's watching us now."

Her eyes shot around her. The sudden thought
of him out there, not dead, but observing them,
was terrifying. Why wouldn't he try to contact
her if he was alive? Sharon was dead. Kate
herself had been wounded. Emily and Justin
needed him. It was too much to accept. She was
his daughter. Whatever this debt, this oath that
he was bound to, no twisted concept of blood
would make him forget that or be so cruel.

"You're lying." She stood up again. "You're
using me to lure him to you. My mother's dead.

You people killed her. You shot up our house. I saw it. I was there. Now you're telling me about this ridiculous brotherhood and that everything in my life was just some kind of cover. A goddamn lie!"

"You know it," Oscar Mercado said softly. "You saw the photograph, Kate."

She wanted not to believe him, but his solemn eyes were clear and unflinching, and she could see in them the man who was in the photograph under that gate with his arm around her father. *His brother.*

"It's still not enough," she said. "I know my father. I know what I felt. You said you can prove it, so show me. *How?*"

"I hope, with *this*." The old man reached inside the pocket of his wrinkled jacket and came out with something in his palm, bound in tissue. He handed it to Kate.

As she unwrapped it, the world shifted for her again. She knew he was telling the truth. She knew he knew everything about her. As she stood staring at him, a sudden rush of tears welled in her eyes.

It was the other half of the broken sun given to her by her mother.

CHAPTER SIXTY-FOUR

It all came apart for Kate there.

An inner quake shook her so emphatically she felt as if it were cleaving her in two. She pulled the chain out from around her neck with the same broken half sun. She placed Mercado's and hers in her palm, side by side.

They formed a perfect match.

"You knew my mother?" She looked at him closely, staring into his clear blue eyes.

"I more than knew her, Kate. We were *familia*."

"Family . . . ?"

He nodded. He took her by the hand. This time she didn't flinch. His hands were hard, but there was a tenderness to them. Then he explained a part of her history Kate had never known.

"It was true what your father told you. He did come here as a boy. But not from Spain. From

Colombia. From our own country. His mother was my father's mistress. After my own mother died of an infection in her lungs, Ben's mother became the love of his life."

"Rose." Kate nodded. Her mind darted back to the pictures she had found of the woman, recalling the face of the man with her, with her father as an infant. Her grandfather.

"*Rosa.*" He shook his head and pronounced it in Spanish. "She was a beautiful woman, Kate. From Buenos Aires. She studied painting. She was full of life. Of course, they could never marry. Even at this time, in Colombia, this kind of union could never be permitted."

Kate understood what he was telling her. "Because she was a Jew," she said.

"*Sí, ella staba judía.*" The old man nodded. "When she bore him a child, it was necessary that she move away."

"*My father . . .*" Kate sat back against the bench.

"*Benjamín.* After her father. So she came here."

All of a sudden, questions about her father's past started to become clear. That was why she knew nothing of her grandmother's life. They hadn't come from Spain. He'd hidden the truth all along. The rest of it seemed to fall in place like the last pieces of a puzzle: Her father had set up his own arrest. He'd gone to meet

Margaret Seymour, just as Cavetti and the FBI had claimed. And that photo of the two men underneath the gate. The chilling name, overhead—MERCADO. That other man in the snapshot was before her now. His brother. Now it all made sense. Her eyes stole to the broken pendant—the gold half suns.

"It holds secrets, Kate," Sharon had said when she placed the pendant around Kate's neck. *"One day I'll tell them to you."*

Her mother knew!

"Your mother gave me this," Mercado said. "She knew one day it would be me to tell you, not him. You must realize now"—the man smiled—"what happened to her, it was not me."

"No!" A wail rose up inside Kate. Her hands trembled, but her voice was firm. "You're saying he killed his own wife. That can't be. He loved her. I saw them. For over twenty years. That was no lie."

"I am telling you, Kate, this bond, it is stronger than what you know as love. All these years inside the program, I've never once divulged what I've just said to you. I never betrayed *him*."

"Why are you telling me this? Why did you show yourself? What is it you want me to do?"

"I want you to help me find him, Kate."

"Why? So you can kill him. So that he doesn't

kill you. Whatever's happened, he's still my
father. Until he looks me in the eye and tells me
he did these things. From *him*, not you . . . You're
saying that everything I've trusted in my whole
life has been a lie."

"Not a lie. A protection. For your own—"

"*A lie!*"

Oscar Mercado took her by the wrist and
gently opened her palm. He picked up the two
pendants of the broken Aztec sun and reached
over and placed them around her neck. The two
halves dangled momentarily, then came to rest
against her chest in a way that made them appear
as one. A single golden sun.

"You want the truth, Kate, here it is. Here is
your chance. The gate is open, Kate. Do you
want to walk through?"

CHAPTER SIXTY-FIVE

Phil Cavetti parked his car across from the blocked-off blue-shingled ranch in Orchard Park, New York, which was ablaze in flashing lights. He dropped his shield in front of a local cop guarding the taped-off walkway leading up to the front door. The cop waved Cavetti through. There was a doggie bed on the landing, and a little plaque nearby that read HOME OF CHOWDER. WORLD'S FAVORITE CANINE.

The door was open.

Stepping into the house, the first thing Cavetti saw was the outline on the floor of the first victim, Pamela Birnmeyer. She'd been an agent with the U.S. Marshals Service, out of the Warrants and Bonds Division, for six years. He'd met her once. She had a husband who taught computer science at a local college and a two-year-old at home. Probably why she'd put in for hazardous duty. Extra cash.

Cavetti swallowed a rush of bile. He hadn't been to a fresh crime scene in years.

He followed the commotion into the kitchen. He had to avoid a couple of FBI crime-scene specialists who were kneeling, trying to lift shoe prints off the floor. The body of the second victim had been removed, but a bright scarlet smear was still visible on the white fridge where her body had crumpled to the floor.

The gnawing feeling in his gut returned.

Alton Booth met his eyes from across the room. The FBI agent nodded for Cavetti to come over.

"And just when you thought you were getting ready to retire . . ." the FBI man said with a cynical snort. He handed Cavetti a stack of black-and-white prints.

They made Cavetti sick to his stomach. In twenty-six years, he'd never dealt with anything like this. He'd never lost a witness. He'd never had an identity uncovered. He'd never, ever been penetrated.

Now this.

The woman had died from a nine-millimeter bullet to the brain, but that wasn't what made him feel like a queasy rookie looking over his first grisly kill. It was her hands. He'd read about it in the report, but the pictures were worse. The palms were charred black. Both. From the burner on the stove. She'd been tortured, just as Maggie had been. One hand was all it would have taken for the killer to be certain she didn't know a damned thing. But two, both palms—that was just for the sport.

"Least now I guess we have an idea what Maggie Seymour may have divulged." Booth rolled his eyes.

Cavetti knew these people. The woman's husband was more than just an asset in an investigation. Cavetti had placed him in his current identity twenty years ago. He'd watched him build a new life. Get married.

He felt responsible.

"What makes it worse is, I'm pretty sure the poor woman didn't even know." Cavetti sighed disgustedly. "She had no idea who her husband really was." He handed back the photos. "Any leads?"

"Dry-cleaning truck," Booth replied. "A woman across the street said one was parked in front of the house around the TOD last night. We found it at a closed water-treatment plant down the hill. The delivery kid took two in the chest. He was thrown in with the dress shirts and sheets. That totals five. Not including the pooch. So tell me"—the FBI man looked around—"who kills like this?"

Cavetti didn't reply. They both knew the answer. The Russian mob. The drug cartels. *Colombians.*

"This Raab fellow." Booth shook his head. "You starting to get the feeling we may have been duped?"

This wasn't just Raab. Cavetti was sure. Raab wasn't a killer. At least, not like this. Still, Raab led to Margaret Seymour. Maggie led to Mercado. Mercado led here.

Raab and Mercado.

Cavetti suddenly had a premonition about who might be next.

He handed the photos back to Booth. "You know how to reach me. Let me know if anything turns up."

The FBI man smiled. "Seen enough? Where you headed?" he called after him.

"Blue Zone," Cavetti answered. "That's where the hell everyone else seems to be, right?"

CHAPTER SIXTY-SIX

Kate listened to the whoosh of a late-night car driving in the rain on the street. The glow of the streetlamp outside her bedroom window had never seemed quite so bright. Her eyes were open. The clock on the table next to her bed read 3:10 A.M.

She couldn't sleep.

Mercado's question kept reverberating in her head. *"The gate is open, Kate. Do you want to walk through?"*

How could she deny it any longer?

Her father had been part of the Mercados. It had been his family, not just his brotherhood but his family—his *real* family—from birth. *Fraternidad.* His own father had been the head of it. He had kept this concealed from those he loved. *If he ever really did love us.* Now he was free to go after his brother for betraying him.

Kate's mother was dead. Her brother and sister were in hiding.

This kind of truth didn't set anyone free.

Her mind kept coming back to the picture of the dark European-looking woman holding her infant son. Kate's grandmother. They had come here from Colombia, not Spain. *"For years, he has been my protector,"* Mercado had said of her grandfather. The grandfather she thought had died in Spain decades ago. Now he had died. The old commitments were gone. It had sent her father on a journey of vengeance and reprisal, so vile, so unbelievable, that every time she thought about it, it felt like a fist in her abdomen. Their family had been sacrificed so her father could get inside the program.

Where his brother had been in hiding for twenty years.

Kate turned away from the window. What was it Margaret Seymour had told them? *"I'm sort of a specialist in the Mercados."*

They had the same case agent.

Mercado's story was true, Kate understood, no matter how it hurt to accept it. No matter how it made the past twenty years of their lives seem like a flimsy façade.

She saw it in his face. He knew about Rosa. He knew Kate's true name. He had the matching half of the broken sun. Her father was alive. It no longer made Kate feel elated; it made her feel sick. She knew that it all had to be true.

We're your family, Ben, not them. You have to choose.

Now she knew the meaning of those words. *Su deber.* His duty. What hurt as much as anything was that he had been lying to her all these years. To them all.

Kate sat up, her nightshirt cold with sweat. Next to her, Greg stirred. She didn't know anymore what was right to do. Take everything she knew to Cavetti. The haunting picture she'd found—Ben and Mercado. What Howard had divulged. How her father had brought himself down. All that the old man had told her in the park.

Why?

WITSEC had never played straight with her. All along, they'd been protecting Mercado. All along, they knew his secret.

It was her father they were desperate to find.

At some point Kate drifted off to sleep—brief, fitful. She had a dream. Her father was in the gazebo where she first told him she wouldn't be coming into the program. He seemed so distant there, so beaten. So small. His touch was tremulous and afraid.

When he turned to her, there was a malevolent glimmer in his eyes.

Kate's eyes flashed open. The clock read 4:20. Her pillow was drenched with sweat. Her heart was beating like mad.

She had misjudged it, his reaction.

All along, Kate had thought it was simply shame pouring out. That was why he couldn't look at her. A shame he'd never had to bear before. But that wasn't what was on his face.

It was the face of the man from her flashback on the train. A nightmare from her childhood. Someone she'd never seen before. With his hand gripping her mother's arm. A foreign glimmer in his eye.

His fist raised!

Who shot up our house that night? Kate suddenly asked herself. *Who killed Mom?* Did Kate really want to walk through that gate?

Why are you in that picture, Dad?

Across the bed, Greg reached in the darkness, fumbling for her.

She wrapped herself in his arms and nestled close to him. He murmured, "Is everything all right?"

She shook her head in tears on the pillow. *"No."*

She didn't know what to trust anymore.

"You'll always be there for me, Greg? Right? I can always trust you."

"Of course you can, pooch." He tightened his arms around her.

"No, I need to hear you say it, Greg. I know it's dumb, but just this once, *please.* . . ."

"You can trust me, Kate," he said softly.

She closed her eyes.

"Whatever happens, baby, you always have me."

CHAPTER SIXTY-SEVEN

The next day Kate went back to work. It had been almost a month. With both her and Tina out of the lab, a lot of things had been put on hold. Kate deflected the inevitable questions as best she could. She said her mother had been sick. She'd dislocated her shoulder in a fall. But it was good to be back. It just felt a little strange.

Without Tina.

Packer had brought in a new researcher to fill Tina's place. He was an Indian Ph.D. candidate named Sunil, who had studied cellular physics at Cambridge.

He seemed nice enough, though at first Kate knew she was probably a little cool to him. It was like saying that Tina was never coming back, and Kate didn't want to feel that way. Packer put him on the project Tina had been working on. He wasn't yet up to speed.

It was just a little weird, not having her around. Work had to go on, though.

Kate came back to a mountain of things to catch up on. There were tons of data to archive, an updated project-status report to complete, lots of government forms to fill out. Packer was applying to the National Science Foundation for a new grant.

Her shoulder was still too stiff to handle some of her old assignments. Kate could only imagine dropping a petri dish and sending a valuable systemic stem-cell line crashing onto the floor in a mess.

But at some point she couldn't hold back. She put the paperwork aside.

She went into the lab and took out two dishes filled with covered slides from the specimen fridge.

Leukemic Cytoplasmic Prototype #3. Nucleic Stem-Cell Model 472B.

Tristan and Isolde.

Kate took them over to the Siemens. She placed the leukocytic cell in the viewing tray and flicked the powerful scope on. The squiggle-shaped cell with the familiar dot in the center shone brilliantly into view. Kate smiled. *Hey, girl . . .*

It was like saying hello to an old friend.

"Haven't seen *you* in a while," Kate said,

adjusting the settings on the lens. Then she wrapped her magnification goggles around her head and placed the tiny catheter over the stem dish, and with the steady touch of someone who had mastered those little ball games that always came in Cracker Jack boxes, she isolated the cell into the tiny glass tube and jiggled it onto the leukocytic slide.

Kate narrowed the magnification of the Siemens. Both cells appeared.

"I see a guilty look in there," Kate said, grinning. "You dudes haven't been stepping out on me with anyone else while I've been gone, have you?"

It felt familiar and exciting to see them again. Kate perceived a minute reproduction of the whole world contained in their tiny clusters. A world of clarity and order. One thing she could always trust: the perfect symmetry of truth in a single cell.

She probed the stem. It was as if the clock had suddenly turned back and everything was just as she'd left it. Tina could be about to stick her head in to declare a Caffeine Emergency. Sharon was alive. Kate's cell phone had never buzzed to say that her father had been arrested. It was nice to hide out here for a moment, even though she knew it was a fantasy.

"Kate."

Kate lifted her head. It was Sunil.

"Sorry. I was told you could show me how to download data imaging onto the digital machine?"

"Sure." Kate smiled. He wasn't so bad. "I was just saying hi to some old friends. I'll meet you in the library in a second, okay."

Sunil smiled back. "Thanks."

As he left, Kate let her forehead rest on the bridge of the scope. Truth was, she had no idea if Tina would ever come back. If she would ever be the same. It was foolish to cling to that hope. The work just couldn't stop.

Carefully, she transferred the cells back to their sterile dishes. She went to place them back in their home, inside the fridge.

Her cell phone vibrated. Greg, she figured, congratulating her on her first day back. Kate flicked it open, kneeling down to a lower shelf of the fridge. She crooked the phone to her ear. "Hey!"

The voice on the other end was one she hadn't heard in months. It used to be a friendly one. Now it chilled her. The petri dish slipped out of her hand, crashing to the floor.

"Hello, pumpkin."

CHAPTER SIXTY-EIGHT

"Daddy . . . ?"

Kate froze. She wasn't sure what to say or do. Part of her was just excited to hear he was alive— hear his voice at last. Another part didn't know what she felt. She had wanted to hear her father's voice for so long—and now it scared her to death.

"Dad, no one knew if you were even alive."

"I'm sorry I had to make you worry, baby. But I'm here. I'm here . . . You don't know how good it is to hear your voice."

Kate stood quickly and pressed her back against the refrigerator door. Her eyes ran down to the shattered dish on the floor.

"I need to talk with you, Kate."

She felt a chill pass through her body.

"Daddy, you know what's happened, don't you? *Mom's dead.*" There was a pause.

"I know that, honey." Her father sighed.

"She was shot. We buried her last week. If you knew, why weren't you there?"

She didn't know what she should tell him. About the picture? Mercado? She held back what she really wanted to say.

"Everyone thinks you've done these terrible things. They think you killed your case agent, Margaret Seymour. They showed me pictures of her. They were horrible . . . Daddy, where have you been? Everyone was so worried about you. Why haven't you been in touch?"

"*Who*, Kate?" her father replied, his tone strangely even. "Who thinks those things?"

"Cavetti. The FBI." Suddenly Kate froze. She had no idea how much she could tell him.

"I need you not to believe whatever they're telling you, Kate. I didn't murder that agent. I didn't hurt anybody. These people killed my wife, Kate. Your mom. I've had to hide. I couldn't be in touch. They've taken away everything I loved in my life. You don't believe them, do you, Kate?"

"I want not to, Daddy, but—"

"You *can't* believe them, Kate. I need to see you, baby. This is me talking now. *Me* . . ."

She shut her eyes. She gripped the phone with two hands.

This was her dad, the same familiar, reassuring

voice she had always trusted. What if it was all part of some plan to frame him? To make it look like he killed that agent? What if it always *was* Mercado, and what they wanted all along was to have him surface, to use her to get to her father?

A spasm of fear racked Kate's stomach. "Dad, you have to go to the WITSEC people. You can't keep hiding forever. You have to turn yourself in."

"I'm afraid it's not that easy, pumpkin. I think the FBI let what happened to Sharon take place. I think there are elements there who are in bed with Mercado. They could even be close to you, Kate. I need to see you, honey. I've got nowhere else to turn."

"Please . . ." Her hands were cold and trembling. "You have to contact them. You have to turn yourself in."

She wanted to tell him she'd seen the photo. How she wanted to say, *I know . . . I know. About your brother . . . About Mercado . . . I talked to Howard. I know you set the whole thing up.*

How she wanted to ask him who had shot up their home that night, while they huddled on the floor so terrified? Who had killed their mom?

Kate waited. She waited for him to say something, *anything*, hoping against hope, her eyes tightly shut. That all of this wasn't true. The words were on the tip of her tongue, but she bit them off, silent. Because she was afraid. She was afraid to hear his answer.

She was afraid to walk through that gate.

Afraid of what he might say.

"None of that is an option, Kate. Not now. What I really need is for you to believe me. What I need is for you to hear it in my voice. I didn't kill that agent, Kate. I didn't torture her. Or anybody. I'm telling you this on your mother's life. On *our* lives, Kate. That still means something to you, doesn't it?"

She sucked in a halting breath and shut her eyes. "*Yes . . .*"

"Whatever I've done, whatever's happened, I'm still your father, Kate. You know me. You know I couldn't do something like that. It was Mercado who killed your mother, Kate. Who killed my wife. Don't let them poison you. You're the only hope I have left."

"I want to, Daddy." Tears massed in her eyes. "It's just that—"

"It's just that what, Kate? Who's been talking to you? I need to know. These are devious people, baby. That's why I couldn't contact you. You were safe from all this. I couldn't get you involved . . . Look at Tina."

"Tina?"

"Look what happened to her, Kate." The question almost had the feel of a threat. And how did he even know about Tina?

She suddenly realized she was petrified of him. The voice she'd grown up with, that she'd always trusted. Now it left her numb with dread.

"I need to ask you something, Dad."

"Anything, Kate. I know I've done a lot of things wrong. Go ahead."

"Your mother, Rose . . ."

"What about Grandma Rose, baby? Why is that important now?"

Kate moistened her lips. "She came from Spain, didn't she? After your father died? A short while after you were born?"

"Of course she came from Spain," her father replied. "Seville. My father was a milliner there. You know the story, Kate. He was run over by a streetcar. Who's been talking to you?"

"No one." Kate felt completely empty and alone.

In the pause that followed, Kate knew. She knew that her father realized it wasn't just WITSEC and the FBI she'd been talking to. Mercado was right. That's what this was about. Why he was calling her now. That's who her father was after.

And he knew.

"I need to see you, Kate. You're the only one I can count on now."

"I don't know if that's such a good idea."

"Of course it's a good idea. When you were sick, whenever you needed anything, I was always there for you, wasn't I? Now I need someone, Kate. You can't just walk away. I'll get word to you. I know how to. But what I need from you even more is for you not to trust anyone until I see you. No one. You'll promise me that, won't you, baby?"

"Dad, please . . ."

"You owe me that, Kate. Until we talk. Not the FBI, not Cavetti. Not even Greg. You know I'd never do anything to harm you, don't you?"

"I know that, Daddy." Kate shut her eyes.

"So I can count on you . . . You promise me?"

Her mouth was as dry as sandpaper. She nodded, and the word dropped off her lips like a falling weight. "Yes."

"That's my little girl." Her father's voice regained its reassuring quality. "I'll be in touch. You know it's just about family now, pumpkin. Like I always told you. Family. That's all we have left."

He hung up. Kate stood there in the starkness of the lab.

No one had ever mentioned anything about Margaret Seymour being tortured.

How would he have known that? How would he know the horror that had been done to her? It was only family now.

CHAPTER SIXTY-NINE

"Kate!"

She had just come home from work. Greg was at some two-day medical conference for the new job. She had stopped at the cleaners on Second Avenue. She had just put the key in the door to her building's lobby.

Kate turned, anxious, expecting to see her father. For the past few days, she'd been afraid he'd be waiting for her around every corner.

Instead she was staring at Phil Cavetti.

"Don't you guys ever just *call*?" Kate exhaled, not knowing whether to feel anxious or relieved.

"I haven't seen you in a while," he answered, coming up with an apologetic smile. "You mind if we talk?"

"Everything's fine, Cavetti. I meant to write, but things have just been a little too hectic lately. I don't need the protection anymore."

He nodded with his chin. "I meant upstairs."

Kate had not forgotten for a minute how they'd used her. How they'd broken into her apartment and tapped her phones. How they'd hidden everything from her—her father's disappearance, pretending to be protecting her—when all along it was Mercado they were protecting, his secrets. Now Kate understood they were hiding a whole lot more.

In the elevator Cavetti looked at her arm and asked how she was doing.

"Better," Kate replied, softer. She gave him a bit of a smile, realizing she'd been abrupt. "Really. Thanks."

"If you don't mind me saying, you don't exactly look so much better."

Kate knew that it had all been taking a toll on her. She knew she looked a little puffy and drawn. She hadn't been eating so well since she'd spoken with her father. Or sleeping. She still couldn't row. Once or twice she'd forgotten to give herself her insulin. Her blood levels were the most elevated they'd been in years.

"Don't feel obliged to continue with the compliments," Kate said. "They're not working."

The elevator opened on seven. "You remember the place, don't you, Cavetti? You remember Fergus?" Kate opened the door, and the dog

372

came up and sniffed Cavetti. The WITSEC agent nodded guiltily at the jab.

"He's been alone all day, so I've got about a minute before he takes it out on the rug. You wanted to talk?"

"I was just up in Buffalo," he said.

Kate nodded as if impressed. "I know the job can be dull, but at least you get to travel to strange and exciting places." She sat back on the arm of the couch. Cavetti didn't sit down.

"A woman was killed there," he said awkwardly. "I was called up to take a look."

Kate snorted. "What, no pictures this time?"

"Kate, listen, *please*." He took a step toward her. "She wasn't just killed. The palms of her hands were burned black. Someone held them over a gas flame until the skin basically sheared away from her hands. This was a fifty-year-old woman, Kate."

"I'm sorry." Kate stared at him. "But why are you here? Are you going to tell me my father did that, too?"

"Two FBI men, a deputy marshal guarding her, and an innocent bystander were murdered as well."

Kate flinched. A pain knifed through the pit of her stomach. She was sorry.

"Kate, I need to ask you something, and you

have to be truthful with me, whatever you may think. When was the last time you spoke with him, Kate?"

She looked down. It all scared her. She knew she should tell him. The photo of Mercado and her dad. The old man in the park. Her father's call from the other day . . . Five more people were dead. The longer she hid it, the more she was part of it. She was afraid that Cavetti could see right through her and it would all come tumbling out.

"Kate, the woman had her palms burned off. First the one. Then the other. By that time she'd probably already passed out from the pain. Then they put a bullet in her head."

"It's not him."

"This was to get her to talk," Cavetti went on. "Just like in Chicago. Three more of my men are dead. Your father's looking for someone. This isn't about protecting him any longer."

"Then what the hell *is* it about?" Kate glared up at him. *I know about Mercado,* she wanted to say. *I know you've been protecting him all along. What do you want with my father?*

"Have you heard from him, Kate? Do you know where he is?"

"No."

"I need you to tell me, Kate, in spite of what you may feel toward WITSEC—or me. I know

I haven't been entirely truthful, but I only wanted one thing when it came to you—as I do now—and that is your absolute safety. I'll put my life on the line for that. If you're holding back, you're getting yourself deeper into something you won't be able to control."

He was right. She was putting herself right in the middle of it. *Five more people were dead.* But what was she supposed to do, meet him and have her father dragged away in cuffs?

Kate looked at him closely. "I can't help you." She shook her head.

The WITSEC agent nodded. She knew he was unconvinced. He reached into his jacket pocket and came out with a folded piece of paper.

Another photograph.

"I knew you couldn't help yourself, Cavetti."

"What I'm about to show you, only a handful of people have ever seen." The way the photo was folded, only half of it was visible. "I want you to look closely and tell me, have you ever seen this man before?"

He handed it to her. Kate's hand trembled as she took it. As she looked, her heart crawled up into her throat.

It was the man in the park. Oscar Mercado. The weathered beard, the flat tweed cap. As if the picture were taken just the other day.

A jolt rippled through her. She didn't know what she was getting herself into, just that it was getting deeper. And she no longer knew who was telling the truth.

Her eyes found Cavetti's. "No."

The WITSEC agent nodded with a skeptical sigh. Kate handed back the photo. He looked at her as though her lie were written all over her face.

"You're a smart gal, Kate, but now I need you to be smarter than you've ever been in your life and level with me. Are you sure?"

"Who is he?"

"No one." Cavetti shrugged. "Just a face." Maybe if he told her, she could do the same. This was his chance to come clean, too.

She shook her head again. "No."

"As long as I'm breaking new ground"—the agent smoothed his salt-and-pepper hair—"I'm going to do something else I've never done before." This time he reached into his side pocket and came out with a solid object wrapped in a white handkerchief.

Kate's heart slowed.

"It's untraceable," Cavetti said. "If it ever comes out I gave this to you, I'll deny it. It can't be tied to me. Put it in a drawer. You may need it. That's all I can say. There's a safety catch on the side. You push it off. You understand?"

Kate nodded, suddenly realizing what he was saying to her. Cavetti stood up and left the wrapped object lying on the chair.

"Like I told you, Kate, what I'm trying to do here is for your own protection."

"Thank you," she said softly, and met his eyes with a tight but appreciative smile.

Cavetti stepped toward the door. Kate stood up. All of a sudden, whatever anger and distrust she felt for him disappeared. *Tell him, Kate.*

"Who was she?" Kate asked. "The woman in Buffalo."

Cavetti reached into his jacket. He took out the photo again. This time he unfolded the side that had been hidden.

Next to the man in the flat golf cap was a smiling, warm-faced, middle-aged woman, a white Lab sitting at her knees.

Kate stood still, staring at the photo.

Cavetti shrugged, stuffing it back into his pocket as he opened the door. "Just someone's wife."

CHAPTER SEVENTY

One good thing was happening amid everything else. Greg agreed to the job up at New York–Presbyterian.

The Morgan Stanley Center was one of the best pediatric orthopedic programs in the city. It also meant they could stay in the city. Greg joked that he'd probably have to be on call every other weekend for a year and, as low resident, work every Christmas and Thanksgiving—probably Haitian Pride Day as well—but the position came with a real doctor's salary—over a hundred and twenty grand, plus a forty-thousand-dollar signing bonus. And an office overlooking the Hudson River and the George Washington Bridge.

Friday night Kate took him out for a celebratory dinner at Spice Market with a bunch of his friends from the ER.

The following morning they borrowed a friend's van and moved all of Greg's old medical texts and other belongings that had been crammed into boxes in the apartment up to his office. They parked on Fort Washington Avenue and wheeled everything up through the Harkness Pavilion to Pediatric Orthopedics on the seventh floor.

Greg's office was cramped—not much larger than a Formica-topped desk with two fabric chairs and a bookshelf—but it had that impressive view. And it was a real thrill to see his name in bold letters on the door: DR. GREG HERRERA

"So"—Greg kicked open the door, exposing the Hudson, his arm wrapped around a carton of books—"what do you think?"

"I'm thinking I want dibs on the new space all this stuff frees up in the apartment." Kate, who was carrying a desk lamp, grinned.

"Knew you were proud of me, hon." He winked.

Greg unloaded his boxes. Kate started hanging his medical diplomas on the wall.

"How about this?" She picked up an old photograph they had taken on a holiday in Acapulco, where, a little blotto and bleary-eyed from margaritas in the middle of the day, they had posed at the table in the local Carlos 'n' Charlie's with a live chimpanzee. The chimp was a shill, of course. Cost them fifty dollars. He was probably the only one in the place who wasn't drunk.

Kate held it up next to the diplomas.

"Nah." Greg shook his head. "Not very Hippocratic. Maybe I should wait until I'm made a full partner somewhere."

"Yeah, I was thinking that, too." Kate nodded, placing it back on the desk. "However, there is something this seems like a good time to give you . . ."

She bent down and took out a gift-wrapped box from one of the cartons. "To my own Dr. Kovac." Kate smiled. They always joked about the likable Croatian doctor on *ER.* Kate thought Greg had the same moppy hair, sleepy eyes, and unique accent.

"I didn't want you to feel left out on your first day of work."

Greg pulled off the ribbon. What he saw inside made him laugh.

It was an old black leather doctor's bag. Circa 1940. Complete with an antique-looking stethoscope and reflex hammer.

"Like it?"

"Love it, pooch. It's just that . . ." Greg scratched his head as if stumped. "I'm not sure I even know what these old things do."

"I got it on eBay," Kate said. "I just didn't want you to feel left out, technologically speaking."

"I'll be sure and bring it on rounds." He took out the stethoscope and placed it against Kate's T-shirt, over her heart. "Say ah."

"Ah . . ." Kate said, giggling.

Greg maneuvered it seductively across her chest. "That's ah . . . Again, please."

"You just make sure the only one you ever use that on is *me*," she said, teasing. "Seriously, though . . ." Kate draped her arms around his neck and edged her leg between his. "I couldn't have held together these past weeks without you. I'm really proud of you, Greg. I know I've been crazy, but I'm not crazy when I say this: You're going to make a great doctor."

It was one of the first tender moments they'd had in a long time. Kate realized how much she missed it. She gave him a kiss.

"You do know I already am a doctor." He shrugged with a sheepish smile.

"I know," she said, resting her head against his, "but don't break the spell."

They continued to unpack Greg's belongings. Some photos and mementos, including a painted wooden block she had given him with the word PERSEVERANCE, in bold, block letters on it. A ton of old medical tomes. Greg lifted himself up onto the counter, feeding the books into the shelves as Kate handed them up, two or three at a time. Most were old clothbound texts from medical school. "Largely unread," Greg admitted. Some were even older than that. A couple of dust-covered textbooks on philosophy from under-graduate days. A few he'd carried with him when he moved here. In Spanish.

"Why the hell are you even displaying these old things?" Kate asked.

"Why all doctors display them. Makes us look smart."

Kate stood up, trying to hand him three more. "Then *here*, Einstein—"

Suddenly one fell out of her grasp, knocking against her shoulder as it tumbled to the floor.

"You okay?" Greg asked.

"Yeah." Kate knelt down. It was an old copy of Gabriel García Márquez's *One Hundred Years of Solitude*. In his native Spanish. Greg must've brought it with him from Mexico. It had prob-ably sat at the bottom of this old box for years.

"Hey, check this out."

The flap was open. There was a name scrawled on the inside cover in faded ink.

Kate went cold.

There was this instant—this time-stopping freeze—where Kate saw her life on one side, a life she knew was now left behind—and something else on the other, something she didn't want to see. And no matter how hard she wanted to keep it from happening, the moment wouldn't stop.

She read what was there.

"Kate!"

It was as if the oxygen had been sucked out of her lungs. Or like the horror of a plane suddenly accelerating into a steep dive—something chilling and life-changing that was way beyond belief, yet real.

Gregorio Concerga, the name read in a familiar, right-leaning script.

Not *Herrera.* Kate knew the name immediately. *Concerga*—he had been one of Mercado's henchmen. Her eyes ran down the page and saw something else.

La Escuela Nacional, Carmenes, 1989.

Kate looked up. At Greg. His face was ashen.

Then it was like she was on that plane—as the whole thing started to blow apart.

CHAPTER SEVENTY-ONE

Kate staggered backward, as if a concussion grenade had gone off and everything was black. Had she read it right? She looked at the book again. *Gregorio Concerga. Carmenes. 1989.* Then back at Greg. The stonelike dread on his face confirmed that she had.

"Kate, I don't know where the hell that came from."

Kate stared into her husband's face. All of a sudden, she saw a person she had never seen before.

"Jesus, no, Greg . . ." She shook her head. Her stomach dropped off a cliff.

"Kate, listen, you don't understand." He jumped down from the counter.

No, she didn't understand.

Suddenly things started to become clear. "How did my father know about Tina?" Kate asked.

Greg acted a little confused. "What?"

"*Tina.* He knew she'd been shot. How would he know that? That all happened after he disappeared. How the hell would he know about that, Greg?"

"I don't know!" He took a step toward her. "Listen, baby, this isn't what you think . . ."

"*What I think . . . ?*" Her blood was buzzing with shock. "Oh, God, Greg, what I think?"

Kate dropped the book to the floor. Her fingers went numb, useless. She backed away from him and toward the door. "How did he know about Margaret Seymour being tortured, Greg?"

Greg took a step toward her. "Kate, please . . ."

"*No!*" She flailed at him with her fists. "Oh, my God, Greg, what have you done?"

She realized she had to get out of there. She continued to the door. Greg's eyes darted toward the book on the floor. Kate started to run. Before she hit the door, she caught a glimpse of him kneeling, picking up the book.

"Kate, where are you going? Please."

She dashed into the hall, flinging aside an idle gurney that was blocking her path. She needed to get out, she needed air. "Don't come after me!" she begged. At the elevator bank, Kate jammed her palm against the buttons.

She heard Greg's voice calling after her, *"Kate, wait, please . . ."* She heard him running after her. She looked around frantically for the stairs, mashing her hand over and over against both buttons. *Please!*

Miraculously, the elevator door opened. Kate threw herself in. It was empty. She feverishly pressed the green "Door Close" button. Greg slid around the turn and tried to force his arm through the closing doors. Thank God, he was an instant too late.

She pressed "Lobby."

As the elevator descended, Kate put her hands over her face and leaned back into the paneled wall. Her stomach was grinding.

You have to think. She flashed through a mental reel of their relationship since they'd first met. It had been four years. They'd met at the temple. In New York. Rosh Hashanah. Greg was in medical school. He didn't have any family here. Her father took a liking to him, and Kate did, too. Then her father invited him out to the house. It was as if she were being set up.

Kate gagged in revulsion. *Was it all part of the fucking plan?*

Finally the elevator door rattled open in the lobby. Kate ran out, brushing by a mother and son about to step in. "Hey . . ."

She sprinted through the high-ceilinged atrium space and out the glass doors, her mind a jumble of thoughts and fears.

All she knew was that she had trusted Greg— and suddenly he was part of it. He had been the *only* thing in her life she could count on as real.

Kate pushed through the revolving doors onto Fort Washington Avenue. She had to get away and think. She couldn't see Greg or hear him explain. He was probably coming down the stairs after her now.

Their van was parked across from the rear entrance on 168th Street. Kate ran the other way, toward Broadway.

A security guard came out of the entrance with a radio and called after her. Kate didn't even stop to think. Halfway up the block, she looked around and saw Greg pushing through the revolving doors, calling, "Kate, listen, please!" Kate kept on running. She didn't know what she would do when she got to the corner. All she could think of was losing herself in a crowd.

Broadway was jammed. Bodegas. Discount clothing stores. A Dr. J's athletic-shoe store. Fast-food outlets. The intersection at 168th Street was one of the busiest in this part of town.

Kate looked frantically for a cab.

There was a subway entrance in front of her.

Kate bolted down the stairs. She remembered the MetroCard in her wallet and groped wildly in her purse, her fingers shaking. She located her card, forced it into the turnstile, and went through.

The Broadway line.

First she headed toward the downtown staircase. Then she stopped. She didn't know how soon the next train would arrive. Not seeing her on the street, Greg might come down here. She might still be on the platform when he caught up to her.

Then Kate remembered that 168th was where the Broadway and Eighth Avenue lines merged. She searched the signs above and spotted the green circle for the IND line. She followed them, running eastward down a long corridor. She didn't know if Greg had followed her. Then she thought she heard his voice behind her, coming down the stairs: "Kate . . . Kate . . ."

Her heart rate accelerated. *Please, just leave me alone.*

There were a few people in the long underground tunnel. A group of teenagers wearing Knicks jerseys and basketball sneakers. Their voices echoed off the low ceiling as Kate brushed by. "Watch it, lady!"

She ran as fast as she could. She didn't know

if Greg was behind her. Then she saw the green circle indicating her train. There was an escalator leading to the platform. Kate took it down.

A handful of people were standing around on the downtown platform. Greg wouldn't look for her there. Kate peered down the dark tunnel, begging for the train. Every second she was sure Greg was going to bound down the escalator and find her. Finally she saw a light in the distance. *Thank God! Hurry, please . . .*

The subway train rattled into the station, and Kate jumped aboard. She headed toward the front of the train, her eyes locked on the escalator. She prayed she wouldn't see him. She couldn't bear it.

Mercifully, the train doors beeped and closed.

Kate pressed herself against the doors, exhaling in a long, deep spasm of relief. Then there was just a weird, uneasy calm.

Her heart was beating like a furnace that wouldn't slow down. Her eyes were raw with tears. The light of her past life flickered out as the train pulled out of the station and into the dark tunnel. She had no idea where she was going to go.

CHAPTER SEVENTY-TWO

Phil Cavetti opened the doors to the dingy, sparsely filled bar, the Liffey, on West Forty-ninth Street. No one even looked up as he stepped in.

An assortment of raggedy-looking old-timers with beers in front of them were yelling at a soccer match on the TV. One wall was covered with black-and-white pictures of famous soccer stars and tenors. Another had a Gaelic national flag draped like a tapestry. Cavetti stepped up to the bar, next to a balding man in a tan raincoat, hunched over his beer.

"Drinking alone?"

The man turned. "Not sure. Brad and Angelina are supposed to drop in any minute now."

"Sorry to disappoint."

"Fuck it." He sighed. Alton Booth removed

the newspaper from the stool beside him. "I have this feeling I'm being stood up."

Cavetti sat down. "I'll have what he's having," he instructed the muscular, ponytailed man behind the bar, sleeves of colorful tattoos running up and down his arms.

"Shirley Temple!" the barman called loudly. A few people turned away from their match to look.

"He knows I'm a cop, right?" Cavetti snorted in an amused sort of way.

"Everyone in here does. You sat next to me."

The barman brought Cavetti a Killian's, with a smirk that let him know he'd had him made as soon as he walked in. Cavetti took a swig of his beer. "So you got me here, Al. I'm kinda thinking it wasn't for the charm."

"Sorry." The FBI man shrugged sheepishly. He slid a manila envelope across. Cavetti unfastened the clasp and pulled out what was inside.

Photos.

He laughed. "Couldn't help yourself, huh?"

"What's the joke?"

"Kate Raab said that to me. Every time I see her, I bring out pictures."

"Wait till she gets a load of these."

Cavetti slid out the contents. There was a cover sheet marked CRIMINAL EVIDENCE, from the Seattle office of the FBI. The top sheet read PIKE'S MARKET. HOMICIDE OF SHARON RAAB, A/K/A SHARON GELLER.

"A team of agents on our field staff were following up on the crime scene," Booth explained. "These were taken by a security camera in a garage a block from the hotel. The agent in charge, ambitious up-and-comer that he was, ran the plates of all vehicles leaving area garages within a few minutes after the attack."

"Thorough." Cavetti nodded, leafing through the photos, impressed.

They were all of the rear of a single car. A Chrysler Le Baron. Years before, Cavetti used to drive one. This one was newer. Michigan plates—EV6 7490.

"Rental," the FBI man said, anticipating the next question. "Two days before. It was turned back in the day after at the Sacramento airport."

Cavetti looked at him impatiently. "Do I have to order another beer, Al, or are you going to give me a name?"

"Skinner."

Cavetti's eyes widened. "Fuckin' A . . ."

"Kenneth John Skinner" was one of the licenses they'd traced to Benjamin Raab.

So it wasn't Mercado after all. It was only made to look that way. Raab was behind it, even if he hadn't pulled the trigger.

The son of a bitch had murdered his own wife.

"Does this photo come with an understanding of what's going on?"

"I understand we've got four agents dead, Phil. And that Oscar Mercado is missing. I understand that we're dealing with a man we've greatly underestimated. Problem is, Assistant Director Cummings is starting to understand that, too."

"*Cummings?*"

"The AD wants this over, Phil. They want Raab, Mercado—this whole thing put under wraps. No more pissing around your little Blue Zone. His directive is, 'By whatever means . . .'"

"Whoever it puts at risk." Cavetti nodded. "Whoever happens to get in the way."

Booth shrugged again. "Your boys are squaring off against each other, Phil." He signaled for another beer. "Either that, or this is one fucking elaborate scheme to get out of paying alimony."

"You're right." Cavetti took a final swig and stood up, patting Booth on the back. "His daughter's not going to be thrilled about this at all."

He looked at Booth, then glanced around the dingy bar. "What is it you like about this place, Al?" he asked, reaching into his pocket for a bill.

Booth stopped him. "I was on Westies patrol when I was cutting my bones back in the seventies." The Westies were the bloody Hell's Kitchen gang whose members were always used as muscle for the mob. "This was the local HQ. I was outside this place so many times on surveillance, one day the manager came out and brought me a beer. Haven't paid since."

Cavetti laughed. He had a few of those stories himself.

But he wasn't happy. He had spoken with Kate Raab yesterday. He was certain she hadn't been truthful with him when he asked about her father.

Now he felt doubly scared for her.

CHAPTER SEVENTY-THREE

Kate stayed on the train for what seemed like hours. She rode it all the way downtown to 59th Street, then wandered through the crowded station in a daze and took the Broadway line all the way back uptown.

Her world had just been cracked in two.

She had seen her mother killed. Her closest friend shot and in a coma. Her father go from the person she loved and admired most in the world to someone whose very voice now riddled her with doubt and fear.

Yet with all that had happened, she had never felt alone. Because she'd always had Greg. She knew she could always come back to him. He made her feel whole.

Until now.

Now she didn't know where to go. To the police? *Cavetti?* Tell them everything. Her father's connection to Mercado. That he had set up his own arrest. That he was after his own brother. That she had spoken with him.

That her own husband might be part of it, too.

The rattling rhythm of the train soothed her. She rode it all the way back uptown, past 168th Street. She didn't know where to go. Only that soon she'd have to make a decision. She couldn't go home. That was where Greg would be. She couldn't face him. Not now.

That was when the PA announced: *"Dyckman Street—next stop."*

It was like something out of a dream. That was the answer. At least for a while. Kate got off there. She ran down the stairs and headed toward the river.

The boathouse was only a short walk away.

In the cold of the November afternoon, Kate leaned against the pier. Only a few staunch rowers were braving the bitter chill out there today. A club-team eight was powering out by the big Columbia C. Kate could hear the coxswain: "Stroke ... stroke ..." She huddled in her sweatshirt, the wet breeze whipping her face and hair.

Had it always been arranged? Had Greg always been part of this? Meeting, falling in love, every time they laughed, danced, talked about their lives, found things for their apartment. Every time they'd made love.

Had it all been part of the same plan?

The nausea came back, the sweeping violent, unstoppable surge. When it subsided, a numbed feeling took its place, like she'd been battered, every bone broken. Enervated.

They've won. They've beaten you, Kate. Give up. Don't try to figure it out any longer. Just find Cavetti. Tell him everything. Who are you protecting now? Why can't you just do the one smart thing?

Let it out. There's nothing to keep inside. She pressed her palms against her eyes and started to cry. They *had* won. Beaten her. She had nothing left. She had no one to trust anymore.

Her phone vibrated again. It was Greg—he'd been leaving frantic messages—for maybe the fifteenth time. "*Kate, pick up, please . . .*"

This time she flipped it open. She didn't know why. A bitter anger was clawing its way through every aching pore.

"*Kate!*" Greg shouted when he heard her pick up. "Please let me explain."

"Explain." Her voice was a dull, derisive snort. She'd scream at him if only she had the strength for rage. "Why don't you start with who you are, Greg? Who am I suddenly married to? Or what your name is really? *My name!* Why don't you start with that? You want to explain, Greg? Explain what I've been feeling for the past four years. Who I'm sleeping next to. Start with how you found me?"

"Kate, listen, please . . . I admit, I was asked four years ago to get to know you—"

"To get to know me?" Nothing he might have said could have sounded quite so cruel.

"To watch out for you, Kate. That's all, I swear. I can't lie—what you saw in that book is real. My name *is* Concerga. And I'm not from Mexico City. I'm sorry, Kate. But I fell in love with you. That part was always real. That part is the truth, I swear it on my life. I never thought in a million years this would ever come out."

"But it did, Greg," she said. "It did come out. So who is it you work for, Greg?"

"I don't work for anybody, Kate. Please . . . I'm your husband."

"No, you aren't my husband. Not now. Who have you been keeping tabs on me for? Because it's over now, Greg. I release you. From the duty. This *deber* of yours—the debt is cleared."

"Kate, it's not what you think. Please, tell me where you are. Let me come and talk to you." There was a desperation in his voice, and it hurt her not to respond, but she no longer had any

398

hold on what was real. "I love you, Kate. Don't turn me away."

"Go away," Kate said. "Just go away, Greg. Your job is done."

"No," he said. "I won't. I'm not going to."

"I mean it, baby," she said. "I can't talk to you now. Just go away."

CHAPTER SEVENTY-FOUR

There was only one place Kate could go.

Even though she'd been expressly forbidden to.

She stood in front of the white-trimmed blue cape in Hewlett, Long Island, and the WITSEC agent who had spotted her approaching on the street and intercepted her now held her tightly by the arm.

She had remained at the boathouse until after dark. It had taken her two trains and the rest of the afternoon to make up her mind. She knew she wasn't followed. But she couldn't chance they'd say no by calling. Where else could she go?

As the front door opened, Aunt Abbie's eyes went wide. "*Kate!* Oh, my God, what are you doing here?"

It took barely a second for her mother's sister

to see that something was really wrong.

"It's okay." Abbie nodded to the agent, hastily pulling Kate in and throwing her arms around her niece. "*Em, Justin*, come down quick!"

Kate realized she looked horrible. She'd been huddled on the bank of the river all afternoon. She was cold and wet, her hair windblown and disheveled, her cheeks raw. Only a blind person couldn't see that she'd been crying.

But the moment her brother and sister barreled down the stairs in a state of happy shock, everything brightened. Em screamed, and they hugged each other joyously, just as they had back at the boathouse in Seattle before everything fell apart. Em and Justin had been staying here since the funeral. Under guard. David and Abbie's own kids were away at college. The plan was for them to remain here for the rest of the semester and start fresh in the spring.

"I need to stay here," Kate said to Abbie. "Just for a day or two."

"Of course you can stay," Abbie said, hesitating only in trying to decipher the troubled cast on Kate's face.

"You can sleep in *my* room!" Emily shouted, gleefully. "I meant *Jill's*—"

"That's okay." Aunt Abbie smiled. "Jill

401

wouldn't mind. It *is* your room now. For as long as you want it. Yours, too, Kate."

"Thank you." Kate smiled back in appreciation.

"Why are you here, Kate?" "What's going on?" The questions from Emily and Justin seemed to shoot at her from all directions. Right now she just felt so exhausted she wanted to collapse. They took her into the living room and let her sink into a chair. "Are you all right? Where's Greg?"

"He's working," she said.

"What's happened, Kate?" They weren't crazy. They could read it in her eyes.

"Let Kate alone," Aunt Abbie told them.

And something did start to revive her. Something Kate had been missing for a long time.

Her sister's happy grin, her brother's slightly dumb buzz haircut. Abbie next to her on the arm of her chair with a gentle hand on her shoulder. There was no confusion here, no doubt. They all looked like home to her.

Her Uncle David came home around seven. He worked in the city as sales manager of a fashion jewelry line. They had dinner in the dining room. Pot roast, mashed potatoes, gravy. It was the first solid meal Kate had eaten in days.

Everyone bombarded her with questions. How were things back at the lab? How was Tina coming along? What was going on with Greg?

Kate deflected them as best she could, telling them how he had gotten the position at New York–Presbyterian and how they could stay in New York now, and that was great.

Justin said they would be going to Hewlett High School for the rest of the semester. With a WITSEC escort. "Then, in the spring, maybe this private school, Friends Academy."

"Jill and Matt went there," Abbie said. "They've agreed to take them in."

"Friends has the third-ranked squash team in the East," Emily announced. "I'll be able to start playing tourneys in the fall."

"That's great." Kate beamed. She looked at Abbie and David. "Thank you for what you're doing. Mom would be proud."

"Your mother wouldn't have hesitated to do the same for us," Abbie said. She put down her fork and looked away.

And Kate knew she was right.

Later Uncle David helped Aunt Abbie with the dishes, giving Justin and Emily time with Kate.

They all went up to Em's room on the second floor—their cousin Jill's room—papered with magazine shots of Beyoncé, Angelina Jolie, and Benjamin McKenzie from *The O.C.* Kate curled up on the bed with a pillow, Em sitting cross-legged at her feet. Justin spun a desk chair around backward and flopped himself down.

Emily looked at her, concerned. "Something's wrong."

"Nothing's wrong." Kate shook her head. She knew her voice didn't sound convincing.

"C'mon, Kate. Look at you. You're pale as a ghost. Your eyes are totally bloodshot. When was the last time you took your medicine?"

Kate thought back. *Yesterday, maybe the day before* . . . What suddenly scared her was that she couldn't recall.

"We're not exactly idiots, Kate," Justin said, "we all know the agreement."

It was a condition of their aunt and uncle's taking them in that Kate agreed not to come here without prior notice until things cooled down.

"Is it Greg? Has something happened? Kate, why are you here?"

Kate nodded. She realized when she walked through that door and saw their faces that they had a right to know.

"All right." She sat up. "I don't know how you're going to react when you hear this. But Dad's alive."

They both just sat there staring at her for a second.

Emily's jaw slackened. *"He's alive?"*

"Yeah." Kate nodded. "I spoke with him. He's alive."

Justin almost toppled over in his chair. "Jesus, Kate, you were just gonna throw that in?"

How much could she tell them? Without telling them everything. Margaret Seymour. Mercado. The picture she'd found. The truth about their grandmother and where their father had come from. How could she just tell them these things? How could she destroy their world, the way hers had been destroyed? Wasn't it right to protect them? If not from harm, then at least from knowing too much.

"Where is he?" Emily asked, dumbfounded.

"I don't know. He said he would contact me. The police want to find him, in connection with some stuff that's been going on. But he's okay. I just wanted you to know. He's alive."

A blush of excitement, then confusion, rushed into Emily's face. "Doesn't he want to see us? Does he even know about Mom? Where, Kate? Where on earth has he been all this time?"

Kate didn't answer. She just kept looking at them. She knew exactly what was in her sister's mind. Something between shock and anger.

"There's something you're not telling us, Kate, isn't there? About why you're here. Mom's dead. We're in the goddamn Witness Protection Program! You can tell us. We're not children anymore."

Justin stared. "Dad's done something really bad, hasn't he?" Kate didn't reply, but it was as if the question had already been silently answered. As if he understood. "We're not just hiding here from Mercado, are we?"

Kate's eyes glistened, and she slowly shook her head. "No."

"Oh, God . . ."

Kate had made up her mind. Before she even came here tonight. What she had to do. She just needed to see them first.

Because they could still be protected, couldn't they? They could still go to school. They could laugh, play squash, hang out on weekends, take the SATs. Live out their lives. They could still feel hope and trust. They didn't fucking have to know.

A pall came over Emily's face. "Are you in danger, Kate? Is that why you're here?"

"Sshhh . . ." Kate put a finger to her sister's

lips. She reached out, and Em just leaned into her. Even Justin didn't resist and joined them. They put their heads against her shoulders. Stared up at the ceiling. She drew them close.

"Remember when we used to sit in your room, like this?" Kate said. "You had those stars. And we'd talk about when you were gonna get that first kiss . . . Or how you told me about the night you snuck out and took Mom's Range Rover after Mom and Dad were asleep—and picked up your friend Ally?"

"You took out the car?" Justin asked.

"Duh!" Em snapped. "If you weren't stuck to your computer all the time like some stupid cybergeek, you might have a clue!"

"I never told." Kate squeezed her shoulder.

"Of course you never told. What are you, some kind of Mom-and-Dad spy?"

For a while no one said anything. They just lay there, looking at the ceiling.

Then Emily asked, "What's more important, Kate, knowing that your family loved you, even if they might not be the people you once thought? Or seeing them as they really are and feeling totally betrayed?"

"I don't know," Kate answered. But for the first time, she actually felt she did. Her father.

Greg. She'd made up her mind. She locked her fingers tightly around theirs. "How can you really love something that's not the truth?"

CHAPTER SEVENTY-FIVE

The following morning Kate dropped some change into a pay phone at a 7-Eleven store in Hewlett. No cell phones now. Nothing that could ever be traced.

During the night she'd thought a lot about what she had to do. She knew she was putting herself in danger. Feeling Emily next to her, the innocent breathing of her sleep, had removed all doubt.

This had to end.

The coins tumbled in. The dial tone sounded. Taking a breath, Kate punched in the number. She waited for someone to pick up.

Her dad. Cavetti. Mercado. Greg ... Each of them was someone who had betrayed her. And each of them was someone she might trust, one last time. All through the night, each had flickered through her anxious mind.

When she heard the voice, she didn't dare hesitate. "Okay, I'll do what you asked," she said.

"I'm glad to hear that, Kate," the voice replied. "You've made the right choice."

They worked out a place to meet. Somewhere safe, public. Lots of people. Somewhere she felt at home.

This had to end. People had died. She could no longer pretend she wasn't complicit now. She thought of the smiling woman in the photo with Mercado. The man's wife. Would she still be alive if Kate had acted earlier?

Would Mom?

Kate fumbled in her handbag for another quarter. At the bottom of her bag, she came upon the gun Cavetti had given her.

"I have to trust somebody," she said, placing her makeup case over the gun. "It might as well be you."

Luis Prado's phone rang shortly afterward.

He was in Brooklyn, in the shabby apartment he rented, with some heavyset, fifty-dollar whore named Rosella straddling him, her large breasts bobbing in his face, the cheap metal bed squeaking and rocking against the paint-chipped wall.

The cell phone interrupted them.

"Don't stop, baby," Rosella whined.

Luis fumbled for the phone, knocking over a photo of his wife and kids back home that he kept on the table. "Shit . . ."

The number said this was the call he'd been expecting all day.

"Bizness, baby," he sighed, rolling the girl off him.

"Luis . . ."

"I need you to get ready," the caller said. "There's a job for you tonight."

"I am ready." Luis ran his hand playfully along Rosella's cheek. "I've been practicing my aim all day."

"Good. I'll be in touch later with the details. And, Luis?"

"Yes."

"This one will require all of your loyalty. Do it well," the caller said, "and you can go home. For good."

His loyalty had never been in doubt. He had always done the jobs they wanted. His wife was home. His children. He had seen his newest boy only once.

Luis Prado didn't hesitate. "I'm here."

PART FIVE

CHAPTER SEVENTY-SIX

Kate waited on the Promenade in Brooklyn Heights, the skyline of Lower Manhattan towering across the East River behind her. Joggers ran along the walk, and young families pushed strollers. Rollerbladers wove in and out of the Sunday crowd. The sprawling span of the Brooklyn Bridge with its steel-gray cables stretched above her. She knew she could count on the crowds. Kate had come here many times. Taking Fergus on a run. Breezing through the shops on Montague Street with Greg. She scanned around. Two policemen were standing nearby. She stepped a little closer to them.

He was somewhere out here.

It was a perfect autumn afternoon, and it made Kate recall how she had graduated from college on such a day. She still kept that picture on her desk—her in her cap and gown on the Green at

Brown—everyone's smiles so bright and proud, her head leaning on her father's shoulder. The sky had never been bluer than it was on that day.

He'd been lying to her—even then.

Kate prayed she was doing the right thing. Her brain was dull from the lack of insulin, and even her blood felt thick and a little slow. She knew she wasn't thinking so clearly. She glanced at her watch: 3:30. He was making her wait. She checked inside her bag for the gun and glanced again at the cops.

Please, Kate, please don't be making the biggest mistake of your life.

Then suddenly she saw him, materializing out of the crowd, as if from nowhere.

Their gazes met. He stood a short distance away, as if letting her grow accustomed to the sight, a familiar yet uncertain smile. He was wearing khakis, an open-necked blue shirt, the ubiquitous navy blazer. His hair was shorter, almost shaved. The tan was gone. His face was leaner than she'd ever seen it. It was like some low-budget sci-fi movie—someone inhabiting someone else's body. A jogger crossed in front of them. Kate's every nerve stood on edge.

"Hello, pumpkin."

He didn't make a move to hug her. If he had, Kate didn't know what she would do. She just looked at him—her eyes drawn to every familiar feature. There was a part of her that wanted to put her face against his chest and her arms around him as she had a thousand times. There was another part that wanted to tear into him with anger. So she just squinted into the faraway regions of his eyes.

"Who are you . . . Daddy?"

"Who *am* I? What do you mean, pumpkin? I'm your father, Kate. Nothing that's happened can change that."

Kate shook her head. "I'm not sure I know anymore."

He smiled fondly. "You remember how I took you down the mountain at Snowmass that first time? How you followed right in my tracks? And how it was me you came to when you got dumped by that jerk from BU, that actor? How I hugged you and wiped the tears out of your eyes—"

"I don't have any tears now, Dad . . . I asked you who you are. What's our real name? It isn't Raab. I know that now. What's the truth about our family? Rosa—where was she really from? It wasn't Spain."

"Who's been talking to you, Kate? Whoever's been telling you these things is lying." He reached out a hand to her.

"Stop!" She backed away. "Just stop, please . . . I know the truth. I know, Daddy. How long you've been working for them. Mercado. How it was that the FBI found out about you. Who turned you in." She waited for him to say something, anything, to deny it, but he just kept staring at her. "Who was it who shot up our house that night? Were you even protecting us, Dad? Were you even afraid?"

"I was always protecting you, pumpkin," he said with a nod. "I'm the person who helped nurse you back when you got sick. I was the one there in the hospital when you opened your eyes. You know that, Kate. Who was the first person you saw? The rest, what does it matter? Anything else is just a lie."

"*No.*" Kate's blood surged with rage. "It does matter, Dad. It's *all* that matters. You want to see what a lie looks like, I'll show you."

She reached into her bag and came out with something and placed it in his hand. It was the snapshot of him and his brother in front of the gate in Carmenes.

"Look at *this*, Daddy. *This* is a lie. This is the lie you've been telling your whole life, you bastard."

CHAPTER SEVENTY-SEVEN

He didn't show surprise or even flinch. He only stared at the photo with some remembrance, as if he'd come upon something intimate and valued that had been lost for a long time. When he looked back at Kate, the edge of his mouth curled into a resigned smile.

"Where did you get this, Kate?"

"Goddamn you, Daddy, we trusted you," Kate said, unable to control the raging inside her. "Em, Justin, Mom . . . We trusted you with our lives. More than our lives, Dad—we trusted you with who we are."

He flicked the photo with his thumb. "I asked you where you got this, Kate."

"What does it matter? I want to hear it from your lips. That's why I'm here. I want to hear you tell me that everything was a lie. What you did. Who you were. Who *we* were."

A few passersby turned and stared, but Kate kept on, her eyes flooding with tears. "What about Greg, Dad? Was that all part of the plan, too? Was that a Sephardic thing, Dad, or just business? *Fraternidad!*"

He reached out, but Kate just drew away. He had become something vile.

"*I know!* I know he's your brother. I know about your father and who he was. I know you set the whole thing up—your arrest, the trial, getting into the program. I know what you're trying to do."

He just stood there looking at her, shielding his eyes against the sun.

"You killed that woman, didn't you? Margaret Seymour. You killed my mother—*your own wife!* That woman in Buffalo. It's all true. *All* of it, isn't it? What the hell kind of monster *are* you?"

He blinked. Suddenly it was as though something familiar shifted. There was a steeliness to his eyes, an icy blankness in his stare. "Where is he, sweetheart?"

"Where is *who*?"

His voice was dull, almost businesslike. He reached for her. "You know who I mean."

And then it was as if the person she'd known her whole life was no longer standing there.

Kate pulled away. "I don't know who you're

talking about. I don't even know what our real name is. Did you bring Greg into my life, you bastard? To do what? Make my life a lie as well? Tell me something, Dad. How long"—she met his hollow gaze—"how long did my mother know?"

He shrugged. "I know you've seen him, Kate. It's *he* who's poisoning you. *He* who's telling you lies. I want you to come with me. I thought about what you said. We'll both go to the FBI. They'll tell you the same thing." This time he reached out and grabbed her. It made her cringe, and Kate wrestled her arm away.

"No!" She took a step back. "I know what you're trying to do. You're trying to lure him with me. Goddamn you, Daddy, he's your brother. What are you going to do, kill him, too?"

Her father went to touch her, but then he stopped. His gaze strangely shifted. Kate felt the eeriest chill come over her.

He'd seen something.

"What are you staring at?" she asked, the shiver rippling down her spine.

"Nothing." His gaze returned to her. A little half smile curled on his lips.

There was something creepy and almost impersonal in his eyes. Her heart was pounding. Her mind went to the gun in her bag. She glanced around for the cops. She knew she had to get out of here. *This was her father!* Suddenly Kate felt scared for her life.

"I need to go now, Daddy."

He took a step after her. "Why are you protecting him, Kate? He's nothing to you."

"I'm not protecting anyone. You've got to turn yourself in. I can't help you anymore."

Kate backed into a woman, knocking a package out of her arms. "Hey!" She started to run along the Promenade. Her father followed for a few steps, people crisscrossing in his path.

"I'm going to find him, Kate! You're not the only way."

She picked up her pace, knifing through the strollers. All she knew was that she had to get out of there. At the Montague Street entrance, she glanced back. He had stopped. Her heart was racing. She caught a glimpse of him through the crowd.

He raised his hand. He had the most impassive smile on his face.

He gave her a one-fingered wave.

Kate ran out of the park, glancing back once or twice on Montague Street. Past a few shops and cafés. She edged through the pedestrians. Kate got a block or two away and looked behind. He wasn't following her. *Thank God . . .*

She found herself in front of a store window, a Starbucks, leaning her palm on the glass to rest, sucking air back into her lungs.

She had no idea where to go.

She couldn't go home. Greg was there. And she couldn't go back to Abbie's. Not any longer. She was petrified of getting Em and Justin any more deeply involved.

Kate's gaze slowly fell upon her own mixed-up reflection in the glass.

She saw what he'd been staring at.

Her pendants. When her father jostled her they must have come out.

Both halves . . .

Her father knew that she had seen Mercado now.

CHAPTER SEVENTY-EIGHT

Greg pressed the speed-dial button for Kate's cell phone over and over.

C'mon, Kate, please pick up.

And for maybe the fiftieth time, her voice mail responded: *"It's Kate. You know what to do . . ."* There was no point leaving another message. He'd left a dozen already. Greg tossed the phone away and put his head back on the couch. He'd been trying her all night.

He had gone to their apartment, praying she'd come home, hoping his pleas would have some effect. He slept on the couch, but barely. At several points he'd awoken, thinking he heard her key in the door, her footsteps.

But it was always just Fergus, shifting or nudging his water bowl during the night.

How would she ever trust him again?

It was true, of course, everything that had

come out when the book fell open. That he'd kept a terrible secret from her. That he'd pretended to be someone he wasn't. *Who do you work for, Greg?* All true, except her accusation that it was some kind of duty or job.

He had never deceived her for a second about what was in his heart.

What could he tell her that he hadn't already? That it was all something out of his control. That it had happened a long time ago, before they met. A part of him he tried to deny by pretending that he was simply a doctor, a faithful husband, her best friend. Supporting her as she lived through the horror of finding out about her father—how many times he prayed that the truth would never be told.

But feuds of blood, they never stay buried. They were his family, too.

Still, he had always loved her. He had always tried his best to protect her. He had never lied to her about that. How could his heart ache so badly if it weren't all true?

He was ashamed of the bloodline that had caused him to do this. Ashamed of the debt he'd had to pay. Yet without them he would be just a boy on the streets. Not a person schooled in the United States. A doctor. Someone free.

How foolish he was to have believed all this time that he was someone else.

Fergus nestled up to him. Greg pulled the dog's face close and kissed his snout. Greg knew that Kate was in danger. And there was nothing he could do.

Suddenly the cell phone rang. Greg lunged across the couch and flipped it open, not checking who it was. "Hello, Kate . . . ?"

But the voice on the other end was the one he most feared. His heart dropped off a cliff.

"Es su tiempo ahora, hijo," the voice said, softly but decisively.

It is your time now, son.

CHAPTER SEVENTY-NINE

There was only one place Kate could think to go. She caught the Number 5 train at Borough Hall back into Manhattan, rode it all the way to the Bronx. It was a Sunday afternoon. No one would be there. She knew she'd be safe there until she figured out what to do. And she hadn't taken her insulin shot in two days.

Kate got off at the 180th Street station in the Bronx. She thought she spotted the same Latino guy in a Yankees cap whom she'd noticed at the station in Brooklyn, but she wasn't sure. On the street she quickened her pace, heading over to Morris Avenue in a blur, weaving through the crowds of Sunday shoppers and families hanging out on their stoops.

Then she saw the three-story redbrick building on the grounds of the medical college, the familiar brass plaque on the door. The riot in her blood began to slow.

PACKER LABS.

She was safe here. At least for a while.

Kate twisted the key in the outside lock and punched in the alarm code. She thrust open the door and shut it solidly behind her. She pressed her back against the wall.

She hadn't been taking care of herself, and she could feel it. On the train she had taken her bloods: 435. *Jesus, Kate, you're off the charts.* Any higher and she could go into a coma. She blinked against the daze to stay alert. Before she made any decisions, she had to stabilize herself.

And then make the biggest decision of her life.

Kate rummaged inside the medical-storage closet until she located a box of syringes. They used them now and then to inject fluid into cells.

She always kept a spare bottle of Humulin in the fridge. Just for emergencies. Kate opened the fridge, kneeling, and searched around. There were trays of solution vials and marked clear tubes on every shelf. *C'mon, c'mon.* She fumbled anxiously through the shelves.

Goddamn it! She sank to the floor in frustration. It wasn't there. Maybe while she was away, someone had cleaned the thing out.

Okay, Kate, what are you going to do? Tomorrow the lab would be open. People would be here. She couldn't exactly go on with her normal routine. Her heart felt twice its normal size. She knew it was her glucose levels. She could go to the medical center—it was only a few blocks away. But she had to call someone.

Cavetti. Aunt Abbie . . . There was no way she could handle this thing herself anymore. She thought of Emily and Justin.

Suddenly a spasm of dread sliced through the haze.

Does he know where they are?

Oh, God, he might. Where else would they be? A panicky thought suddenly gripped her.

If her father had done what he had to Mom, why couldn't he hurt *them*?

She remembered what he said: *"You're not the only way . . ."*

She ran over to the counter and fumbled through her bag. She found her cell phone and scrolled awkwardly through her speed-dial list. What had he told her? Anywhere, anytime. Who the hell else did she have to turn to now?

She found Cavetti's name and anxiously pressed the button, holding it the whole time it connected. Who knew where he would be? Kate didn't even know where he lived.

It took three rings, but he answered. "Cavetti." Thank God!

"It's Kate!" she shouted, exhaling in relief at the sound of his voice.

"Kate." He heard her agitation instantly. "What's wrong?"

"I've seen my dad. I know what he's done. But listen, it's a lot deeper than that. I know about Mercado. I've seen him, too. And I think my father is trying to find me. He thinks I know where he is."

"Where *who* is, Kate?" he asked.

"*Mercado!*" She was barely keeping it together now.

"Okay," he said. He asked where she was calling from. Kate told him, and that she was safe. He said to stay where she was. Not to go out. For anything. He was in New Jersey. He was going to call Booth and Ruiz from the FBI.

"Don't open the door for anyone until one of us gets there, you understand? Not your father. Your husband. No one. *Do you understand?*"

"Yes. But there's something else."

She told him about Justin and Emily and what her father had implied. *He had other ways . . .* "I'm afraid he's going to go there, Cavetti. He might be on his way there now."

"I'll take care of it. But like I said, Kate, not

for anybody, except the FBI. *You understand?"*

"Yes," she shouted. *"I understand!"*

After Cavetti clicked off, Kate found the number for Aunt Abbie's. She quickly dialed, and, to her dismay, the voice recording came on. *"We're not at home . . ."*

Then she tried Em's cell phone. No answer as well. Kate was getting scared. She left a frantic message. "Em, I need you and Justin to get somewhere safe. Not in the house. A neighbor's, a friend's. And quick. And whatever you do, please don't go near Dad. Don't even talk to him if he calls. I'll explain when you reach me. You've got to trust me on this. The police are on the way."

She sat there on the floor. She kept redialing Aunt Abbie's number with the same result. What if he'd already gotten there? What if he had them? There was nothing she could do but wait.

At the bottom of her bag, Kate once again came across the gun Cavetti had given her. She held it in her hand. It was almost like a toy. Could she use it if she had to? Against her father? She closed her eyes.

Suddenly she heard the outside door buzzer. *Thank God—they're here.*

Kate leaped up, put the gun on top of the counter, and ran down the hallway toward the front door.

"Who is it? Who's there?"

"Agent Booth," a voice replied from outside. "FBI."

There was a video monitor to the front entrance behind the reception desk, and Kate went behind and checked. She saw Booth on the black-and-white screen, his familiar balding head, and another man behind him in a baseball cap, holding up his badge.

She ran over to the door and punched in the code. The green light flashed on. Suddenly her cell phone started to ring. *Em!* Kate twisted the inside bolt and flung open the door into the face of the FBI agent.

"Thank God—"

Booth's eyes were strangely blank, lifeless. Then, to Kate's horror, the agent just sank to the floor, two red blotches on his chest. There was another body behind him.

The man who'd been propping Booth up tossed aside his badge and ID.

"Put down that phone, pumpkin."

CHAPTER EIGHTY

Kate screamed.

She stared down at the two inert bodies on the floor, then back at her father. Behind him was the Hispanic figure in the Yankees cap whom Kate had noticed leaving the train. Her father glanced at him conspiratorially, saying, "Wait here."

"Daddy, what the hell are you doing?"

He stepped inside the front hall, letting the door shut gently behind him, careful not to engage the lock. "Where is he, Kate? I know you've seen him." There was no longer even a pretended softness to his voice.

"*I saw them, Kate*—the pendants. Both. Now there won't be any more lying. You're going to tell me where he is."

Kate backpedaled down the hallway. She dropped the cell phone. That's when she saw the gun at his side. "I don't know—that's the truth." The FBI agents were dead. Cavetti was somewhere, but she didn't know where. He could be dead, too. And what they did to her mother, they could do to her.

"You know where he is, Kate," her father said, pushing her deeper inside the lab. "Don't make me do something I don't want to. You have to know, I'm going to kill him whether I have to harm you or not."

She shook her head, terrified. "Why are you *doing* this, Daddy?"

"Why are you protecting him?"

She racked her brain for what to do. She kept moving backward. Her lab . . . There was a lock on the inside of the door. She could call someone if she could get inside.

"Don't make this harder than it is," he said.

Kate took off, sliding down the long hallway. She threw herself inside and tried to slam the door. But he reached it just before it shut. He braced his weight against the door, trying to force it open. Kate strained against it with all her might.

But he was stronger and forced it open.

"No, Daddy, no!"

She grabbed anything she could find— Beakers, vials, jars of chemicals, specimens—and threw them as hard as she could. He shielded himself with his arm as he advanced, glass shattering all over the floor. She grabbed a large Pyrex beaker, smashed the base against the counter, and held out the jagged glass neck to fend him off. She couldn't believe she was doing this. That this was the man she had grown up with and trusted, and now all she could think of was how to protect herself, hold him off.

"I'm your daughter!" she screamed, her eyes ablaze. "How can you be doing this? How can you want to hurt me?"

He came toward her.

Kate tried to bring the jagged beaker down at him, but he caught her by the wrist, squeezing it until the blood rushed into her face and the makeshift weapon fell from her grasp, splintering on the floor.

"Why did you kill my mother? She loved you. We all loved you. You broke her heart, Daddy. Why?"

Her father didn't answer, just backed Kate against the counter until the edge dug deep into her back. She didn't know what he was going to do. She searched for anything she could use against him. An instrument, a phone, anything. Then she saw the gun on the counter. All the way across, on the other side.

With one hand her father held his own gun, and with the other he took Kate by the neck and pushed her back, applying pressure with his forefingers, cutting off the air to her lungs. She gagged, disbelieving.

"You're hurting me, Daddy . . ."

Then, just as suddenly, he released her. In the same motion, he brushed his hand across her face. He reached inside the top of her sweatshirt and took out the pendants and smiled.

"Where is he, baby? No more lying. No more running now."

That was when the voice came from directly behind them. *"Estoy aquí, Benjamín.* I'm right here."

CHAPTER EIGHTY-ONE

Luis Prado waited outside in the hall. He had done his job well, following the girl back to the office. Taking care of the two agents when they came. Now there was only one more job to do. And he could go home.

It was a little creepy just hanging there in the narrow space with these two bodies on the floor. Even for him. What was Raab doing inside?

Luis stepped outside and lit a cigarette. He glanced at his watch, waiting for Raab to emerge. This was a medical office. It was a Sunday evening. Only a few people passed by on the street. He looked away from them. He wasn't worried someone would come in.

Luis was thinking that this job would be his last. He had given everything to the brother-hood. Now he could go home. Back to his family. They would set him up with a little operation, a bodega, maybe a package-shipping outlet. Something legitimate. He could coach kids— maybe football, baseball. He liked kids. Maybe he even had enough money to move his family here.

Things were taking longer than he imagined. It was pointless standing out here. Maybe he could be of use inside. The jefe, he wasn't used to getting his hands dirty, Luis laughed to himself. He tossed away his butt, pulled the outside door back open. The office door was ajar. Maybe he'd just go and check it out.

That's when he felt something slam into his back. Was it a fist? A knife? Without even realizing it, Luis was on his knees.

He groped behind him at the pain in his back. When he brought his hand around again, there was blood all over it. Another thud hit him, and now he keeled forward, his face pressed against the cold tile floor.

Blood seeped out of his mouth. His vision was filmy. He glanced behind him. There was a bearded man standing above him, wearing a flat cap.

Luis chuckled—more like a sharp coughing spasm, razor blades in his chest, gurgling on his own blood. He always knew that it would end like this. In this way. It was right. Everything else—his silly dreams, baseball, the solace of his wife, his family—was just a lie.

The man knelt down and said in Spanish, "Time to go home now," pressing the barrel of his gun against the back of Luis's head. He pulled the trigger, and Luis no longer felt anything.

"*Su deber es pagado aqui, amigo.* Your duty here is done."

CHAPTER EIGHTY-TWO

"Right here, Benjamín," the voice said again, calmly.

Every line in her father's face stiffened. It was as if he saw who was standing behind him in the reflection in Kate's eyes.

Mercado took a step forward, into view. "Turn around, brother. Put the gun on the counter."

Her father did as he was told. As he turned, the two brothers stood facing each other for the first time in twenty years.

"You wanted me, Benjamín." Mercado smiled, the gun just hanging loosely at his side. "So here I am."

"What are you going to do?" her father asked.

"I'm not going to shoot you, Ben, if that's what you think. Your man outside is dead. Along with the others. There's been enough killing, don't you think? Sharon, Eleanor, my wife ... Like you said, no more lying."

"Then what do you want?" Her father eyed him balefully.

"What do I want?" Mercado's gaze shifted toward Kate. "What I want is for Kate to hear."

Mercado took a step closer, his gaze steady and penetrating. "What was Sharon going to tell her, Ben? It's just the three of us now. What was it you didn't want Kate to know?"

Raab's eyes darted around. He moved toward Kate. She could see he was desperate. He might use her as a hostage. He would do anything now.

"You're the one with the pendant, Oscar. You're the one who seems to have truth on his side. And the gun."

Then Mercado did something that shocked Kate. He put his gun on a stool nearby. He just stood there, hands empty.

"Now it's only the truth, Ben. Tell her. What were you afraid she would find out? That's all she wants to know."

Kate could see that he wasn't expecting to come out of this alive.

"Tell me what, Dad?"

Her father didn't reply.

Mercado smiled. "No, I don't think that even mattered to you, did it, Ben? Because it was never Sharon you were after, was it?" His eyes were firm yet calm. "*Was it, brother?* This is the time for truth, Ben. Tell her! She deserves to know."

There was a haunting silence.

Kate was transfixed by Mercado's gaze, unsure what she had just heard. Then suddenly it hit her. She turned back to her father.

"*Me . . . ?*"

The word came out as more of a stammer. She stared at her father, trying to fight back her confusion.

"You were trying to kill *me*? Why?"

At that moment her father reached behind him, grabbing his gun. Mercado just stood there, staring back at him. He never made a move to defend himself.

Kate screamed as the gun went off, "No!"

The bullet struck Mercado in the right thigh. His knees buckled, and he went to the floor.

"*Tell her, Ben*. It was because it would hurt *me*—isn't that right? That's all you were ever trying to achieve. Because it would hurt *me*. Blood washes away blood, isn't that the creed? So what was Sharon going to say? Go on, tell her, Ben. *It's time.*"

Mercado looked up almost tenderly at Kate, who stood there mesmerized.

"Tell her about the pendant, Benjamín. It's time. *It's true. . . .*" He smiled at Kate as her father leveled the gun at him. "It does hold secrets, Kate. Your mother wanted you to have it one day . . . Didn't she, Ben? Your *mother*, Kate . . ." He kept looking up at her, eyes glistening.

"It just wasn't Sharon, child."

CHAPTER EIGHTY-THREE

The emptiness Kate felt in the rush of that moment was like nothing she had ever felt before.

Did she hear it right?

For an instant she just fixed on Mercado. Then she looked down, in the silent manner in which a bomb victim looks down, numbed by the shock of concussion, staring at a limb suddenly not there, trying to comprehend if what had just happened was real.

"Tell her, Benjamín." Mercado gazed up at him. "Tell her how you can hurt someone that is family. Something you pretend to love."

Kate's father pulled the trigger again. The gun flashed, hitting Mercado again, this time in the shoulder.

Kate lunged to stop him. "No, Daddy, no!"

Mercado keeled backward. He steadied himself with one hand. Kate pulled off her sweat-

shirt and wrapped it around him like a tourni-
quet.

"What is he talking about?" She turned to
Mercado. "What do you mean about my mother?"

"She was a beautiful woman, wasn't she, Ben?
Of course, I didn't have the life to raise a child
properly, did I? I was going to prison. I was
going to be away for a very long time. And, my
wife, she was sick. Isn't that right? *Diabetes*,
wasn't it?"

He looked softly at Kate. And she suddenly
recalled how the first time they'd talked, in the
park, he had spoken about a wife who'd died
of diabetes many years before.

My mother . . . ?

"I had to make a choice, didn't I, Ben? How
could I leave my child alone, without a mother
. . . or a family?" He put his hand over Kate's.
It was cold. "And you were always the consum-
mate family man, weren't you, Benjamín?"

"In all regards."

The muzzle flashed again, and Mercado rolled
backward, grasping his side.

Kate realized she was watching her real father
slowly being killed.

"I thought I did the right thing for you,"
Mercado said to Kate. "And you were protected,
all these years . . ."

"Until you started betraying our family," Raab said. "Until you forgot who you were."

"I had to make a choice." Mercado looked toward Kate.

Raab pulled the hammer. "And so, brother, *so do I!*"

"No!" Kate lunged at him, catching his arm. He took her by the wrist as if she were a piece of wood and flung her aside. Kate fell against the lab counter, a tray of tubes crashing to the floor. She reached up to the counter and pulled herself up.

"*I* sent Greg." Mercado looked at her. "Not to spy, child. To watch over you. To protect you, Catarina. Now you know why."

Kate nodded. Suddenly her gaze shifted to the counter.

"See, Benjamín, look at what you've lost," Mercado said. "Everything in your heart. Look at her . . . Was it worth it? This oath of yours. Where can you go now?"

"I can go back," Raab said, placing the muzzle of the gun in front of the old man's eyes. "But you, brother, your time is up. You have nowhere to go but hell."

"No, Daddy," Kate said firmly.

It made him turn. Her gun was extended. Directly at him. She shook her head. "Not just yet."

446

CHAPTER EIGHTY-FOUR

Raab held the gun at his brother's head, his finger on the trigger. And Kate steadied *her* gun with both hands. She had no idea what she would do.

Then, slowly, Raab released the hammer and lowered the gun.

"You're not going to shoot me, are you, pumpkin?"

"Kate, get out," Mercado said to her. "*Run.* Let him do what he has to do."

"No!" Kate glared at Raab, trying to fight through the vision of everything she once trusted and loved. All the pain he'd caused. It was going to end. Here. She shook her head and leveled the gun at his chest.

"I'm *not* running."

"Put it down," Raab said to her. "I've never wanted to hurt you, Kate. He's right. You can get out now."

"Oh, you've already hurt me, Daddy. Nothing in the world could undo the hurt you've caused."

There was a calculating pause in Raab's eyes. And then, with a smile that sent a chill through her, Raab slowly brought the gun back up to Mercado's head.

"You wouldn't shoot me, would you, baby? Not the person who loved you all these years? Who raised you? You can't undo that, Kate, whatever you now feel. Not for *this*—"

Raab nudged Mercado with his foot and he rolled on the floor.

"Please don't make me do something horrible, Dad," Kate said. Tears were streaming down her cheeks.

"Go," Mercado said. *"Please . . ."* A pool of blood began to spread onto the floor.

"If you can do it, go ahead, Kate . . . *shoot!"* Raab turned toward her. "We both know I'm going to kill him in a minute. So go ahead, pumpkin." He raised his gun up at her. "Kill me, baby, if you can do it. *Now's the time . . ."*

Kate's fingers froze. She fixed on the thin, gray barrel of his gun. She didn't know what he would do. *Squeeze, squeeze,* a voice inside insisted. *He's not your father. He's an animal.* She leveled her own gun toward his chest and shut her eyes. *Squeeze.*

Then she opened them again.

He was smirking. "I didn't think so, Kate. But he's right. Get out, Kate, *now*. I won't come after you." He turned back to Mercado and put the muzzle inches from his head. "I've got what I want."

A shot rang out. Kate screamed, shutting her eyes. When she opened them, Raab's gaze was still fixed on her, but his expression had changed.

He staggered back. He glanced at his shoulder in a state of shock. He put his hand inside his jacket, and when he drew it away, it was covered in blood. He looked at her, disbelieving. Then he pointed his gun at Mercado.

"No!"

Kate squeezed the trigger one more time. This time Raab spun and grabbed his right arm, his gun clattering across the floor. He looked confused. For a second, Kate didn't know what he was about to do.

Then he took a stubborn step toward his gun on the floor. Kate pulled back the hammer one more time. "Please, don't make me do this . . ."

Her hands were trembling. Tears burned her eyes. She took a step and leveled the gun at the center of Raab's chest.

"What are you going to do?" Raab stared down at the blood on his palm as if unable to believe what she had done. "Kill your own father, Kate?"

Kate steadied her hands. She slowly shook her head. "You're not my father, you son of a bitch."

Raab stopped, bent over the gun, breathing heavily. His wounded arm dangled at his side. Then he reached down.

Kate's fingers quivered on the trigger. "No!"

Raab leaned a little further, his fingers wrapping around the gun. He slowly brought it back up.

"Please, Daddy . . ." Kate cried.

"You always were the fighter in the family, weren't you, pumpkin?" He steadied the gun until it pointed toward her. "I'm sorry, baby, but I just can't let him live."

A shot rang out from behind. Raab pitched forward, a spatter of blood erupting from his chest. Then another—more blood spraying, his gun clattering across the floor. Raab spun, his fingers still wrapped around an imaginary weapon, pointing it at the air, legs buckling, fixing on the shooter.

He fell.

Greg stood in the doorway, white as a ghost, his arms extended. He turned to Kate and shook his head. "I wasn't going to let him hurt you, baby. I told you, you could always count on me."

CHAPTER EIGHTY-FIVE

The police arrived at the lab within minutes. The EMS teams were close behind. It looked like a war zone, with flashing lights and sirens as patrol cars and emergency teams screeched to a stop outside. There were three dead bodies in the exterior hallway. Blood was all over the place. Kate sat with Greg, his arm around her, while the medical teams looked after Mercado. She told the police that she'd speak only to Agent Cavetti of the WITSEC Program. He was on his way.

Raab was dead. Mercado was still alive, but barely. As they waited, Kate kept stroking his face, urging him to hang on. And somehow he did. He kept muttering in a sort of semi-conscious state that there was still something she had to know. Kate just squeezed his hand. *"Please, don't die . . ."*

Cavetti arrived at the scene a few minutes

later. As soon as Kate saw him, she broke away and hugged him.

"*My father* . . ." She sobbed on his shoulder. "My father came . . . with that man outside. He killed those agents . . . I had to—"

"I know, Kate." Cavetti nodded, patting her on the back. He made no move to pull her away. "*I know* . . ."

"It was all about revenge," Kate said. "Our whole life was just a lie—about revenge. He destroyed our whole family, to get back at Oscar Mercado for having betrayed them. *Fraternidad.* His own brother . . ." Kate's eyes flooded with fresh tears. "*My father* . . . Mercado is my father, Cavetti." She pulled away and looked over at Raab. "My whole life, he always said it was about family. That was the only thing that wasn't a lie."

The EMS crew treating Mercado lifted him up onto a gurney. Cavetti cast them a nod to take him away.

"Where are you taking him?" Kate asked, panicked. She wanted to come along.

Cavetti took her by the shoulders. He shook his head, ever so slightly. "I'm sorry, Kate, but that's something you can't know."

They started to wheel him toward the entrance. Kate suddenly saw that it was happening all over again. "*No!*"

She rushed up alongside the gurney and clung to his hand. This was her father they were taking away.

"I did the right thing," he uttered, turning to look at her.

"Yes." Kate nodded, squeezing his hand. "You did."

He smiled.

They carried him through the corridor leading to the reception area and down the stairs to the sidewalk. Kate kept up, alongside. A crowd had formed on the street. Several EMS vans, lights flashing, were blocking off traffic.

"He loves you," Mercado said. His hand reached out and firmly took hold of her arm. "He was only there to protect you all this time. You have to know that, Kate. He was only there from me . . ."

"I know." Kate nodded. She glanced back around. Greg was standing in the entrance. Later there'd be a time to sort out where they stood. But not now.

"There's something in my pocket," the dying man said. "Take it."

Kate reached inside his jacket and came out with something in her hand.

A locket.

"It holds secrets, Kate . . ." He wrapped her

453

fingers tightly around it. "Beautiful ones." He smiled. "Just like your sun."

"I know." She reached out for his hand and she held it as long as she could while they lifted him into the van. The EMS crew climbed inside. Sirens were wailing. They were taking him away, Kate knew. Not just to the hospital but back inside the program. Back into darkness. She was never going to see him again.

"Good-bye . . ." She smiled, holding his gaze until the doors were shut. *"Daddy . . ."*

The two lead vans had already been loaded. The lights began to rotate, and they took off with a police escort down the street. The two vehicles made a left at the corner. She was sure they were heading to Jacobi Medical Center, just blocks away.

But at the intersection the one carrying Mercado continued straight onto Morris Avenue, through the light.

Cavetti came up and put a hand on her shoulder.

"What's going to happen to him?" Kate asked, Mercado's van disappearing into the sea of flashing lights.

"To *whom*, Kate?" He smiled, knowingly. "To whom?"

She followed the trail as long as she could.

Then finally she looked down and opened her fingers. In her hand was the locket Mercado had given her. It was an old, polished silver frame, with a filigreed clasp.

"It holds secrets, Kate," he had told her. *"Just like your sun."*

Kate pushed it open.

She was staring at a photo of a beautiful woman with braided light hair and sunny green eyes that almost took her breath away. For the first time, Kate realized, she was looking at her mother.

She smiled. She held back tears. There was a name engraved under the picture.

Pilar.

CHAPTER EIGHTY-SIX

It took several days for Kate to feel she could see him again. Days for her to get back on track with her medication and regain her strength.

And she had several meetings with the police and the FBI to go over what had happened at the lab. *Everything* that had happened, this time. She replayed those last moments over a hundred times. *Could she have pulled that trigger? Could he?* It made her sad, in a final kind of way. At least it had all come to an end. Raab's debt had been paid. He had raised her. There was a part of her that still felt tears for him. Whatever he'd done.

He was right. *You can't just erase twenty years.*

Kate and Greg decided on a cup of coffee at the Ritz, a café around the corner from their loft. "This time no secrets," Greg promised, and Kate agreed. She wasn't sure how she felt. She wasn't sure if what Mercado had told her made any difference. All Greg said was, "I just want the chance to show you how I feel."

How did she feel?

Kate got there a few minutes late, taking the train in from Long Island. He still looked cute to her there, with his messy brown hair, a long woolen coat and scarf. Kate smiled—his Latin blood. And it was only November.

When he saw her, Greg stood up. She came over.

"You're a sight for sore eyes," he said, and smiled.

She smiled back. The first time he'd tried to use that phrase, their second date, he'd said, "You make my eyes sore."

They ordered, and he brought the tray to their table. "A little cinnamon, yes?"

Kate nodded. They'd been doing this for four years. He finally got it right. "Thanks."

They talked about anything at first: Fergus, who was missing her, of course. As she was missing him. The electric bill, which had come in high this month. One of their neighbors down the hall had delivered twins.

"What's your name?" Kate stopped him. She looked in his aqua-blue eyes. They were hurting and a little guilty, as if saying, *Kate, this is killing me . . .*

"You know my name," Greg answered. "It's Concerga. My mother's sister married into the Mercado family ten years ago. She is Bobi's, the youngest brother's, wife."

Kate nodded, shutting her eyes. All these years she'd been living with a stranger. These were people she'd never heard of or met.

How do *I feel?*

"I swear, I never meant for anything ever to hurt you, Kate." Greg reached for her hand. "I was only told to watch out for you. I'd been sent here to school. It was just a favor at first. Not to your father, Kate, I swear, but to—"

"Greg, I know." Kate stopped him. "Mercado told me. He told me everything."

Everything she had to know.

Greg wrapped his fingers around her hand. "I know how corny this may sound, but I've always loved you, Kate. From the first day I met you. From that first time I heard you say my name. At the temple . . ."

"I butchered it, didn't I?" Kate said, blushing. "*Gray-ghoree* . . ."

"No." Greg shook his head. Tears glistened in his eyes. "It sounded like angels to me."

Kate stared at him. She started to cry and couldn't stop. It seemed as if everything she'd held inside over the past year—her father's fall from grace, her mother dying in her arms, Raab twisting at the end—came uncontrollably pouring out. Greg moved from across the booth and sat next to her. He wrapped her in his arms. She just let it go, unable to stop.

"Kate, are you ever going to be able to trust me again?" Greg squeezed her, resting his forehead against her shoulder.

She shook her head. "I don't know."

Maybe what the old man had told her at the end changed things, just a little. How he'd looked up at her with nothing left to protect in his life and said, at peace, "*I had to make a choice*."

Maybe we all had to make a choice, Kate thought. Maybe we all had a place, a space between certainty and trust, truth and lies. Between hatred and forgiveness.

A Blue Zone.

"I don't know." Kate lifted Greg's face up to hers. "We'll try."

Greg looked at her, elated.

"Promise me, we never keep anything from each other ever again," she said. "No more lies."

"I promise, baby, no more lies."

He hugged her. Kate could feel the emotion in his embrace. "Please come back, Kate," he begged. "I need you. And I think Fergus would like to say hi."

"Yeah." She nodded. She wiped away the tears with the heel of her hand. "I think I'd like to say hi, too."

They left and went outside, to Second Avenue. Greg put his arm around her. Kate let her head fall to his shoulder as they walked. Everything was familiar. Their life. Rosa's Foods, their little bodega. The Korean dry cleaner. It felt like she'd been away for a long time, and now she was home.

As they turned onto Seventh Street, Kate stopped. Smiled. "So is there anything else you'd like to tell me before we go in, now that it's all out on the table?"

"'On the table'?"

"Before we open that door, Greg. Because when we do, we start over. Who we are. Where we go from here. We can never take it back. It's a freebie, Greg. A chance to turn the page and put the past behind us. A last chance."

"Yes, there is something." Greg bowed his head. He took Kate by the shoulders and looked deeply into her eyes.

"I'm not sure I ever told you," he teased. "I actually *hate* dogs."

CHAPTER EIGHTY-SEVEN

"So that's how it is." Kate shrugged, her fingers wrapped around Tina's curled fist in her private room. "It's been a couple of weeks. We're working on the trust thing. He came through for me, Teen. I don't know, I think maybe it's going to be okay."

Kate brushed her friend's smooth, white face. Tina's eyelids quivered. Her mouth twitched every once in a while. But that was something they'd come to expect. Over the past weeks, her condition had improved. Her intracranial pressure was down. The bandages were gone. The breathing tube as well. She was breathing on her own now. Her Glasgow reading had risen all the way up to 14. She was going to wake up, of that the doctors were fairly sure. In a month or in a day.

But then what? That was the question no one could answer.

"I'm back at the lab," Kate said. She stared blankly at the monitors by Tina's bed: the steady yellow wave of her heartbeat, the reading of her BP. "It feels good. Packer's got me finishing up on Tristan and Isolde. Two hundred and sixty-four trials, Teen. Can you believe that? We're starting to write it up. The *P & S Medical Review*'s agreed to publish it. And I've even been working on my thesis. You better get your ass in gear. Any longer, you're gonna wake up and have to address me as 'Doc'—"

Kate felt a tug on her hand. Just a reflex, the doctors said. It happened often. Kate looked. Tina's eyelids twitched.

So much had gone by, how could Kate possibly tell her everything?

"It's weird, Teen," Kate said, staring out the window, "but I'm okay with it, what happened to Dad. At least it's over. In a strange way, Greg probably did me a favor. Dad got what he deserved. But I asked myself, would I have pulled it, Teen? That trigger. If Greg hadn't come.

"And I think the answer's yes, I would have. That was my father lying there. I would have— *for him!*"

Still, when Kate thought of it, it always came with tears. "You knew him, Teen. He was quite

462

a guy. And he was right. You can't just erase twenty years . . ."

Kate felt a tug again. She just kept staring.

But this time the finger wrapped around her thumb.

Kate shot Tina a glance. *Holy shit!* She almost jumped out of her skin.

Tina was staring back at her.

With open eyes.

"Oh, my God, Tina!" Kate leaped up, starting to scream for the nurse. But before she could, Tina's mouth moved ever so slightly and the faintest smile of recognition edged onto her lips.

Kate could barely contain herself. "Tina, it's me, Kate! Can you hear me? You're in the hospital, baby. I'm here!"

Tina blinked and tugged on her hand again. She moistened her lips, as if she wanted to speak.

Kate bent close, her ear inches from Tina's lips. They barely quivered, releasing only a single, murmured sound.

Kate couldn't believe what she heard.

"Leukocytes . . ."

Tina's eyes locked on Kate's. There was a flicker of life in them. Of laughter. Then the corner of her mouth curled into a familiar smile.

"Yes, *leukocytes*." Kate nodded, giddily. *Leukocytes!*

She leaned on the green nurse's button. Tina squeezed her hand again, motioning Kate to come close again. Her eyes darted around, struggling to sort out where she was, why the tubes were in her arm. Clutching Kate's arm, she mouthed, "You still watch them? *All day?*"

"Yes." Kate nodded, her eyes filling up with tears. "All fucking day!"

Tina blinked at her and whispered, "You gotta get a life, Kate."

She was all right! Kate could see it in her eyes. Her friend was going to be okay!

EPILOGUE

THE FOLLOWING OCTOBER . . .

"Life is not fixed or owned. Our bodies are merely rented for a short while. When the time is up, like all things, they must be returned."

The rabbi's voice wound through the sanctuary. It was a Friday-night memorial service. The rows were dotted with a few, mostly older worshippers. Kate sat in a seat near the rear, Justin and Em by her side.

None of them had been here since the funeral.

Their mom had died a year ago.

"Oh, Lord, let us be truthful and worthy," the rabbi intoned. "Let us see who we really are through your watchful light."

He smiled, catching Kate's eye.

Kate's work on the stem-cell research project had landed her a couple of full-time prospects.

Greg was doing well at the hospital. But he was right—one science geek in the family was quite enough. Emily had applied for early admission—to Brown—and planned to play squash there. The coach was hot on her tail.

And the best news—Kate smiled silently under the prayers—Tina was back at work full-time. She and Kate took coffee breaks together. Kate promised she wouldn't freak out at the sight of strangers across the cafeteria.

In the past year, Kate had struggled to come to terms with all that had happened. She wore her pendants close to her heart. Both of them. And now they meant more to her than ever. A few months back, she'd received an envelope sent through the WITSEC office with no return address. All that was in it was a card—half a card, actually—intentionally torn in two. There was no message. No address.

It didn't need any words.

On the other side was a halved picture of a golden sun.

It was okay. Better to think of him that way. She didn't have to see him. Just to know that he was alive. *"I had to make a choice,"* he'd said. Kate would remember that choice for the rest of her life. And when she did, there was no way she could think of him as anything other than her father. A bearded man in a flat hat whom she'd met only a couple of times. Because that was the truth. He *was* her father. He had proven that. And the truth was something she couldn't hide from anymore.

Kate kept the locket, too. In a drawer by her bed. From time to time, she opened it and looked at the pretty face inside. The caring green eyes and the light brown hair in braids. And Kate realized how much a person must have loved her to give her up. And how much of her birth mother she carried in her own blood.

She realized it every day. *Twice a day.*

They were connected. That was something that could never be reversed. That would always be true.

Kate looked up. Greg was standing at the end of the aisle. He'd said he would be there as soon as he could break away. He came and sat beside her and reached for her hand. She smiled. He winked and mouthed under the rabbi's voice, *"Pooch . . ."*

The service had arrived at the closing prayers. The rabbi asked the congregation to rise. He recited the Mourner's Kaddish, the hallowed memorial prayer for those who were gone. Greg squeezed her hand.

Then the rabbi said, "We think on those who

have recently departed or been taken at this time in past years. Or those who just need our prayers, relatives and loved ones who have meant so much to us and remain part of our lives." He looked out. "Feel free to honor them now by speaking their names."

Someone in the second row stood up. "Ruth Bernstein," he said. Then someone in the rear, "Alan Marcus." And a woman near the side with a shawl draped over her shoulders, in a hushed voice, "Arthur Levine."

Then there was silence. The rabbi waited. He looked around to see if there were any more.

Kate stood up. She took Em and Justin by the hand.

Sharon would always be that to her. No matter what had taken place. No matter whose blood ran through her.

"Sharon Raab," she proclaimed loudly. "Our mother."

Because that was the truth, too.

ACKNOWLEDGMENTS

They say that every person has a story inside them. The problem sets in when they actually begin to believe it.

And when my first story, written after fifteen years in business in an unrelated field, made a final clunking sound on the last publisher's floor, a senior editor whom I had never even heard of happened to pass it along to their top-selling author with a note: *"Read this."*

Thank God, he did! I figured I would do one book with Jim Patterson—I'm sure he thought the same thing too—and hoped it would leave me off somewhere inside the circle I was peering into, unable to nudge my way in. But the one turned into many, all number one bestsellers, and I got to catch murderers in San Francisco, find holy relics in fourteenth-century France, chase bad guys from Palm Beach to Tierra del

Fuego—the greatest postgraduate degree a thriller writer could have.

So here at last is my chance to say thanks to a few of you, some unsuspecting, who guided me along the way.

To Gerry Friedman, a friend who convinced me over lettuce wraps, in what now seems a lifetime ago, that I'd be chasing that dream the rest of my life if I didn't, like the commercial says, just do it!

To Paul Sidey, senior editor at Random House UK. Everyone needs a first believer. A long-overdue case of wine will be at your door!

To Holly Pera, homicide sergeant of the San Francisco Police Department, my real-life Lindsay Boxer, who so graciously shared her time and experience, and taught me to think like a female cop.

To Dr. Greg Zorman, my brother-in-law and chief of staff at Lakeside Hospital in Hollywood, Florida, my medical editor-upon-demand who, for years, has been making me appear a whole lot smarter and medically savvier than I really am.

To Amy Berkower and Simon Lipskar of Writers House, who took an outline I had noodled together in the lull between Patterson books and transformed it into a full-fledged career. Simon, your keen insights for what is on the page and steady advocacy for what is beyond it made this transition a fabulous ride.

To Lisa Gallagher and David Highfill of William Morrow/HarperCollins, for believing so strongly in that outline—and in *me*! David, *The Blue Zone* is a far better story for its ebb and flow along the way. And thanks most of all for, I hope, permanently taking the prefix "*co-*" out of my job description for the rest of my career. Also to Lynn Grady, Debbie Stier, and Seale Ballenger, for their commitment and energy in advancing the book along the way.

To my sister, Liz Scoponich, and my friend Roy Grossman, early readers of *The Blue Zone*, for taking that responsibility seriously and for your truly constructive thoughts. The same to Maureen Sugden, copy editor *par excellence*, a person I've never met, yet whose imprint found its way in big, red ink onto every page. (Every goddamn page!)

And a long-overdue thanks to Maureen Egen, former deputy chairman and publisher of the Hachette Book Group, USA, for seeing something in that first heavily rejected manuscript and passing it along to Jim, almost ten years ago.

But mostly this book contains the spirit and belief of three people who set me on the road and kept me there solidly—in books and in life:

Jim Patterson, whose call, completely out of the blue, changed my writing life.

My wife, Lynn, whose belief in me never wavered, and who's kept my direction on course for twenty-five years.

And my mom, Leslie Pomerantz, for her faith too, and who stood by patiently while my credits went from tiny to small, from small to a little larger with each passing book, and who, I suspect, is probably carrying this around and showing it off right now.